Candy: you are really the Best!!!

The Written

Stories by

Eddie Lee

PublishAmerica
Baltimore

First printing

ISBN: 1-60441-769-2
PUBLISHED BY PUBLISHAMERICA, LLLP
www.publishamerica.com
Baltimore

Printed in the United States of America

This book is dedicated to the loving memory of
Eddie Lee Gates Sr. and Alreatha Gates
Two of the most wonderful people who ever lived.
This is for you from your only son
EDDIE LEE!

And also my family who has heard me talk about doing this forever it seems, and never gave up on their little brother Jr.
I love you all, this is it!
Mae, Doris, Edna, Joanne, Evelyn, Janie, Jonie, Jackie, Terri.
Latonya Jada and Aleah
I love you!

And to all my dear friends and supporters,
The Gates Family, the Miles Family, the Spring Family, the Howard Family.
P. Williams and Family, C. Sims and Family, D. Smith and Family.
D. Adams and Family, R. Edwards and Family, H. McKenna and Family.
A. Fisher and Family. J. Lucas and Family.

Love and peace.
So let it be WRITTEN!
So let it be done!

This is my first book and I am so proud, I would like to ask
That you look out for my new upcoming
novel
"UNDER THE WINDOW SEAT"
Please enjoy.

Chapter One

Never Testify

Part I

My name is Tom Walker. I'm a lawyer at Park and Walker Associates in L.A. I had a long drive to Arizona this particular morning. Not something I really wanted to do, but anyway I had to go. I got dressed, put on my blue four button suit, white shirt with cuff links, and my silver-gray tie. It was hot and getting hotter by the minute. My briefcase waited for me by the front door. I grabbed it as I walked out. I felt good. It seemed like any other day, but this day would prove to be the most horrifying, life changing day I would ever spend here on earth. I stopped for gas and water and picked up a bite to eat. The only reason I was somewhat okay with the drive was that I was driving my brand new mustang GT. 5.0.

I loved this car, and couldn't wait to get out on the open roads of Arizona.

It was a murder case I was prosecuting. This case was one of the worst I had ever seen and the defense had only the plea of insanity to convince the jury of the defendant's innocence. In my briefcase I carried the only piece of paper I would need to convict this man; a subpoena for a woman who eye-witnessed one of the killings. This woman was terrified. I knew I had to go and bring her back myself; she had fled the state praying to get away from this man and never testify!

The man's name was Frank Morehouse, a brutal cold blooded killer. I knew where she was going. In the interview tapes, she spoke about a cabin out in the middle of nowhere. She wanted to relocate in our witness protection program. She said this was the only place on earth she would feel safe.

And I planned to make sure after she testified that this is where she ended up, but now she's already gone, and who could really blame her for being afraid? I couldn't, but I thought I could bring her back.

The victims were all women in their late 20's early 30's; raped and mutilated.

Only dental records could identify the victims. The hands of Morehouse had killed 3, and I was determined to make sure there would never be a 4th.

I left L.A. around 8am. It was after 3pm now. I was well into the mountains and open roads of Arizona. It seemed as if I was the only person in the world all alone in the deserted mountain regions of Tucson as I opened up my 5.0, moving effortlessly, watching the scenic view change and then change again. But my mind was still on the case, remembering the crime scene photos; the bloody twisted work of a killer. Those pictures stuck in my mind; they had me and wouldn't let me go. But Linda Fax, she saw what no one would ever want to see; the murder as it happened.

I was getting close, still all alone on the road, or at least I thought I was.

Out of nowhere, right up behind me, was an eighteen-wheeler moving very fast. It scared me. I didn't know where it came from. All at once, it was all over me and the driver started laying on the horn. My car swerved left and back right as I tried to quickly get the hell out of this truck's way. It came past me so fast it was like a blur, and quickly faded out of sight far ahead of me. I had never seen a truck move so fast, I thought to myself.

After my heart rate returned to normal it was right back to my thoughts and the seemingly endless road ahead. I started to feel a little stiff and needed to stretch my legs, and then I noticed that I was really low on gas and needed to stop soon. I hadn't seen any signs for food or gas that I could remember at least for the last 50 miles or so. There had to be something close by. I put in a jazz CD to pass the time and to try to take my mind off the case. As I moved through the breathtaking mountains, I noticed a small bent over sign. The sign which you could barely see said "gas."

Yes! Just what I needed. Well, I really needed to use the restroom as well. The CD had played its last song and now the car was silent as the gas station came into view. The place looked deserted and dusty, like no one had been there for years. There were two red pumps in the middle of a dirt and gravel yard. Four cars, old and broken down, lined the right side of the yard, and a large dog was tied to a very big old tire rim. The dog was very loud running back and forth, but only as far as the chain would allow him to reach. As I came closer, a cloud of dirt had lofted up from the dog's excitement. The station itself was old and run down, but this place was bigger than most filling stations out in the middle of nowhere, like this place had been used for something else in the past. My bladder was full and I was starting to squirm in my seat as I slowly pulled into the lot looking for any signs of life, other than the big barking dog. As I looked around, I noticed a big sign at the end of the lot that read

"FILL UP"

Now I was at the pump. Even though I had to go to the men's room, I didn't get right out of the car. I looked around and waited. Still no sign of anyone. I hit the horn a few times, and then started to go through my pockets looking for my credit card. The dog was still barking running back and forth launching more and more dust and dirt into the air all around my car. When I looked up from my glove box, I could see the door of the station slowly opening. Finally! I breathed a sigh of relief, and looked back to my glove box to find the credit card that had somehow grown legs and walked away. As I was digging through the box, I glanced up to see what seemed to be this tall, dirty, long haired man walking out to my car. The dust made it hard to make him out. I kept digging; he was almost to my window now, although it was bright and sunny, the dust and dirt obscured his face. There it was: my card in the back of the glove box.

I reached over to let down my window and dust rushed right in I looked over and said,

"Fill it up please."

Just as I started to give him my card, through the dust a light mist was sprayed. It came through my window and up into my mouth and nose. The card fell from my hand outside the car door to the ground. Then everything went black. I was out cold. Was this really happening? Or was I just dreaming? In my mind I was in complete darkness. Flashes of all three murder victims. Flashed like bright lights then back to blackness. Smoke mixed with a very bad odor surrounded me, with the sound of a mad dog growling and barking in the background. What was happening to me? Somebody, anybody please help me!

I started to wake up, but I was no longer in my car. My eyes tried to focus, but this was very hard to do. In and out of consciousness, nothing but darkness and flashes of light and naked bloody images. Finally my eyes started to focus. I was no longer in my car, but inside. I must be inside the old station. It was very dark and wet with no windows and one big door to the outside. Small leaks of light made their way through the cracks. I looked around. The room was huge and I was on the floor still very dizzy and when I tried to get to my feet, I noticed the chain around my ankle. I was chained to the wall; my leg had already started to turn black and blue. I tried to scream, but I was still so out of it from whatever he sprayed into my face that nothing really came out. I was terrified, starting to panic and hyperventilate. What is this? Why is this man holding me here? I had no answers, just the fear of what this man had in mind for me, but why?

This was the most terrifying situation I could ever imagine being in. I had tried many cases where people were beaten and even killed in unspeakable ways, but it had never chilled my blood cold and tightened my chest to the point where I found it hard to breathe, but now this was happening to me. It was getting late. The light that had filled the cracks around the door started to fade dim. The cold wet room was even colder now. I tried to pull the chain from the wall but there was no way this could be done. I was trapped with no hopes of being freed tonight. I could hear the big dog starting to bark, and the sound of his chain that kept him from freedom, moving back and forth against the dirt and rocks of the yard. I was starting to feel just like that dog, wanting to be freed maybe needing food and water. So just like a dog I stood up to relieve myself. The smell was so bad in this room; the scent of my urine went unnoticed. Then I heard a noise; not from outside the room, but in.

I turned slowly to where I thought the sound came from; my eyes had somewhat adjusted to the darkness of the room. There were three large crates side by side in one corner of the room. Whatever it was it was coming from the big crates. I stood still not making a sound trying to hear if there really was something or was I just imagining the whole thing. Then I heard it again.

It was real. It was something, but I wasn't sure if I really wanted to know.

I was afraid but I tried to move as close as the chain would allow me to get to the crates. It was close but not close enough; I went back to the wall and started to work on the chain anchored to the wall. As I fussed with my chain, I heard footsteps starting down the hall outside the big doors; I stopped and sat back down on the floor not making another sound. Now he was right outside the doors. I could hear him messing with the lock and shaking the doorknob. I knew for sure he was coming in, but then he stopped and walked away. I took a deep breath and put my head in both my hands, trying to understand what the hell was going on. I started to lose control, hitting my head against the wall slowly at first and then faster, until I knocked myself out. Out cold, I laid in a puddle of my own urine, dreaming of a man whose face I've never seen breaking through the big doors and cutting my fingers off one by one, then my ears one by one, and placing them in the crate and sealing it shut, leaving me on the floor still chained to the wall bleeding looking up at the crates in terrible pain and shock. Slowly, the crate would open as my own fingers started to crawl their way out and down the crate slowly moving towards me, as I screamed in great terror.

I woke up. I must have been out for twenty minutes or so. I felt bad and my head was bleeding down the right side of my face. The smell was getting even worse. My white shirt was now gritty black and golden brown from the dirty wet floors and my urine mixed all together. I noticed one of my cuff links was missing. I started to look around for it, and there it was over on top of one of the crates. My father had given these links to me before he died years ago so they were very important to me. I sat back down against the wall. The cuff link made me think back to when I became a prosecutor, and the reason I wanted to be one.

My father and I were very close; he was a police officer for the LAPD. He was a good cop; he served for 22 years on the streets of L.A. Then he was accused of shooting and killing an innocent man in the line of duty. My father was not guilty of any of these charges; the case was being dragged out, and it didn't look good for him. I was there as the prosecutor destroyed my father and brought his reputation to nothing, and there was nothing I could do about it.

I felt helpless and alone, as I watched my father going down for something he never was guilty of. But I guess his being found guilty was not enough for the victim's brother, who waited on the steps of city hall as we left the courthouse on sentencing day.

This man was dressed like one of the press when he pulled a 45 out of his pocket and shot my father dead right there on the steps of city hall in cold blood right in front of my eyes. I would never be the same after this day, my life had changed. I decided to study law and become the best prosecutor I could be for my father, or was it really for me?

Was it all for this? Is this what I set out to accomplish? Now I'm here not knowing if I'm going to live or die by the hands of a cold blooded killer just like my father was.

It's funny something as small as a cufflink can hold all the meaning mine does.

Time was passing slowly. It must have been close to midnight by now. I could hear coyotes howling at the moonlight, and the big dog joining in, like a doomsday ritual or something. I was tired, but too afraid to sleep. I was hungry, but there was nothing for me to eat. I started to think about dying here. I felt I had no hope. But what was this man waiting for? Why not come in and kill me and get it over with? Was this some type of torture? Maybe he wanted to make me suffer, but for what?

Then I heard it again; the noise from the crates. It seemed to be a little louder now, like maybe a rat gnawing at the crate. I jumped to my feet trying to see, trying to see anything if I could. Then came the footsteps back down the hall. I quickly moved up to the door. There he was again, right outside the door. This time he didn't touch the lock, he just stood there.

I was on one side and he was on the other. It was quiet, and then he walked away.

Slowly I put my hand on the door and started to pull on it, but then I stopped, afraid he would hear me, so I moved back from the door. I looked back over at the crates now it was quiet. The sound had stopped again. I sat back down on the floor near the wall.

I was tired. I was expected back in court at ten a.m. tomorrow morning and if I didn't show, they would start looking for me.

But for me, it no longer mattered. I didn't know if I would make it through the night.

Here I was, trying to put a killer in prison to make our streets safe to walk on, but here sat another that no one even knew about. I was doomed. We all are. There's really nothing anyone can do to change things.

I fell back to the floor and pushed my self back up against the wall were I was chained, grabbing both my knees into a fetal position, like a small scared child would do.

It was quiet with nothing moving but my trembling body. I had to get out, but how?

I tried to think as I sat up looking around the room, trying to see something, anything that would help me get free from the chains. But the room was so dimly lit that it was hard to see anything. Just then, I heard footsteps coming in my direction from just outside the big doors. I yelled out, "Help me!! Somebody help me!!!"

The sound stopped right in front of the doors. I went silent trying not to breathe.

The person stood there for a minute and then just walked away.

I knew it was the same man that had put me in here.

Maybe I didn't want him to come in. I had no idea what he was prepared to do.

I would always have this dream as a prosecutor, where I was in front of the jury giving my closing argument,

"None of us was there to save the victim from this man; we couldn't hear the screams or pleas for mercy.

The victim was alone. This man had all the power of life and death right in his very hands. He alone decided if this person would live or die.

He chose death and ended this innocent human life.

When a man is capable of taking innocent life, we define this person as being a cold blooded killer! Take a look at his face."

As the jury and I turn to look at the defendant, I notice that the defendant is me.

Then I wake up.

I found myself drifting in and out. I was afraid to sleep, not knowing if I would ever wake up again. The smell seemed to be getting even worse now; it was starting to make me gag, but nothing would ever come up. I felt like I had all ready started to die. I was weak and disoriented. My mind was mush. Maybe I was still feeling the effects of what he had given me in the car. I didn't know, all I knew was I felt like shit.

As I sat on the dirty, cold, wet floor, my eyes half closed, I could see the doors starting to open. I didn't move. I couldn't move. I started to breathe heavily. My heart started to pound. This was it; I was about to die, then the door slowly started to close again, and I passed out.

My eyes started to open again. And I noticed the door to the room was now open. Then I heard a noise over by the crates. When I looked over, there he was.

I didn't move, trying to appear that I was still asleep.

I could only see his legs. The room was still very dark. What was he doing?

What was in those crates? And what was he going to do to me?

He moved around very slowly, opening and closing the crates. I closed my eyes just for a second; at least that's what it felt like to me.

I was afraid and didn't want to see what was really in there.

But then I opened my eyes. He was gone and the door was closed.

The room was quiet and dark again. What was that real? Or was I dreaming?

I didn't know, but it sure felt real to me.

My head was pounding and my hands were hurting as well. I guess from pulling on the chains that held me to the floor. I started to feel like I couldn't move, like I was paralyzed.

I tried to move my legs, but they would not respond. I blacked out again.

Somehow I got to my feet and moved over to the crates.

Standing over them, looking down, I put my hand on one corner of the crate and tried to pull the cover off. It seemed to be nailed shut. I couldn't move it.

My hands hurt. This made it harder for me to apply real pressure to the top of the crates.

When I moved my hands from the crates, my bloody handprint remained.

So I moved from one crate to the next. It was nailed shut as well; no way could I open it.

I moved slowly over to the next one, and this one opened right up.

I pushed the top to the floor and peered down into the crate. I couldn't see anything but blackness. It was still very dark. So slowly I put my hand down into the dark crate to feel around for something, anything.

I had no idea what I might find. Then, right when I was sure it was just an empty crate and pulled my hand back, is when it grabbed me, and jerked me back in.

It had me, whatever it was. I screamed and tried to pull away, but it was stronger than I was. Whatever it was, it wasn't just going to let me go. It was a tug of war.

It wanted to pull me in, all the way into the crate, but I wasn't going without a fight.

I pulled with all my might and somehow it let me go. I fell back very fast and hit the floor hard. I quickly moved back over to the wall, very upset, my heart rate was very high. I had to calm down as I was just staring back at the dark crate, not taking my eyes off of it, not even for a second.

Was this it? What he had in store for me? To let whatever is in here kill me?

I couldn't believe this was really happening to me. My head started to spin and I woke up, or did I pass out?

The chain that had me anchored to the floor was starting to give a little from all the moisture in the room; it started to work its way loose. I didn't have much strength, but whenever I could build some up; I would pull my arm as hard as I could to free myself.

One crate was open; two were still closed up tight. What was in the open crate? I still didn't know. I was still afraid to find out. Something dark and very strong. Something that meant me harm. How long would it wait to come out and kill me? How long?

Part 2

Every man has his own breaking point, his own line to cross. Once this line has been crossed, there's no turning back. This limit must be respected at all times.

As we know, the Bible said,

"Man is incapable of directing his own footsteps."

Now imagine this same man past his limit or breaking point.

A man that kills has his own take on reality. In such a mind, he feels his thinking is clear and his motive is true. Such a man has no remorse and sometimes no recollection of his terrible actions. What really defends a cold blooded killer? You? Me? We all are human and all of us are capable of many things.

The night continued. I was ready for this all to end. Not knowing the day and time you die; you can find some comfort in that, but when you expect it or see it coming, you die a thousand times over.

Right now, that's how I felt. Like being buried alive, slowly dying.

I started to gag again from the smell that kept growing worse and worse.

I tried to use my tie to cover my nose and mouth, but nothing could stop the smell from poisoning my system.

I needed water desperately, but I tried not to think about it. Then there it was again; the sound from the crate.

I moved closer to the wall pulling on the chain, trying to break it free from the wet rotting floor it was screwed to.

Still it was not ready to release me. I kept my eyes fixed on the crate, expecting at any moment for whatever it was to come out.

The noise continued longer this time, louder, but still I could not see anything.

Was there anything in there? Or was it just in my mind?

At this point I didn't know.

I started to doubt my mind and thoughts. I could no longer tell what was real.

The chain that held me to the floor was working its way loose. Soon I could break my way free. Even though I was still very weak, I needed to try and focus so I could really understand what was going on.

Now I knew for sure the one crate was open. The other two were still closed tight. But was I dreaming? Did something grab me and try to pull me in?

This made no sense to me after I calmed down enough to think about it.

If so, whatever had me surely would have come out for me by now.

But now, I had to be sure. So I started over to the crates. Slowly I moved, still terrified of what I might find.

Still the room was dark and the open crate looked a lot like an opened grave.

My hand was shaky, unsteady as I reached up for the side of the crate.

What would I find? What would find me?

No matter what the cost, even if I paid tonight with my life, at least I would know!

Now I was standing right over the crate, my hand clutching the wood tightly.

My eyes were closed shut and afraid to open, but slowly they did.

What did I see? What did I see???

NOTHING.

Once again the crate was black, dark and empty.

I guess I felt relieved, but at the same time somewhat disappointed.

I mean, I was happy to be alive, but felt cheated.

By now, I had built myself up to face whatever was going to happen to me, facing my fear head on, but the crate was just—Empty.

Now I found myself back on the floor, crying like a baby.

The crate may have been empty, but somehow it couldn't be.

I continued to cry until I passed out again. Not only was this situation not right, but I was starting to realize that something was not right with me.

Fighting with myself, trying to understand what was really happening, I tossed and turned until I came to.

I sat up with my back against the wall. I stared at the chain that had me confined to the floor. Why can't I free myself? Is it really this hard? There must be a way.

I slowly turned back to the three crates. I sat and stared at them all for a while. And then, at the door, there he was again.

Now he shook the door like he really wanted to come in, but for some reason he couldn't get the door to open. I watched the door; no longer did I feel afraid.

There was no panic or heavy breathing. I was calm. The door shook hard for a moment or two, and then it just stopped. My eyes went right back to the crates. It was like a game of chess, me against the madness. At this point I was in no hurry to move again. Strategy was the plan from here on out. Position myself to move in for the kill.

I started to crawl around on the floor, feeling my way through the darkness. My hands burned from the open wounds when they came in contact with whatever filth covered the wet, dark floor. I was looking for something to free me from the chains. Then, there it was like clock-work; the sound from the crates again.

I stopped instantly to listen even closer.

It was getting stronger now and lasting a bit longer before it would stop. By now, I had crawled to the far corner of the room where my left foot struck a lead pipe.

It brought a loud sound to the dark and wet room.

I pushed it a little out of reach, so I felt around with my feet and hands until I moved it again. I quickly picked it up and walked back to the wall. The sound from the crates had stopped. It was back to quiet. Now, with the lead pipe I sat and waited to make my next move. One crate was empty, the other two still closed.

The sound had to be coming from one of them, but which one? They all appeared to be the same size; very big and very old.

From what I could see, the crate right next to the open one looked like something was coming out of the side and the bottom. Something wet and runny.

It was too dark to see what it was.

Like I said, I was taking my time, thinking about what I was going to do before I did it.

I stood up and started to walk to the crates, but the chain would not let me go.

As I moved, the chain grabbed me, almost making me fall flat on my face.

I was pissed. I raised the lead pipe over my head. As I opened my mouth, out came a loud scream of madness I didn't think I was capable of making. I crashed the pipe into the chain as hard as I could, over and over, then again and again, like I was out of control.

Then I started to feel sick, and I passed out.

Dreaming

Is my mind friend or foe? As I slept, I had visions of a stream of water out deep in the woods. The blood-red water moved around my legs, as I stood over a female deer that was the victim of a hunter's hand.

Looking down at the deer as it lay there dying, I felt responsible, but why?

I reached down to touch the animal, my hands both covered in blood.

I woke up.

Where am I? For just a moment I didn't realize what was real.

But yes. Not the woods, but the dark room and the crates.

Now what was I going to do? Just wait for this guy to come in here and kill me? And then put me into crate number 3?

Victims are made to be victims, but what can I do not to become the next one?

Trying to be as calm as I could, I started to look around. Where did I set that lead pipe?

I would now use it to protect myself when this man came for me.

I could hear the dog out in the lot starting to bark again, but I could not hear the chains that held him.

Maybe he was now free from the chains as I was, but I'm still locked in this room, so how free is that?

Then out of nowhere, there he was again, beating on the door harder than he ever did before. The whole room started to shake like an earthquake.

The walls were moving and everything was falling from the shelves.

The crates were starting to move, hitting each other. But I kept my eyes on the door.

He didn't get in and then he was gone, and once again the room returned to silence.

But then the crates. The sound from the crates.

I started to sit up, but it was hard. Everything on my body hurt really badly.

Why? I don't know; it just did.

Then I noticed. I looked down and the chain was gone.

It shocked me; I didn't remember what happened before I fell asleep.

But it was gone, I mean completely gone. Nowhere could I feel it lying on the floor.

Maybe he came in and took it?

The first thing I did was to grab the pipe again, and then I moved over to the big door.

I wanted to see if it was still locked. It was locked and no way could I get it open.

Then I heard the crates. I turned and faced them, gripping the pipe tightly in both hands.

Now I moved to the crates, slowly, still not afraid and my thoughts were very deep and focused.

I chose the crate that was leaking from the sides and bottom.

As I got close, I could still hear the noise coming from one of them. I wasn't sure which.

But now, I had made up my mind that it would be this one.

I raised the pipe and hit the crate. I stopped, stayed quiet to listen, but now the sound had stopped. Then I went all out trying to open the crate. It was hard at first then it started to give. I dropped the pipe. Now I was breathing heavily. I put my hands on one corner of the crate and pushed as hard as I could.

It started to open. My feet were slipping in whatever was leaking from the bottom of the crate and the smell was overwhelming.

I was choking badly, so I took a deep breath and pushed.

The top fell to the floor and I looked in.

It—oh my god!

It was the remains of an old man. I fell to my knees vomiting.

I could no longer breathe.

Finally I pulled myself together and got up on my feet. I put both hands over my mouth as I tried to balance myself.

I stood in a puddle of human blood. It was unbearable to look at.

Maggots were crawling in and out of the man's flesh; a sick and bloody nightmare.

There was a patch I could barely see on the man's shirt as it too was covered in blood.

The patch said, "FILL UP."

Which I remembered was the name of the station I had stopped at for gas.

I picked up the lid of the crate and placed it back on top, trying to cut the smell the best I could. I had to sit back down. Whatever fear I had overcome before now had just returned to me, but now it was ten times worse.

This man was dead, someone had killed him and I was alone with no way out.

My skin was white as snow. I was close to going into shock, but after seeing that dead body I wanted to live even more now. I had every reason to want to live. I started to think, this man worked here. He was killed by that crazy man in cold blood and put into this crate. Was the empty one for me? And what is in the other crate? I really didn't want to know now.

But now I knew for sure that the man who locked me in here was a killer.

Who knows how many may have died? And will he kill again? The fact that I'm still alive and in here against my will would say him killing again is a very strong possibility.

Part 3

I had made up my mind I was not going to open the third crate, but clearly now this was where the sound had been coming from the whole time. It had to be, there was nothing left. I had the pipe in my hand and I started moving back to the crates.

Deep Inside

The longest journey one could take is deep inside one's self.

No matter how well you think you may know yourself and what you would or wouldn't do. The mind is uncharted territory, so it would be impossible to really know, truly know,

What lies deep inside.

My mind started to play tricks. I was seeing things that could not be there, images of myself walking through the doors and going over to the crates. And just sitting in a chair on the other side of the room.

I closed my eyes. I didn't want to see any more. It frightened me.

The sound from the last crate was louder now. I was afraid to move. Afraid of what I might find in the last crate or this man outside trying to get in or of the man inside trying to out.

It all started to drive me mad. I put my hands over my ears trying to stop the sound coming from the last crate, rocking back and forth hitting my head on the wall every time I rocked back. But I still could hear it, so I rocked harder until I knocked myself out cold once again.

I woke up lying on my back on the floor. It was still dark in the room. I had no idea what time of morning it was, but I knew dawn was not very far away. As I started to sit up, I noticed that the door was wide open. I asked myself, is that real? I was still a bit out of it.

I got up and started slowly over to the door. With every step, the door seemed to be farther and farther away, but somehow I was getting closer.

Then I could hear the noise from the last crate start up again. I looked over for just a second. I looked back to the doorway and there he was. The same man who had kept me here against my will, a killer, someone I despised.

As I got closer to the doorway, it all became very clear.

I could no longer hide from myself.

There I was, standing face to face with no one but myself.

But it was all so real. I could see myself standing in the door way holding the chains that held me, but the image of myself wasn't really there in the doorway. It was only me.

But then I thought, what about the crates? Is that real? I turned to go over to the crates.

Everything looked the same. Two were open and one was still closed.

But now I felt different, like I'd been here before. I looked in.

The dead man was still there. That had not changed. Then it hit me; I killed him.

It was like standing outside yourself, but never knowing what the other side of you is doing. Never feeling yourself going through these situations, and having no control over yourself at these unspeakable times.

So now I know. I was never kidnapped and held here.

There was never a locked door to hold me and there were no chains to keep me in one place. It was all in my mind. I stood there in the middle of the room with a blank look of horror on my face.

Who was I? I no longer knew. It was all unknown to me, at least half of me.

The sounds continued from the unopened crate. As I turned and started over to it, it felt like my other self was shown to me for the first time; what I had kept from myself for so long.

It was strange to feel that, but I seemed to go right along with it.

I dropped the lead pipe. I no longer needed it. I knew just how to open the crate.

All at once, things were so clear to me. I knew just what I needed to do.

The morning was coming and I was running out of time.

The darkness was the key. It made it all so easy for me. Now it was time for me to do what needed to be done.

I opened the crate. She was still alive; hog-tied, hands to feet, bloody and close to death; one Linda Fax.

When she saw my face, a look of knowing death appeared on her face.

Her mouth was duct-taped. So she could not make a sound. I stood over her looking down at her. I sat on the edge of the crate.

Then I told her, "This must be done. One must clearly understand that by taking someone's life you get nothing in return."

She looked up with bloodshot eyes,crying dirt-filled tears of pain and desperation.

I felt for her at the same time.

She was a victim of being at the wrong place at the wrong time.

But I knew how to make it all right, how to make it all go away.

I moved in close to her, and looked deep into her eyes I said,

"Don't judge me."

She shook in great terror. As I reached out my hand slowly, she closed her eyes.

"LOOK AT ME!!!"

I demanded. She opened her eyes slowly. I removed the tape from her mouth, and she said, "Oh my god!! Oh my god!!" She repeated it over and over again. She was going into shock. Linda said, "Please! I'll never testify! Please!"

"I know what you want." Just as I put the tape back over her mouth.

The morning was coming fast. I continued back outside past my car which was right where I left it, over by the row of cars. In the lot sat two big gas cans, which I picked up and carried over to the red gas pumps.

I filled them both and I struggled with the cans taking them back inside. One I put right in the center of the room. And the other I took over to the crate.

She was out cold, but not dead. I unscrewed the gas cap and started filling the crate with gas. Then with the other can I poured a line of gas from the crate to the big doors of the room and before I lit the match, I said,

"You'll never know who you truly are until you know what lies deep inside you. Never Testify!"

The Ring of Deception

Part 1

Intricate dreams come cascading down over me, with faded visions of malice, or redemption. This is my world, even though a mere dream, complicated and shameful. I am puzzled, unsure of the life that is my own, insignificant to the careless world around me. A man should be strong. I am not. Although I am a man, I am cursed, tainted to the true life granted to every other man.

My name is Leonard Butterfield; even my own name mocks me, I bear not say it. Always fearful of the laughter that would surely almost always follow. Somehow I survive, alone without family or friends to go to for the much needed love and affection.

I did feel this way, but I never pitied myself. What kept me going was fear and anger. For what I thought I should have and should be. So every day I faced the world afraid, but with madness in my heart. The more afraid I became, the more hate burned inside me, pulling me down deeper and deeper into this hellish world of existence. I wanted love. I wanted respect. I wanted to be happy, if there was such a thing. And if there were, would there be any for me?

I worked every day at a law office, where I was a clerk for the past two years. I am a very methodical individual, so I was very good at my work. Everything I've ever wanted always seemed to be dangling right in front of me, teasing me. I worked very hard for the past two years, hoping to become Jim Thompson's legal assistant.

The practice was called Thompson and Jones at law; Sarah Jones was Jim's legal partner. She enchanted me. She was beautiful in every way, and my dreams often included her, my thoughts haunted by her scent and sound. Just like the job, Sarah was one of the many things I wanted, but could not possess. I could never find the words, along with the actions; to reach out for the things I desired in life, hence my reclusive existence.

Sarah knew of my feelings for her. She was unkind in a very presumptuous way, but no matter how thoughtless her actions may have been many times, I loved her and wanted her still. I was starting to think less of myself as time passed. Just as no one else cared for me, I started to feel the same way. Maybe I do deserve this life not being life at all. Who will stand for me if I continue to fail to stand for myself?

Sarah would tease me. One night when we were working late, she called me into her office for dictation. As she spoke, she walked from her desk over to the window, opening her blouse, exposing herself to me in the reflection of the window. I became overwhelmed, instantly frozen, and sweaty. She stopped talking and began to smile, looking at me in the reflection of the window. I jumped up and ran from the room in embarrassment, as her smile turned to laughter.

The next day, as I passed Jim's office, I could hear Sarah, telling Jim what she had done to me just last night. They laughed together, just before they began to make love in his office. As I listened to them though the door, my body began trembling, but it was not out of shame for me that I trembled, but out of desire for Sarah. I longed for her still.

They toyed with me, as if I were a child, the both of them. But I did nothing; I thought what could I do? At least I would be close to Sarah.

Some time had passed, and things mostly stayed the same. Well, for me, anyway. Jim was working on a big case, and I knew he really needed some help. Somehow I got myself up and unconsciously made my way into his office. As I approached the door, my insecurities as a man almost turned me away, but this time somehow they didn't.

"Jim, excuse me, but do you have a second?"

"I'm really busy right now, Leonard. What is it?" As I stood there in front of him, fighting to control myself from exploding, I took a deep breath.

"Jim, I know how busy you are with this case, and I would really like to help you, if I could?" He looked up at me, from his work very intimidating, also with surprise.

"You want to help me?"

"Yes, I would like to show you firsthand what I can do. I know I can be helpful, as far as the gathering of information you may need."

"Well, Leonard, you might at that." He sat back in his chair, looking at me with a smirk emerging on his face. And just then, in walked Sarah.

"What's going on, boys? Am I not invited?"

"Sarah, Leonard has just come in to let me know that he would like to help with the workload on the case. Do you think he's ready?"

"I think he's been ready, Jim. Leonard, you know you are very special to us. I know you will do just fine."

"Thank you, Sarah. I won't let you down."

Jim smiled and said," Sarah, I think this calls for a celebration. Tonight, why don't we have Leonard meet us for drinks at the pub?"

"You know, that sounds wonderful. I have a few of my girlfriends meeting me as well. How does that sound, Leonard? You up for some real fun?" She said as she looked over at Jim.

"Well, I think so?"

"Don't think so, Leonard; know so. You have to learn to let your hair down sometimes and have some fun."

"Maybe you're right, Sarah."

"I know I am, so be at the pub around seven." She ran her fingers through her long brown hair as she passed me leaving the room. I couldn't take my eyes off of her, lost deeply in her magic I was. As I left Jim's office, I began to smile for the first time in a very long time. Maybe this was it, the changing of good things to come.

I couldn't wait for the day to be over so I could go home to get ready for what I thought would be the biggest night of my life.

Finally I made it home. I tossed off my clothes, running to the shower to get ready. I was more than excited. I had just over an hour to get to the pub by seven. As I walked up to the front of the pub, I stopped and a very cold breeze made its way around the corner, swirling around me. I pulled up my collar, looking up at the neon sign flashing, THE PUB.

I closed my eyes and made a wish that this would be the change I needed in my life, making me the better, stronger individual I so desperately needed to be. As I walked in, there they were, up at the bar, drinking and laughing. There were two other women with them whom I had never seen before. Then Sarah turned and saw me standing there looking quite nervous.

"Leonard, there you are. Come on over here. I have some friends I'd like you to meet." I was terrified. The two women were very pretty, but not even close to the beauty that Sarah possessed. Sarah took my hand and guided me over to the bar.

Jim smiled at me and said," Leonard, nice of you to come."

"Thank you all for inviting me."

Then Sarah said, "Leonard, this is Tina, and Joanna."

"It's nice to meet you both." I said, as I tried my best to be brave. They then decided that we should get a table, so we could all sit together. As we sat at the table, I noticed that the two women were all over each other; they found it hard to keep their hands off of one another.

We ordered drinks and talked for hours. I didn't do much drinking; I never was much of a drinker. But the little I did have, made me feel really good. I was having a really good time. Then Sarah came over to me, sat on my lap, and said to me, "Leonard, my friends and I have a room around the corner and we would like you to come by tonight." I looked up at the two of them. They were looking at me; smiling. Then Tina reached over and fondled Joanna's breast. I couldn't believe what was happing, but I liked it.

I had only had a few drinks, but even that was way too much for me.

The girls all got up to leave. As they passed me, Sarah put a key in my hand and kissed me on my lips. Jim was just returning from the restroom,

"Where is everyone, Leonard?"

"They all just left."

"They did? Well, that's okay. I want you to know that I think you will do a great job. Don't let me down. I got to get home; I'll see you in the office."

"Thank you, Jim. I won't let you down, you'll see." I said, as he was walking away. I looked down at my hand, and tried to focus my eyes on the key. It had the number 102 on the other side.

I went to the restroom, and put cold water on my face, to try to wake up, and prepare for what was going to happen. Or for what I wanted to happen.

As I walked out of the pub, the cold breeze came back around the corner to meet me. I walked on down the street. This was it, what I'd always wanted. Respect from Sarah. To finally touch her skin, and feel her body next to mine. This was the whole reason that I continued with this miserable life of mine.

Now, just across the street I stood, looking over at the hotel. Just then, it started to rain. I headed across the street, and to room 102. I was standing right outside the room. The rain had soaked me from head to toe, as I put the key into the lock and opened the door. Rain came running down my face as the door swung open.

I wiped the rain from my eyes with both of my hands and when I opened up my eyes I could see a woman standing in the room. This woman was not Sarah or one of her friends. She said to me,

"Leonard, come on in out of the rain." I stood there for just a second, before I slowly walked into the room. "Close the door behind you."

I closed the door, and said, "Where is Sarah and her friends?"

"Well, I'm one of Sarah's friends."

"Who are you? Is Sarah here?"

"Sarah is on her way right now. My name is Cat. Why don't you let me help you get out of those wet clothes?"

She started over to me, and walked slowly behind me. And then she pulled my coat off, and moved close to the side of my face. She said, "Don't be afraid. Let me take care of you." Next my shirt hit the floor, as she made her way back around me. She was now standing right in front of me.

She started to take off her clothes very slowly, dancing for me. But when her dress slipped to the floor, nothing could have readied me for what I saw. The Cat was suddenly a Dog.

I grabbed my mouth, trying to keep myself from throwing up as I tripped over my coat, picking up my shirt, trying to get the hell out of this room. As I struggled, putting on my coat without my shirt, Cat grabbed me, and tried pulling me onto the bed. We started struggling, fighting. I was trying to get away, but Cat wanted me to stay. Then I kicked her/him, with all my might, and shot out the door into the rain like a rocket.

I started down a long alley. It was still raining very hard. I was crying, and my tears mixed with the rain.

"Why me?" I screamed stumbling down the long alley. I knew they had set me up. The rain was blinding and I could not see two feet in front of me. Then I tripped. I fell hard and hit my head, and then everything went black. I was out cold. Visions of Sarah, naked with her two friends, flashed in my head. They were calling me, saying,

"Come to us, Leonard. Come to us."

As I reached for them, something had me and I couldn't move. I pulled harder, but I couldn't break free; then I heard those words again, "Let me take care of you." It was Cat. She had me, and then I woke up.

I was face down in a long, dark alley; rain was still coming down hard. I pushed myself back up against a wall and looked around.

I was cold, wet, and alone, not to mention scared to death. Then I heard a noise, it came from deeper into the blackness of the alley. I was afraid, but I got to my feet and started down the alley. Something made me go. I couldn't stop myself, even if I wanted to. Then I just stopped, and looked down, and saw an old man looking up at me. I said, "What do you want from me?" He was very old and drenched from the rain. His beard was white as snow, but his clothes were torn and dirty from the ground that he lived on.

He said, "I want nothing from you, but you need something from me."

"Do you know me, old man?"

He laughed out loud, and then said, "I know you, Leonard. You're a man who is in desperate need."

"How do you know my name?"

"I know your life is not a life at all. You need something from me that can change the unwanted path you walk."

"What do you know of my life, old man? I've never seen you before."

"Just sit down with me, Leonard, and let me help you change your life, for the better." I was confused, and still very much afraid. I started to run away, but something told me to sit with him, so I did.

I looked at him, and said; "Now, how can you help me, old man?"

"I was once like you. I too felt I was less than a man with no woman of my own to love, and no respect that I knew I deserved and then one day I found it."

"Found what? What did you find old man?" He looked at me, and slowly put his hand into his pocket, and pulled out a ring. It shined even in the darkness of the alley. Then I said, "A ring? How can just a ring help me, old man?"

"Is that all you see? This is much more than just a ring."

"How can this ring change my life?"

"This ring is everything you're not. Once you wear the ring, it will fill all the gaps in your troubled life, making you better in every way."

"If this is true, old man, why hasn't the ring done for you what you say it can do for me?"

"You must remember that the ring is everything you are not, the good, as well as the bad. This you must always remember."

He reached out his hand, holding the ring. I opened my hand and he gave it to me.

"Now it belongs to you, Leonard. Be wise in your time to come." I stood up, clutching the ring in my hand, and backed up, never taking my eyes off the old man, until the darkness of the alley was all over him.

The next morning was a Saturday. I had the day off. I was just waking up from my incredible night. I had put the ring across the room on the dresser, and as soon as I opened my eyes, I looked over at it. The ring was glowing, without the presence of light in the room. Normally this would be strange, but oddly enough, it didn't strike me that way. I got up, and walked over to it slowly, and stood looking at it. By now I felt hopeless, but for some reason I started to speak aloud to the ring. I said, "What can you do for me? How can you change my life?"

At the end of my rope, I was surely going mad, standing there talking to a ring. But this is what my life had come to. How could I go back to work and face them? What would I say?

Just standing there, looking at the ring, something started to happen. The ring was glowing, even brighter than before, drawing me closer, until I picked it up, and placed it on my finger.

And just as the ring slid down my finger into place, I could feel it: something strange. I felt different, instantly better than when I first opened my eyes this morning.

Looking at the ring on my finger, I noticed that when I first put it on it was very big, and did not fit at all, but now, just a few minutes later, it was just right, like it was made for me.

I smiled. I liked the way it made me feel. It made me like me, something I could not do for a very long time.

I took a hot shower and got dressed, and as I stood looking in the mirror, I was not the same. It was me, but better, I thought.

What was happing? Is it the ring? As I held my hand up to the light to take a closer look at it, I smiled again, and grabbed my coat and headed out the door.

All my troubled thoughts were not with me as I walked down the street this day. The insecurities were gone. I wasn't sad. I felt good, like I could do anything.

I looked at the ring as I walked, and smiled again. I felt charged with power, confident, something I had never felt before.

This was it, the change I had always prayed for, and I was going to take full advantage of it. "**What will I do first**?"

To Be Continued?

Taxi

It was starting to rain, and I had to get home. I was tired and starting to catch a cold. Over cast gray cloudy sky moved slowly overhead as I walked clutching my coat down the dimly lit street. I was a man dealing with life one day at a time, and every day was hard and unkind.

I was a working man, but the money I made was nothing to speak of. I was struggling to pay the bills I had, so a thing like having a car was not going to happen for me. I was alone with no one to talk to after the workday was over and I really didn't like talking to the people there anyway. The cars sped by me as I walked and the rain started to fall harder now and I had no umbrella, "Damn."

I hated not having a car; it made me feel less than a man; like I wasn't good enough to have one. The water was starting to run down the streets and into the gutters as the cars came past splashing me, taunting me. "ASSHOLE!"

I walked faster. I was pissed, but the rain came down harder then, like it too made fun of me. And a street that was not so busy became very busy. They all lined up one by one to have their chance to spray me not with just more rainwater, but dirty, muddy gutter water from the street. I stopped and looked back down the now dark street at all the cars coming, my eyes blurred by the rain, making the headlights of the cars all run together.

Slowly I turned and back up the street I went with my head down, just taking it from them, what else could I do? Much like my life, I just took it.

I lived on the other side of town. I had missed the last bus and it wasn't my fault!

My asshole boss made me stay late. I told him I had no ride but the son of a bitch didn't care. He had a brand new car, but he never offered me a ride.

So it rains. What a fucking life! Is it just me? Or is somebody else as miserable as I am?

My whole body was starting to ache; my nose was running all down my face, but I didn't give a shit; I let it run. I was weak and getting tired and the cold was getting worse the later it got.

I saw a bus stop, so I stopped to sit just for a second. The rain was still coming down hard, but all the cars that had lined the street were all at once gone.

Only the sound of the rain hitting the street and me remained. I was alone. Again, like always.

But then, just before I got to my feet, I looked back down the street, and that's when I saw a lone pair of headlights coming up my way.

I don't know why, but I stood there watching it come closer, and closer, and before long it was right next to me, but it didn't splash me.

It stopped, a "TAXI".

Now I never ride in taxis, but I always hear you can never catch one when you need one. But this guy stopped like I had flagged him down or something.

Maybe the driver felt sorry for me? Maybe there are still some good people in the world? Or maybe he just smells an easy fare.

Slowly the window came down, and I leaned down and looked in.

He was a thick-haired and bearded man; he wore a yellow rain coat that matched the cab. I thought to myself, why wear the raincoat in the cab? But whatever. I looked at him and him back at me so I said, "Why did you stop? I didn't flag you down."

"It's a shitty night there, fella. There won't be another bus till tomorrow. This rain is going to dog you all night if you don't get your ass in here."

I was tired. I thought this guy was weird. But I did have a long way to go and I was soaked and just then it was like the rain heard what he had said. It started to come down harder than ever. I said, "Well, I wasn't waiting for a bus—I only have about ten bucks on me. I don't think that's enough to get me home."

The cabbie replied, "Is that right. Well where's home, fella?"

"Wilson Park." I answered.

Then he said, "Fella, you'd be surprised how far ten bucks will get you. You just gotta want to get there, you know what I mean?—Now just get on in here, that rain don't like you at all."

I just wiped my eyes and looked at him, then slowly climbed into the back of the TAXI.

The taxi had an old smell, like from somewhere in my past. It was weird and so was he. I was wet from head to toe, but as I wiped my face I looked out the window and the rain had stopped. I was surprised. "Son of a bitch. It stopped raining."

He said, "Yeah, but soon as you stick your head out of this taxi it's gone start dogging you again, you can believe me, fella. I know. Yes sir, I know all about the dogging rain. It's a lot like life just waiting to soak you in shit."

"I guess you're right," I said as the taxi drove slowly down the still wet street off deep into the night.

The cabbie spoke, "Feels like I've been driving this cab forever and it's always raining on people. The good people. The hard working ones like yourself."

I asked, "How do you know if I'm a hard worker?"

He said, "I can tell. I see it in your eyes—I would have left you at that bus stop and let the rain dog you if you wasn't who I thought you was. I know. I always know—It's my job to know."

I thought about it. "So you only stop for people who you know to be good people?"

"That's right," he said. "This is my cab and I do like I like!! People don't understand what it means to have a ride where you're going. They can't see. They're too busy thinking about everything else they want. But you understand."

"I guess I do? Without a car I feel like I don't have control of my life. Things are so bad sometimes that I don't know what I'm going to do."

"That's right!! A car can keep you dry when the dogging rain comes. Get you there when you need to be there. You know. Some people were meant to get other people where they need to go, and some don't deserve to get anywhere. I see all kinds of people. Some I stop for and others I leave behind."

I told him, "Well if I was driving, I wouldn't want to stop for nobody. Ain't nobody ever stopped for me—other than you tonight."

"You ain't like them. You know what the dogging rain feels like. Everybody ain't the same."

I started coughing really hard. The cabby said, "That cough sounds bad, fella. Here. Take this. It will help that cold the dogging rain gave you."

I took the pills the cabby gave me. For some reason I trusted him now. It was quiet in the taxi for a minute then I said, "I don't know. The rain seems to have stopped. I hope it never comes back.—I'm tired. I'm sick of the rain."

The cabby said, "Go on and rest, fella. The dogging rain won't bother you no more. You can believe me. I know all about the dogging rain, just like you."

I fell asleep right there in the back of the taxi, but when I woke up I wasn't in the taxi anymore. I was back at the bus stop where I first got in. The taxi was parked right in front of me, but the cabby was not at the wheel.

I looked around for him, but I was all alone in the night. In my hand were the keys to the taxi. I understood as I walked around to the driver's side, opened the door and found a yellow raincoat on the seat. I put it on, started my taxi and drove slowly into the night.

And just then the dogging rain started once again.

1801 Through Philly Park

Philadelphia 1999. It was the end of a cold and brutal winter that appeared to have aged this great city to an old Gotham city comic strip.

My name is Trina Williams; I had just relocated to Philly for a new job at an advertising firm. I had applied here several times in the past, but never could seem to land a position. And now this was it.

The city was rough and dark, with sharp, dirty edges that spiked up into the gray mixed with orange skyline. And the chill of winters past stayed ever present, not willing to as of yet, make way for the spring. I was a stranger in a strange place, not knowing anyone or anything. But I was thrilled and growing even more intrigued about my new surroundings.

I was holing up at a pretty nice hotel right in downtown Philly, but the prices wouldn't let me keep this up much longer. So with no car of my own, taxicabs, buses, trains, or good old fashioned walking would soon become my new found reality. But I didn't mind; this it was all so excitingly new. A lifestyle that I had never lived was now mine.

Free from all the people and places of the past, this was something I really wanted and I was determined to succeed.

It was Monday morning and my first day on the new job. My stomach was shaky and unsettled from excitement as I walked down Thread Street to 1700 Sky Tower.

This is where I would start my new career; make the name for myself that I always promised myself I would. Now why should I be afraid of the unknown? Without the courage to move forward, what would I live for?

But this is why I was there, to prove to myself that I would not be afraid. I would not be the kind that would let fear stop me from reaching my goals in life. So I breathed in a deep breath of this cold and dusty atmosphere as I walked into the Sky tower. I found the directory and learned that the Sky Advertising was on the thirtieth floor, the penthouse. So as I walked over to the elevators, I watched all the bustle of all these seemingly important people on their way to work with only one thing on their minds; business. At least that's what it looked like to me.

"Good morning. My name is Trina Williams. It's my first day and I'm supposed to see a Kim Wright?"

"Yes, why don't you have a seat and I'll let her know you're here, Ms. Williams."

"Thank you very much."

As I sat down to wait, my alarm on my cell phone went off, reminding me it was time to take my insulin shot. I was a diabetic my whole life and on insulin as long as I could remember. My cell phone I used as a reminder to take my shot because I was always doing something that would steer me away from this life-giving responsibility. I asked the lady behind the desk for a restroom close by, letting her know I would be right back.

As I returned, standing right by the front desk was Kim Wright. She said,

"You must be Trina Williams. My name is Kim Wright. It's a pleasure to finally meet you in person."

As I looked at her, I smiled, but I was somewhat shocked by her at the same time. Kim was tall and skinny with sandy brown hair and big brown eyes. She was very beautiful but sounded nothing like she looked. Her voice was high pitched and her speech would lead you to believe she was Caucasian, but she was of African American descent.

"It's nice to meet you as well. I'm really excited to be here finally."

"That's great. Let's use David's office. He's out of the office for the whole day and that's good news. Maybe I'll be able to get some real work done, you know what I mean?"

As she started to laugh out loud, I smiled not really knowing what to make of her. I sat with Kim for about twenty minutes, and then she gave me the tour of the whole place. It was wonderful and I knew I was going to love working there. And after all of that was done, she left me at my desk to get settled and start right in. Kim had told me she would come back for me at lunchtime so we could grab some food and get to know each other better.

She was really nice. I liked her, even though she was a little high strung. She was kind which is just what a new person needs when everything is brand new. As the morning continued, I met lots of people in the office who stopped by to welcome me to Sky-tower. Things were going better than I had hoped they would. I was very happy, and then before I knew it, it was time for lunch.

Kim grabbed me by the arm and dragged me to the elevators, talking a million words a second without ever stopping to breathe. She was funny and starting to grow on me even more, but I was starting to realize any hopes for a two-sided conversation was not likely to happen.

She took me to a nice deli where we ordered to go. We walked about a block to the park, Philly Park.

It was really nice as far as I could see, and big as I had ever seen a city park be. Kim began telling me how she comes to the park with people from the office all the time. How much they love coming out here to eat, and to watch all the people coming and going. And I knew what she meant. It was really interesting; all kinds of people from all different walks of life. I felt like the super happy kid in the candy store, trying to take it all in and put my hands on every-thing in my reach. I sat back and smiled as Kim went on telling me about the city and the park, but then came the warning.

"But listen to me, Trina. The park is wonderful for lunch, but not for just strolling through it. This place is a whole different place once the sun goes down."

And just as she said that, a cold breeze rustled through the trees near us, and the papers from our lunch started to blow away.

"But it looks so friendly, so green. How could it ever be so bad?"

"Trust me on this one, Trina. I know. There's been stories I hate to even think about that has happened to people, especially women. So don't go walking around alone in there, you hear me?"

I looked again to the tall trees rippling from the icy wind moving past them. I said,

"I got it. I'll be smart."

"Good. Now, where do you live? Are you close by?"

"I'm right downtown here, at the Tillman hotel."

"Wow that can cost a lot of money, you must be doing well?"

"Not really, it was close to Sky Tower. That's the reason I took it. But I can't stay there much longer. I have to find somewhere to go."

"Really, I wish you could stay with me, but I stay with my boyfriend. But you know what? There may be an apartment open in our same building."

"Really? Can you find out for me?"

"I will. I'll call you tonight and give you all the details and if there is one open, you're going to love it. I mean, they're to die for."

"How far away do you live? I have to be able to get to work every day."

"Well don't forget, I live there too and I make it to work on time every day."

"So you have your own car?"

"No, but my boyfriend does. Mostly I take a cab and if you came too, we could split the fare."

Now that was starting to sound good. I wanted to know more, so I listened as she told me more about the place. She told me it was at 1801 Philly Park, at the very back of this huge park. She told me we could walk to work if we went through Philly Park, but she would never do that. She would always call for a cab. It was funny how she talked about the park in the daytime at lunch, but any other time, like nighttime, was a whole other story. By day, you felt the happiness, but by night, you could feel terror inside Philly Park.

That same night I got a call from Kim; she told me that there was an apartment available for me. And on the weekend, I could come take a look at it, as well as apply for the place if I liked it. So one week more at these high prices and hopefully I would have my own place. I was very happy about how everything was going. I took a hot shower and poured myself a drink.

There I was at the beginning of my new life, hoping to be all I knew I was capable of being and not being afraid of change or of things unknown. I was ready for whatever life had in store for me, or so I thought.

My first week was great. Everything was going well and I met a lot of people who I liked and I knew it wouldn't be long before I would have a lot of new friends. Kim talked a lot about Philly Park, getting me more and more excited about living there. I was really looking forward to Saturday and going to see the place for the first time and being settled in my new place.

The only thing that I thought might be a problem was getting a peaceful moment without Kim beating down my door to visit, but even that I could handle, she was my new good friend.

Saturday morning I woke up like a kid on Christmas day, popping up and running to take a shower and getting a cab to 1801 Philly Park. I was so excited as the cab pulled up in front. It was a six-story building with a red brick front, with black fire escapes from top to bottom. The front doorway was black and oval shaped like that of an old church. It looked to be hundreds of years old.

But this place was in good shape; I couldn't wait to get on the inside. I paid the cabby and headed in. Kim was in 204 so I hit her buzzer.

"Hello. Who is it?"

"Kim, hi it's Trina. I'm here."

She hit the buzzer to let me in and as I walked down the hall to the stairs I looked around. It was old but in good shape just like the outside. The place had charm and I could tell it was built a long time ago. I made my way up the stairs to Kim's door and before I could knock, she opened the door.

"Trina, hello! Come in here. Let me show you my place first."

I followed her around her place and it was nice. I really liked it. The only difference was that hers was a two bedroom and mine would only be a one bedroom. Soon the tour was over and she took me back downstairs to meet the landlord. The landlord showed me the apartment on the third floor, and there I fell in love. He told me I could have it today if I wanted it and you know I did. I signed the lease and paid in cash to move in the same day.

Kim and her boyfriend Nick drove me to get all my things and help me get settled in.

Now everything was in place. I still needed some things but in time I would have them all. I was very happy.

Over the next few months, things were going well at work and at home, things were coming together as well. I would ride into work with Kim by cab and back home in the evening with her by cab, or with Nick if he came to pick us up. There was a cold day I'll never forget. The winds blew hard through the park and rattled the windows of 1801 Philly Park. Today was Kim's boyfriend Nick's birthday, and she had planned to take him out on the town for a night of fun. She wanted me to come home after work and do up the house in birthday balloons and streamers. And take the cake out of the icebox so I could light the candles. That way, as they came through the door, it would be all ready for them.

This was no problem; I wanted to do it for them. After all, they had been so good to me. At work she came by my desk to leave the key with me and to tell me she was leaving early so she could meet up with Nick. I was excited for her. I knew just how much he meant to her. She loved him and would do anything for him. I continued to work when my cell phone rang. It meant time to take my shot, but I figured I would finish up what I was working on and then go and take my shot. As the cold gray sky outside turned black, it opened up letting out a downpour, followed by thunder and lighting. So as the rain came down outside my window, I hoped it would stop before it was time for me to leave for home. This took my mind off my shot. I had forgotten. The work day passed slowly, but now it was time for me to head for home. As I looked out to see if the rain had let up, it had, but the sky still looked as if it would open up to cry down once again.

I put on my raincoat, grabbed my bag and umbrella, and headed out to get a cab for home. I stood outside on the curb trying my best to get a cab, as the cars and cabs passed me by splashing me, drenching me. Now wet, cold, and shivering, I was running late and needed to get home. I had a lot to do for Kim and I didn't want to let her down.

As I stood there hoping for a cab, a light rain began to fall; just what I needed. I turned and looked to Philly Park. This was probably my best chance to get home in enough time. Despite the many warnings I was given about Philly Park, I had to take it. There was still daylight; I could make it before dark if I hurried.

So I pulled my bag up onto my shoulder and started up into the park, every step splashing in puddles of water. My feet were already soaked.

Once in the park, I noticed it was darker than it looked from out on the street. The trees shielded the park from what little daylight there was left.

It was quiet with the sound of soft spraying rain landing gently on the treetops and a light foggy mist hung just above the grass line giving the park a gloomy, dimly lit setting. No wind was present. The trees did not move as they received the light rain. I picked up my pace as I started to feel the discomfort of this place, just hearing the sound of the rain drizzling on the trees. And then the dim park lamps began to flicker, trying to come on, giving the park a whole new look of gloom.

Then it hit me, a wave of dizziness came all over me. It was then as I was walking very fast, that I realized I had forgotten to take my shot. I fought to shake off the dizziness taking a deep breath, but it wasn't really working. I told myself to stay calm and not to panic. I was alone in this place and was not about to stop and open my bag and try to give myself a shot. How could I be so stupid? How could I forget?

It was hard to keep up at that same pace, so I slowed down trying to relax myself and make it all the way home. I started looking around, "What was that? Did I hear something?" Now I was becoming paranoid. Was it real? Or was it the fact that I hadn't had my shot? Now I was starting to think that this was not a good idea, but it was too late to turn back now. I was too deep in.

I moved on, but it became harder and harder to focus my eyes. I was breathing heavily like I didn't have enough air and my legs were getting heavy like I was lifting heavy bags of wet sand. What was happening to me? I was starting to feel like I would never make it to 1801

Through Philly Park.

As I fought to stay conscious and keep moving, the rain started to fall a little harder against the treetops. It was getting darker now. I had slowed down a bit more; far more than I needed to. And then, not too far ahead of me, I could see a park bench. I wiped the rain from my face as I came closer and then I saw him; a man sitting on the bench in a black raincoat and black rain hat. Just sitting in the rain and not moving. I was afraid, but I needed help. I knew now that I would not make it without stopping to take my shot.

As I tried to focus my eyes through the foggy rain mist, I was terrified as I approached this man on the park bench. I started to call out to him. I said,

"Sir, can you help me? Please, sir, can you help me?"

He never looked up; he just sat there with his head down not moving.

Now I stood right in front of him on the bench, and just as I said,

"Sir, can you—"He jumped up and grabbed me, and just as I he did, I blacked out.

Out cold and surrounded by blackness in my mind. I must be dreaming?

I saw images of a black sky with rain coming straight down at me, as I lay on my back helpless, unable to move any part of my body.

My eyes blinked rapidly to shield them from the falling rain's attack. Breathing heavily, I start to panic, and then suddenly, I was awake!

Now as I tried hard to focus my eyes, with rain and leaves mixed with dirt passing by me on both sides, I was moving. I wasn't walking but being dragged by my feet deeper into the darker areas of Philly Park.

This man had me, taking me, but where? Oh my god, he is going to kill me!

Before long we were inside and out of the rain, but it wasn't a house. It was more like a cave, muddy and wet and with a foul odor. I was so weak I couldn't really move. I needed my insulin; my bag was still strapped around my shoulder and chest. I could see the man on the other side of the cave, looking through a big pile of boxes, throwing one after the other out of his way frantically. What was he looking for? And what was he going to do to me? More water ran down the sides of my already wet and dirty face, but this was not rainwater. This was the tears of my terror.

Then he turned to me, walking over and looking down at me. He knelt down next to me, looking at me. I tried to speak, but it was hopeless. His face I could barely make out under the big black rain hat he wore down and almost over his eyes. This was it; I was about to die. My eyes were wide open and fixed on the blackness which would be his face under the hat. My breathing was shallow and I was close to passing out.

He started to run his dirty hands over my face and then down my neck and across my breasts. He squeezed hard and began to breathe heavily as he started to undo my coat and blouse.

Then he pulled off my bra with a hard tug. I was now exposed to him, as he started touching my bare skin with his wet and dirty hands, leaving behind his dirt and smell which was more than I could bear.

Then he heard something from outside the cave. Whatever it was, it saved me from what he was about to do to me. He stopped and went out to see what was going on, leaving me there, cold and wet, on the ground.

With all the strength I could muster, I tried to cover myself. I desperately needed my insulin. And if I was going to live, I had to have it to give me the strength I would need to run away from this man.

I had to fight, so I told myself to start fighting. I moved my hands enough to cover myself before he came back, but this took everything I had. Then he came back into the cave. Whatever he saw out there spooked him and he no longer felt safe in the cave. It was time for us to move. He picked me up this time and said to me, "Walk or die, walk or die."

He put my arm over his shoulder, and his around my waist, and out into the rain we went. My legs felt like steel rods, but I did my best to make them move. As he held me close to him walking in the park with the rain falling on us, the smell that surrounded him was worse than that of death. I was close to throwing up. As we moved, every few feet he would turn to look behind us to see if we were alone, like someone may be following.

By now hours had passed; I didn't know what time it was, but it was getting close to morning. Now I knew he wanted to get me to another spot to rape and even kill me, and before daylight returned. Then, as we moved along slowly, my cell phone started to ring, and this scared him. He jumped back dropping me to the ground and looking around very crazily. Then he turned and ran off into some heavy bushes and out of sight.

Now I lay there in a big puddle of water. This was my only chance to take my shot. I didn't know how far away he was or how fast he would be coming back, but I didn't wait a second. I started to open my bag and get the needle ready looking around in every direction, and just as I was about to take the shot, I dropped the syringe into the puddle of rainwater.

So very quickly I slammed my hand down into the water, feeling around for the needle. And as I did that there he was, less than fifty yards away, looking at me. Then I felt it; the syringe. I quickly pulled it out of the water and gave myself the shot and then he walked toward me. As I put the needle back into my bag, Kim's house keys fell from my bag and into the water. And I started to think that they must have been looking for me by now.

As he came closer, I felt around in the water for her keys. He wasn't moving very fast but he didn't take his eyes off of me as he came closer.

There they were. I pulled the keys from the water. I looked at them, and hanging from her key ring was a small black pepper spray. I clutched in one hand as I watched him come and pick me up from the water.

This was crazy. I was always being the brave one, not afraid of anything, and would never carry pepper spray on my key ring.

But there I was, moving with this man once again. I had taken my shot, so shortly I would start to get my strength back. Hopefully it would happen before this man found a place for me. I was going to use the spray when I was strong enough to run from him. That was my plan.

But I was running out of time. Daylight was coming fast and I knew he wasn't going to keep moving around much longer.

Slowly I started to feel better. My eyes started to focus and my legs began to feel lighter. The rain had passed; the park was silent as he started pulling me into a patch of tall bushes.

As we moved through the wet bushes, they kept slapping me in my face as he was now pulling me behind him. I had to make my move. I had to make it now, or I was going to die.

So all at once I let myself fall down, like I couldn't go on anymore. My eyes closed as I cried out for the first time. He stopped and looked down at me and when I opened my eyes, he started to remove his pants. I looked away and that's when I saw her. She was dead and naked, her body was decaying, and she was a bloody, twisted mess. This was one of his victims, the one before me. I screamed as he came down on top of me. I readied the pepper spray and shot him right in the face.

He fell back screaming and holding his eyes. I got up as fast as I could and started running back through the bushes to the main path and he gave chase

Staggering and trying to see, he was having a hard time, but he kept coming after me. Somehow he did.

Daylight was starting to make its way through the trees of the park. Moving as fast as I could, I could see 1801 up at the end of path. I was almost there.

When I turned to look back, there he was, running up behind me.

I screamed, hoping that somebody would hear me. I was almost there, but he was right behind me now. I didn't think I was going to make it out.

But just as I came to the end of the path, and right in front of 1801, he reached out and grabbed me, and I fell hard to the ground.

When I looked up he was gone! That's when I heard someone say, "Are you alright?"

It was a young man with his dog, returning from an early morning walk.

It was over.

He came running over and helped me inside. I had made it, but I don't know how I did. How could something like this happen in a place as beautiful as this park? I had learned why some people fear the unknown, or the uncertainties of change. Now I know, and for the rest of my life, I would fear it as well. I felt after that like I could make it through life and survive. I could do it. Since I was able to make it **Through Philly Park!**

The Back 9

It was a warm, beautiful, early morning summer day at Hillside Green, which was a private country club for members only. The men and women who played golf at Hillside were very wealthy indeed, people like Doug Fenton. Doug had been a member for over five years now and he loved to play early morning practice rounds alone to get ready for the weekend matches with his friends. They were all very wealthy as well, and gambling for money was always the thing to make a good round of golf a great round.

And the dollar amount of the wagers was always more than the blue-collar worker could ever dream of making all year. This was what he did, they all did, and it was fun to them and very private.

#1
489 par 4

This particular morning Doug had the whole 18 to himself, as he hurried to the first tee. Taking out his Wilson driver, he started to stretch, loosening up before teeing off the 489-yard par 4.

Out of nowhere, a man walked up to the first tee. Doug had never seen this man before and he knew everybody who played here. The man approached him with a warm, friendly smile just like most golfers, and said,

"Mind if I go around with you?"

Doug was surprised to see anybody, especially a man he had never met before. He was set to go off alone and get in his practice for the weekend. But it would be rude to just say no, so Doug said,

"Sure, why not."

The man was middle-aged with gray hair, a little overweight but neatly dressed as he puffed on a cigar.

The man said, "The name's Newman. Carl."

"Doug Jones. It's nice to meet you."

"I'm new here, don't know anybody yet. As you can see, I'm looking to change that this morning." He laughed out loud, shaking Doug's hand firmly.

Newman said, "You just trying to get a little practice in this morning?"

"Yes, just trying to get ready for the weekend." As he got himself ready to tee off.

"Nothing like this game. Don't know what I'd do if I couldn't play, I just love it."

"Yeah, it's a great game." Doug was already wishing he had left a little earlier then maybe he would have missed Mr. Newman. Doug was trying to tee off, but this guy just wouldn't close his big mouth.

Newman continued to talk, "Look, you're a wealthy man. I'm a wealthy man too. Let's make this round interesting, what do you say?" Doug looked at him. He already told him he was just practicing, and this guy just didn't get it. But he went on saying,

"See, it's like this to me; money is no big deal, but playing golf is, and I like a challenge. It makes the game fun, and that's all we're really doing, right? Having fun**. It's just a game."**

Doug started taking a few practice swings, thinking to himself,

"This guy is an asshole." And then Doug said,

"All right, what do you want to play for?"

"Now, that's what I wanted to hear. Let's start slow and work our way up as we go around. That way you get to see my game, and I get to see yours."

"Sounds fair to me."

"Good, how about we make it a **skins** match. We'll put something on every hole as we go."

"All right, first tee will be worth $500.00."

"Come on, Doug old boy, surely you can do better than that? Let's make it $5,000."

"I thought you said start slow?"

"Doug, old boy, that is slow." Doug looked at him and agreed to play; they shook hands and Doug teed off first.

Doug set up to hit his first shot. Newman was finally quiet as Doug hit a nice drive right down the middle of the fairway. Newman said,

"Nice shot, Doug old boy. It's right down the middle."

Doug just smiled looking at the shot, thinking he was about to take all this man's money.

"You're up, Newman. Hit a good one." Doug said as he walked to the side of the tee. Newman pulled out a shiny new driver, which looked like he had never used it and walked up to the tee. Newman took a slow back swing and ripped one straight down the middle about 40 yards past Doug's.

He said, "Now that's a tee shot, old boy." Doug said, "Good one." As he frowned and grabbed his bag and headed up the fairway.

Doug hit a pretty nice shot onto the green about 30 feet from the hole; Newman hit one right at it, about 5 feet.

Doug missed the putt, but Newman made his and won the first hole. He was up $5,000.

The next four holes, Doug lost every one to Newman, and was very upset with the way he was playing. But Newman was good, better than Doug thought he would be.

Newman started talking a lot of bullshit about the fact that Doug had not won one hole. $25,000 is what Doug was down, and was tired of hearing Newman's mouth. He started to lose it. He said,

"It's no big fucking deal. I've been down a lot more and still came out on top, so if I were you, I wouldn't talk so much shit."

"Hey, Doug, old boy, don't get upset. It might take you out of your game, but that might not be a bad idea, because you're playing like shit." He laughed out loud.

Doug said, "Is that so? Well, let's make it $10,000 a hole for the rest of the front 9, since I'm playing like shit. What do you have to lose?"

Newman smile dropped real fast to a put up or shut up look. Doug just stared him down, letting him know just how serious he really was. Then Newman said,

"Well, why not? You just might not have enough left to play here after today." Then he walked past Doug to the next tee.

#6
566 par 5

Newman drove the ball once again straight down the middle, about 289 yards. Another great shot. Doug was trying to concentrate on his shot when Newman started jumping up and down saying how he had never hit a better shot than that. Doug was losing it, not the game but his mind. He said,

"Would you please shut the hell up so I can hit!!" Newman stopped and looked at him. He said,

"Don't forget, old boy**, it's just a game."**

Doug walked past him and got ready to tee off; he was trying to calm down to hit the ball. He stood over it longer than he normally would, but this ass had really gotten to him. Doug swung hard and the ball started off right down the middle, but soon started to turn, slicing hard to the right going fast into the trees. Doug screamed,

"God damn it!!" and then walked fast down the fairway after his bad shot, with Newman following close behind. Newman smiled and said,

"Would you like me to help you find your ball, old boy?"

But Doug didn't say a word. He just kept walking.

Doug really wanted to kill Newman as he looked through the trees trying to find his ball, and before long, there it was. It was close to a tree, and all he could do was punch it back out of the trees into the fairway, so that's what he did. Newman's second shot was good as well, right on the green about 15 feet from the hole, Doug was sick, he couldn't believe it. Doug hit his third, and it was good, about 15feet left as well.

Newman was set to putt. He looked at it closely, reading the putt. If Newman made this, there would be no need for Doug to putt his in this game of skins.

Newman hit the putt, and Doug's eyes opened wide as the ball looked like it was going to miss on the right side of the hole, but at the last second it turned back, and fell right in the hole.

"YES!" Newman screamed, "Thirty-five big ones, old boy!!"

#9
155 par3

The game went on, but it wasn't good for Doug. He lost the next two holes. They were now ready to hit the last hole of the front 9.

Newman went first, and hit a nice shot onto the green about 20 feet from the hole. He said, "Not my best, but I'll take it."

Doug set up and hit a shot that flew straight at the stick. It was good, I mean real good. The ball hit about 10feet right in front of the hole and rolled right up and…IN!!!

A HOLE IN ONE!

Newman couldn't believe it. Doug said, "This is where it all changes, OLD BOY." And Newman had nothing to say for the first time in the round.

Doug felt good going to the back 9. He thought he was ready to take the money he lost on the front back from this crazy man. Doug looked at him as they walked up to the first tee of the back 9. He was ready. Newman had a strange look on his face, almost like he hated Doug.

Doug said to him when he noticed the look,

"What is it Newman? You ready for the back 9?"

Newman slowly started to smile looking right at Doug, and then it turned to laughter. He said,

"Do you think you're ready, old boy?"

"I know I'm ready." Newman pulled out another cigar and lit it up, as Doug got ready to hit his first shot on **the back 9.**

#10
401 par 4

This was a very private club, very secluded. No homes lined the fairways. There were no people anywhere; it was just the two of them.

Golf is a gentleman's sport, but truly is a game of pressure. Sometimes this pressure can make the difference between winning and losing, but we know when the stakes are high pressure can kill you! Doug had no idea how much pressure this back 9 would hold for him, and even more, his LIFE.

Doug was ready and just about to hit his shot when Newman said,

"Hold on there, old boy. I think it's time to raise the stakes a bit. You know this is a big golf course, very secluded. We're all alone out here on the back 9. A man could do just about whatever he wanted to out here. Nobody would hear or ever know."

Doug stopped and looked at him and said,

"Just what the hell are you talking about now, Newman?"

"I think I'm done playing. I'm just going to watch you play to 18."

"So what, I win one hole and you want to quit?"

"Oh no, old boy, I'm not quitting. We still can play for money and even more."

"What the hell are you getting at, Newman?"

"Well, we have nine holes left. What's more important than money to you…your car? Or let's say your house? Maybe your wife and kids?"

"Look, you son of a bitch, I don't know where you came from or what the hell you're talking about, but I think you should leave. Our round is over."

"See, there you go again, old boy. You're getting yourself all upset again. You have to try and remember, it's just a game and it's not over until I say it's over." Doug looked at him for just a second, then started over to his bag to put his club back in and leave. As he passed him he said,

"Fuck you!"

And just as Doug was about to put the club back into his bag**, it happened**. A gunshot rang out and hit his bag knocking it over, and scaring Doug to the ground.

Newman started laughing as Doug frantically looked around to see where the shot had come from. It wasn't Newman, so Doug said,

"What's going on?!"

Newman said, "Like I said, it's not over until I say it is."

"Who are you? What do you want from me?"

"I just want you to play, that's all." Newman said, as he sat back in his golf cart puffing on his cigar.

"I don't understand. Who shot at me? Why are you doing this?"

"If you don't play, you die. And if you don't play well, your wife or your kids will die. And if you play like shit, they all die."

Doug's expression now turned to terror as he looked at this man. He couldn't believe what he was saying or why?

Newman said,

"Look up the fairway. There's a man, a friend of mine, in the trees with a high-powered rifle pointed right at you. He will kill you if you try and run. He will kill you if you don't play, so calm down, old boy. Your life and your family's lives depend on your game today. How's that for pressure?" He laughed out loud again. Doug slowly got to his feet and said,

"Please don't kill me. I'll give you whatever you want."

"All I want is for you to play, so get your club and get your ass on the tee. This is a par 4. You must par this hole and the next one, so try to think about the shot and nothing else. I would if I were you, old boy."

Doug was now shaking with fear, as he walked up to the tee, looking down the fairway, not knowing what to do. What could he do? Nothing, but…PLAY. Newman sat back and watched as Doug got set to hit his shot. He was sweating heavily, trying to hold it all together, not knowing if at any minute he could be killed.

Somehow he hit the ball. It was going right, but stayed fair. Newman said,

"Nice one, old boy." They started down the fairway to the next shot. Doug made it on the green with his second shot and made the putt in three strokes. The next hole he pared as well, somehow he did**, but it wasn't over yet.**

Two down with seven more to go, it was like walking through hell on a sunny day. The birds were singing, but all Doug could hear was silence. How could this be happening? Who knew? It just was. Then Newman said,

"Look, old boy, you're doing well. I thought you would be dead by now, shows how much I know. The next two holes must be birdies or better. Don't let me down, old boy."

"Please don't do this! I can't go on, I can't do it!!" Then a second shot rang out at Doug hitting a tree right behind him.

"Oh my God!! Please, I'll do it! Make him stop, please!!!"

Newman, laughing, said,

"You make him stop when you play, old boy." Doug was in tears trying his best to pull himself together to hit the shot.

Doug somehow pulled it together and got through the next two holes. He did it and was a little more confident after that.

Four down with five to play. He was starting to feel like he wasn't ever going to see his family again, but he had to try. All he had left was just this game.

Newman looked to him again and said,

"The next hole is a long par 5 you must make it on the green in two. If not, you'll pay with your wife's life.

Doug started to cry once again. He had played this course many times and had never gotten on the green in two shots ever before.

As he set to hit the shot, his mind left him and he couldn't see the ball right in front of him. This game he loved had turned on him. It had him and would not let him go.

Doug hit the shot hard and long, but the ball found a fairway bunker of sand, leaving a long second shot of about 160 yards. From the sand it may as well have been longer. He wasn't Tiger Woods. He knew he couldn't get it there in two. Standing in the sand, he looked at Newman and said,

"I can't make this shot, not from the sand. There's no way I can."

Newman said, "So you're not even going to try, old boy?"

And before he could answer, a third shot rang out hitting the sand and spraying it right in Doug's eyes. Now he couldn't even see.

Doug was on his knees holding his eyes, and Newman said,

"If it was my wife, I would try. I would think about her."

Doug jumped up and grabbed his club and hit the ball all the way on the green in two. Newman couldn't believe it, and neither could Doug. He survived another one.

Five down and four to play. With his eyes still burning from the sand, he made it through the next two holes, and had just two left.

The next hole was another par 3.

Newman said, "You must put your first shot on the green, or you'll pay with your kids' lives." Slowly Doug pulled his club. This point exhausted him, but now he wasn't going to give up.

Doug hit the shot, and right on the green it went, then it happened: another shot rang out and just grazed his arm. Doug screamed out,

"Why? It's on the green! Why did he shoot me?"

Newman laughed and said, "That's just a scratch, old boy. You're not shot. This will just make the last hole one to remember."

Doug was bleeding, and his arm was hurt but not badly enough to stop him from hitting the last hole on **the back 9.**

The last was a par 4. 369 yards was all he had left. Newman said,

"Well, Doug, old boy, this is it. You think you can do it? All you need is a par here."

Doug closed his eyes and prayed. He knew that this man was going to kill him; he could see it in his eyes. But he had come this far, so he was going to finish.

Doug's drive was good, and his second shot made it on the green. All he had left was a 20-foot putt. Then Newman said,

"This is it, old boy, last putt of the day, but it's not going to be easy."

Doug looked at the putt as his hands shook, sweating as he gripped the putter. He took a deep breath and hit the putt. It looked good as it came close to the hole. Doug's eyes opened wide as he watched, thinking he was about to die if it missed. The ball slowed as it came closer to the hole, and as it rolled up it stopped, and Doug closed his eyes tight. He had missed it.

It was silent as he stood in the middle of the green with his eyes closed, not moving, just waiting to hear the next gunshot that would end his life.

But it never came. As Doug opened his eyes he could hear the birds singing, and the trees waving in the wind.

What happened? Doug looked around and Newman was gone, but he had left a note on the golf cart for Doug.

The note said,

> *Thank you for letting me go around with you. I had a ball. Found this out about you today, money really isn't the most important thing to you, the front 9 proved that.*
>
> *But your family is, don't ever forget that. Whenever you come to the back 9 for the rest of your life, I'm sure you'll do well.*
>
> *P.S. Now it's over, but remember,*
> *it's just a game.*
> *NEWMAN*

Reflection

When you look into the mirror, what do you see? Do you see yourself?

Or is it just a "Reflection."

May 1967. A soon to be father races through traffic with his expectant wife, who is at any second about to give birth to their twin boys. He presses hard on the gas in a panic, moving in and out the way of cars, trying to get his wife there in time. Sweating and breathing heavily she was, in between the horrible screams of labor pains.

Somehow they made it. Just as they were taking her from the car, the first of the two boys started to crown. He was coming fast. And after a long full day of child labor, they both were born: Simon and Shawn King.

The boys were strong and healthy and their parents were very proud.

This time was a happy time, growing and learning, just being together. And as the boys grew, they became very close, and to look at them you couldn't tell one from the other. The only way even their own mother could tell them apart was that Shawn had a small deformity of his left ear, and even that was almost impossible to see. When the boys reached their late teen years, they went their separate ways. Simon went to college and Shawn went into the Marines. Simon went on to become a powerful businessman, while Shawn also did well in the service.

Simon later in life fell deeply in love with the girl of his dreams. Soon they were married with two kids of their own. Life was good for

Simon and getting better every day. Shawn wrote to his brother off and on, just to say hi and to tell all his around the world stories he had to tell, but Simon never wrote back. He still loved his brother, he just would always find himself rushing off and working. He could really never find enough time to sit and write his brother back. This bothered Shawn, but he tried to understand his brother was a busy man. Shawn's last letter to his brother was to let him know that he was coming home in one week and that he couldn't wait to see him and meet his new family.

Simon never responded, but Shawn was still excited to get home.

Simon told his wife Rose all about his twin brother Shawn and how they looked exactly alike. He also told her how close they where growing up. Rose found the whole thing interesting. She had seen pictures of the two of them together, and couldn't tell one from the other. He told her that the only difference was Shawn's ear. It alone separated the two. Sometimes she would tease Simon saying, "If you keep making me crazy, I'll trade you back for your brother." And they would laugh; it was all in good fun.

It was a Saturday. Simon was out front cutting the grass when the cab pulled up in front of his house. It was his brother Shawn, whom he hadn't seen for the past eight years. As Shawn stepped out of the cab, Simon stopped the mower, and they looked at each other. It was just then that they both realized how much they really looked alike.

"Shawn?" he said as he began to smile, walking toward him.

"How are you brother?" He said, as they embraced each other.

"How are you? You look great. Well, you look just like me." Simon said,

"Well some things never change, man." As Simon grabbed his bag and started with his arm around his brother into the house.

"Rose, where are you?" Simon called, as they walked into the house.

"I'll be right there, honey." She said from upstairs where she was getting dressed.

"You have a very nice home, Simon."

"Thanks, it took a lot of hard work. It was a mess when we first got here."

Then Rose came walking down the stairs, and her mouth dropped open. She was without words, as she stared at the two of them.

"Rose, I would like you to meet my brother Shawn, and Shawn, this is my wife Rose."

"It's nice to finally meet you, Rose. You are as beautiful as my brother has told me you were."

"Thank you, Shawn. I'm sorry, it's just unreal, but welcome home."

As she walked over to him and gave him a hug, she captivated Shawn. His eyes glazed over as he looked at her.

"Are you hungry? I'll make something good for dinner. You are staying for dinner. Right, Shawn?"

"Well, I don't want to impose on my brother the first day I get home."

"You're nuts, man, you have been gone too long. Of course he's staying for dinner." Simon said, as he pushed Shawn into the living room to sit and talk.

They sat and drank, talking and laughing about old times for hours, waiting on dinner. The kids came home and met their uncle Shawn; they too couldn't believe how much he looked like their dad. They all got acquainted and had a wonderful dinner. It was a real homecoming for Shawn, he was happy to be with his brother once again. But as they ate, Shawn looked at Rose with lust in his heart. He tried not to, but he couldn't control how he was feeling.

After dinner they sat talking and drinking. Simon got pretty drunk and passed out on the sofa, leaving Shawn up with Rose talking. Shawn took the opportunity to ask all about their lives, and what his brother had been doing over the last eight years, and she told him all kinds of things.

Shawn was staying at their parents' house, where they both grew up. Their parents had passed away some years ago, but the house was still theirs. He had been home over a month now. Everything was good. He and Simon and his whole family got together almost every day, doing things, going places, having all kinds of fun. It seemed like things were going to be all right, but Shawn still was fighting the way he was feeling about Rose. Some days Shawn would drive by the house in the evening and park his car close to the corner, so he could see the house and Rose going in or out. He was beginning to be obsessed with the thought of her.

One night Shawn called Simon over to their parents' house where he was staying. He said he needed Simon to help move a big dresser into the basement.

Simon told him he would be right over. It was evening; the day had already gone to darkness, as Simon pulled up to the house he and his brother grew up in. He walked in and called to Shawn, and Shawn said,

"I'm in the basement. Come on down here." So he started down the stairs. He said, "Shawn, it's dark down here. Don't you have a light?"

"I know it's a little dark, but I'll get us more light."

So Simon went on down. As he came to the bottom of the stairs, he looked around. He said, "Shawn, where are you? I can't see anything."

And just as he said that, out ran Shawn, up from behind, and with a shovel in his hand. He smashed his brother in the head, knocking him unconscious.

Simon started to come around. His eyes were trying to focus, but he still could not see. The room was completely dark, and his hands and feet were tied tightly.

He was in a lot of pain; the back of his head was cut open and bleeding badly. At this point, he had no idea what had really happened.

But the truth was, his brother had done this to him, put him here and left him alone. Shawn wanted what his brother had: his family. And this was his plan to take it all from him. Simon called to him once he got himself together and remembered why he had come there in the first place. But there was no answer. He was alone. He thought that whatever happened to him must have happened to his brother as well, but Shawn was now home with Simon's wife, in bed making love.

The night went on. He tried to get free, but he was tied up too tightly. There was no way he was going to get himself free. Simon was losing a lot of blood, and getting weaker by the minute. He closed his eyes to deal with all the pain he was in. Night had become day and the sunlight squeezed though the gaping paper on the basement windows. Now the room had some light, enough to make out what was in the room. Simon started looking around and was sick to his stomach at what he saw: all kinds of pictures of Rose and the kids, but mostly of Rose. Pictures of people he worked with and friends, dates of business meetings that were coming up, and more pictures of cards and letters he had given to Rose and her to him.

He started breathing heavily as he broke out into tears mixed with screams of terror. He started to pass out as he realized that this was his whole life in this room, a puzzle of pieces being put together which revealed his whole life, but why? Then he was out cold.

That day came and went. It was night once again. Simon was in and out of consciousness, and he was in worse shape now and badly needed water, not to mention medical attention. As he lay there bound tightly, he stared at the big picture of Rose, praying that she and his children were okay.

Shawn was no longer Shawn King. He was Simon King. He had replaced his brother in every way. Simon's life was now his family and all the rest, and there was nothing Simon could do.

One whole week had passed. With no food or water, he was close to death. It was evening and Shawn was sitting down to dinner with Simon's family.

They ate dinner laughing and talking about the day's events just as they always did, and no one had any idea that the man sitting at the head of the table was not who they thought he was.

Not even Rose, who had slept with him every night for the past week.

After dinner, they all settled in for the night, and Shawn sat in the living room in Simon's chair looking out the window. Rose walked up to him, putting her arm around his neck and said,

"Is everything all right, Simon?" he didn't answer right away. As he looked out the window and not back at Rose, he said,

"I want it to be…but I think I need to do it another way." Rose looked at him strangely. She said, "What are you talking about?" He turned to look at her and ran his fingers though her hair. He said,

"Don't worry, Rose, everything is going to be just fine. You still believe in me and love me, don't you?"

"You know I do. You know how much I love you, Simon." She moved to him and kissed him on the mouth with passion. He then jumped up and said,

"I'll be right back. You get yourself ready for bed and I'll be right back."

Then out the door he went, straight over to his parent's house where he had left his brother to die.

He walked in and down to the basement, turned on the light with his back to his brother. He called out to him to try and wake him up.

"Simon…SIMON!" Simon slowly tried to open his eyes. He was still alive, barely. Simon opened his eyes trying to see, but he was so weak that this was really hard. Shawn stood at the end of the couch that his brother was still tied up on with his back to him. Simon looked.

He could barely see, but could make out that someone was standing there. He said with a very weak voice,

"Who are you…have you done this to me?"

"Yes, I have done this to you."

"Why?"

"I'm not the same anymore. I'm not who you remember."

"What are you saying? WHO ARE YOU?" As fear and terror started to build out of control, Shawn said,

"We may carry the same blood, and even look alike, but we're different. We're nothing alike."

"Oh my God, is that you…Shawn?"

Shawn slowly turned to him, showing his face the same face Simon knew so well. Simon was mortified. Shawn looked down at him on the couch and said,

"I was going to leave you here to die, but I can't do it. You're still my brother."

Simon just looked at him, shaking and not saying a word.

Shawn put water and some food on Simon's lap, and made it so he could drink and eat, but he still could not get up on his own. He was bloody, wet and soiled by his own bodily waste. Simon then said,

"Let me die now. I'm going to die anyway; you're not going to keep coming back here to feed me. Why are you here now?"

"I wanted you to know it was me. It will all be the same, Simon. No one will ever know or feel bad. Your family will still be happy."

He turned and headed up the stairs, but stopped and looked back at his brother. He said,

"It is not you I see lying there, Simon. I see myself." Then he was gone.

Another two weeks had passed. Shawn was leading his new life as his brother Simon, and he had not been back to see his brother. He figured he was dead by now. One night, it was about two in the morning. Shawn was asleep in bed with Rose. The kids were spending the night at a friend's.

The house was silent as Shawn slept, and then something woke him.

"Simon...Simon!"

Shawn opened his eyes quickly out of a sound sleep, looking around. Rose was still asleep. He thought it was a bad dream so he lay back down to go back to sleep. Then he heard it again.

"Simon...Simon!" Now he knew he wasn't dreaming, so he got up without waking Rose to see what it was. A storm was coming, outside as well as in. Shawn made his way out of the bedroom. Then from down at the end of the dark hall, and coming from inside the bathroom, he heard it again,

"Simon...Simon!"

Now Shawn slowly walked down towards the bathroom, looking, trying to see in the darkness of the house.

Now he was right outside the bathroom door. The door was almost closed, but not all the way. He reached out to push the door open, and looked in.

He walked in slowly, and right in front of him was the mirror. He looked at the mirror. Staring at it, he said,

"Is that you Simon?" he looked and then he heard,

"Yes...it is me!"

Then, all of a sudden, the glass from the shower door burst into a million pieces, as Simon came crashing out, and onto his brother Shawn.

They fought, rolling on the floor. Simon kicked Shawn out of the bathroom and back down the hall to the stairs. Rose jumped up screaming as they fought, and they tumbled down the stairs.

Then Shawn got up and grabbed a lamp off the table and hit Simon in the head, knocking him out cold, but just for a few seconds. And just as Simon woke up, Rose ran down the stairs. Shawn straddled of Simon and began to strangle his brother to death. Rose stood on the steps looking down. It was dark and hard for her to see whom Simon was fighting.

She screamed,

"Stop it! You're going to kill him!" She ran and turned on the light, and now she could see it was his brother Simon was fighting against. She repeated,

"Simon, stop! You're going to kill your own brother!" He said calmly,

"He must die…it's the only way."

Then as Rose stared down at him on top of his brother, her eyes opened wide. She gasped out, "Oh, my God!" And she ran from the room.

Shawn was just about to choke out Simon's last breath, when Simon asked him,

"Who is it, my brother? Who is about to die? Is it me or is it you?"

Out of nowhere came Rose with Simon's gun. She cocked the trigger and said, "It's you, Shawn." And she pulled the trigger, killing him right on top of his brother.

Months had passed. It was all over. Simon was back with his family, and trying to rebuild their lives. They were sitting in the living room, looking out their window when Simon asked Rose,

"That night, how did you know which one was Shawn?" She smiled and said,

"It was his ear. As I stood over him, I could see it clearly. He wasn't you, he was just…a bad REFLECTION."

Make Believe

Do you believe everything you see? Touch, feel?

The human mind is the world's most powerful instrument. But it is also very easily manipulated. How good is your perception? And how well do you rationalize? Some people feel strong when it comes to these things, and others feel weak.

I could paint a picture in your mind, and make you believe whatever I want you to believe. But only if you truly would—Believe!

Nathan Wade was an extraordinary young man: the world's youngest scientist of experimental technology. Also, he was the youngest man ever to be considered for the Nobel peace prize.

He was a young man with all his dreams being realized one by one. His life and future seemed bright and certain. He was very charismatic in his ways and lovable to all who knew him well, with his realistic principles on life and times. Nathan was strong, athletic, and very handsome. What a catch he would be for any young woman lucky enough to possess him.

So dedicated to his work he was, he never took the needed time for a lover; fearful of the distractions it would bring. Nathan was working on a top-secret project for the United States government. This involved animal testing with the use of experimental drugs. The process was long and tiring causing him tremendous stress and anxiety. And because of the kind of man he was, he handled it very well. But everyone has his breaking point, and so did Nathan.

During this kind of testing animals died. Not something Nathan was proud of, but it is a price that must and will be paid. Nathan's goal was to create something beneficial to all mankind. At least this was Nathan's goal, but as for everyone else, who can really say? We know this; it was supposed to be for the good of all mankind, but not to his downfall.

Nathan worked alongside other top scientist on this project for two years. And as they came closer to completion, something went wrong. There was an explosion in the lab that caused deadly chemicals and gas to spill. Two scientists were killed. Nathan was badly injured. He was infected by the chemicals used in the experiment; he fell into a coma for months. The doctors had no idea if he would ever regain consciousness. They had only prayer and hope.

Some how their prayers were heard, and Nathan came back from the darkness, and opened his eyes to life once again. Only now his life had changed. He no longer had the ability to walk. Being sentenced to a chair with wheels for the rest of his life was a hard obstacle to overcome even for a man like Nathan. Retired at such a young age, he began to rebuild his life. It was different way of life, far different from what he was accustomed to.

As time moved on, Nathan would have massive migraines. They knocked him unconscious for minutes at a time. This was a very emotional time for him. This made it very hard to deal with what had now happened to his life. Not only his lifestyle, but the man himself had changed. So much so that he started to hide his true feeling and emotions from all those who knew him well, but why?

Nathan lived in a beautiful neighborhood in a huge home and all alone, with the exception of his animals. It was in Dallas Texas. In the small community of people, just a few knew Nathan personally. His routines on a daily basis were often the same. Some said they could set their watches by it and never miss a beat. He was loved and respected by everyone and he in return did the same. But all the while he was fighting what he was now feeling on the inside. Not knowing what to make of his new focus and perceptions of things he never seemed to be able to lock onto before.

The migraines would come to haunt him unexpectedly time and time again. Nathan was always a lover of animals; this is what made the experiments of his past so hard to do. In his home, he had fish, birds, and a monkey named Sam. The monkey was like the son that Nathan never had. He loved Sam so.

Sam was always on Nathan's shoulder when Nathan would take his morning ride in his chair down his street every day. They would stop to talk to everyone along the way. Nathan and Sam were inseparable; you never saw one with out the other.

Nathan spoke to Sam as if he was another human being. And Sam responded to him as if they understood one another. Not in words, but a form of understanding that was unreal. The way in which they communicated was incredible to say the least. It was unforgettable after seeing it. Nathan also had a lab set up in his basement, where he worked on ideas; he never seemed to be able to work them out before. But now his focus and the clarity of thought were sharper somehow. He was driven to places in his mind that frightened him, but also intrigued him at the same time.

It was one in the morning. Nathan lay asleep in bed, twisted in a nightmare that only his mind could create. Suddenly his eyes opened and his body was covered in sweat as his heart raced in great terror. No longer could he sleep after such a dream. He got up and rolled himself to the kitchen with Sam on his shoulder. He opened the icebox, and poured himself a tall glass of milk. He sat in his chair with Sam. He held the cold glass of milk in his hand in the middle of his dimly lit kitchen. His eyes and head locked on the glass and he wasn't moving.

It was silent without a sound. Then Sam screamed, he jumped off Nathan's shoulder and ran from the kitchen. Nathan remained very still as he began to take a drink. As soon as he took his first sip, he returned the glass to the arm of his chair. His eyes closed tightly and his body began to shake.

The glass slowly slipped through his fingers, and fell crashing to the hard kitchen floor. His body returned to calm and the shaking had passed. He then placed his hands on the arms of the chair and started to stand, unsteady at first and then sound. Now he stood in the puddle of spilled milk on his own for the first time since the accident. He left the kitchen, walking on his own, and also leaving the chair behind.

He dressed and went out to his van, started the engine, and drove away. Nathan was driving and driving, not knowing where or why he was driving. Then bright lights blinded him from one side of the road: it was a bar, a topless bar. He walked in and took a seat far back in the dark corners of the bar. He watched the dancers taking their clothes off and stripping down to nakedness.

Nathan was now lost within his own mind, as he sat watching the naked bodies' images appear and disappear in flashes of light in this smoky, dark place. Before long, one of the girls made her way back to his table.

"Hi, I've never seen you here before, my name is Angel." Nathan looked at her as if he was seeing a woman for the first time.

"My name is Nathan; it is nice to meet you, Angel."

"You look sad. Is something wrong? You can talk to me, Nathan. I'm a really a good listener."

"Somehow I do believe that you are, Angel." He replied as he began to smile.

"Do you enjoy this, Angel?"

"What? Dancing? Not really, but it pays the bills."

"So why are you here?"

"I guess this is my easy way." She said.

"I appreciate your honesty, Angel. It means a lot. Since you have been so honest, you deserve the same from me. If I told you I don't have the ability to walk, would you believe me?"

Nathan then looked deep into her eyes. The girl was motionless as she stared back into his. The room seemed to slow down. Everything and everyone was now moving in slow motion, but only to the both of them.

Angel stood and began to dance in this dreamlike state. Nathan eyes stayed glued to her now naked body. Nathan had never even seen a woman in this way. He was taken at this moment. He was gone.

The music stopped and so did Angel as she moved in close to him. Placing her hands on both of his legs she said,

"I believe you."

Nathan then gave the girl his card and a one hundred dollar bill. He told her to meet him at that address tomorrow night. Then right in her plain sight, he stood up and walked out of the club. The next morning, just like clockwork Nathan and Sam headed down their street for their morning workout. Nathan was not walking or running, excited to have the use of his legs again, but in his chair with Sam on his shoulder as always. It was as if last night never happened, but did it? Maybe Nathan wanted it this way? Or maybe that's what he wants us to believe?

The next evening at about eight o' clock, his doorbell rang. It was the dancer from the club. Nathan opened the door, still in his chair.

"Come in, Angel. It's nice to see you."

"It's nice to see you, Nathan." He turned in his chair and moved to the living room with Angel following close behind.

"Have a seat and make yourself at home."

They sat across the room from each other for a few moments, no one saying a word as they looked at each other. Then Angel asked,

"How long have you been in that chair, Nathan?"

"Not that long really, but it feels like its been forever."

"It must be hard not being able to walk. I feel really bad for you."

"That's really nice of you to say, but I don't want you to feel bad for me. Sometimes things happen for a reason, and I'm starting to understand my reason for being in this chair."

Nathan then looked deep into her eyes, from across the room. He then looked down at the coffee table between them. There was nothing on the table,

"Do you see the flower in the vase on the table in front of you?"

"Yes I see it."

"Do you know what color the flower is?"

"It's white."

"And what kind of flower do you see?"

"It's a tulip."

"Isn't it beautiful?"

"Yes it is."

"Come with me, Angel."

Nathan was still in the chair rolling back to one of the bedrooms; with Angel following close behind once again. In this room there was a huge bed and one table with two glasses on it. One glass was filled with only water, but the other was clearly filled with ammonia. The smell was very strong. There was no way this could ever be mistaken for anything else.

Nathan moved his chair over closer to the table; Angel was seated on the side of the bed.

"What would you like me to do, Nathan?"

"What do you want to do, Angel?"

"I don't know, but I would really like to make you happy."

"You would like to make me happy?"

"Yes."

"Do you really know what it means to be happy?"

"I think I do, but I've never been truly happy, so how could I really know for sure?"

"So how could you do this for me? Make me happy, that is?"

"You could tell me, just show me how."

Nathan then looked deep into her eyes. He said to her,

"Do you see the two glasses of water on the table?"

"Yes"

"It would make me happy if you took one, and drank it down. Will you do that for me?" Angel took the one glass and drank it all the way down.

"How do you feel? Was it cool and refreshing to you?"

"Yes."

"Now it would make me happy if you take the other glass, and drink it down as well. Will you also do that for me?" Angel reached for the last glass. She picked it up and started to drink it. She gagged as she drank, but she didn't stop until the glass was empty.

She fell back on the bed with her mouth and eyes wide open. Nathan then stood up out of his chair once again, and walked over to the bed. He climbed up over her body and looked into her eyes. She started to gag again, and had trouble breathing, and then he said to her,

"Was that also good and refreshing to you?"

"Yes."

Then she closed her eyes to die.

A few weeks had passed and things were the same for Nathan. He was still in his chair, going on with his everyday life. It was a Saturday. Nathan went to the local library to do some research. As he sat in his chair at a table, a young woman came with books and sat down across the table from him,

"Hello, how are you?" Nathan said with a nice welcoming smile. The woman started her work and Nathan continued to read. An hour or better had passed now. The woman stopped to stretch and rub her neck and shoulders.

"Are you ok?" He asked her,

"Oh yes, I'm sorry. I'm just fine. I have a problem with my neck and shoulders. I can't sit for long periods of time anymore."

"Unfortunately, I have no choice." As he smiled jokingly, looking down at the chair.

"Oh my goodness, I'm so sorry! That was inconsiderate of me. Can you please forgive me?"

"There's no need for that. It's not a problem. My name is Nathan Wade, what's yours?"

"Nathan Wade the scientist?"

"Well, not anymore."

"Oh my goodness! I read all about you. It's really nice to meet you Mr. Wade, my name is Silvia Tucker."

"Call me Nathan", as he shook her hand.

"So, Nathan, what have you been doing since you left Washington DC?"

"Just trying to understand myself, you know, in this really unfamiliar way."

"I can imagine how hard it's been for you, but you look good, much better in person than you do on TV." Silvia rubbed her neck once more.

"How long have you been having this problem?"

"Oh, for a few years now. Although a woman hates to admit her years, they have their own way of speaking out, don't they?" She laughed as Nathan smiled.

"What is it that you do, Silvia, if you don't mind me asking?"

"I'm an attorney. I'm trying my best to protect the rights of others, but it's really a tough thing to do these days."

"Why is that, do you think?"

"Rights. Everybody has them, even those who don't deserve them."

"How would you like to come by my place tonight to have a drink? I could really use the company." She smiled and paused for just a second,

"I think that would be nice."

"That's great. Here's my card. Let's make it around eight o' clock, is that okay?"

"That's fine. I'll see you then." She said as Nathan gathered his things to leave.

Next door to the house, he saw a big moving truck. The house had been empty for some time now, but now it looked as though he would have new neighbors very soon. Nathan took care of Sam and prepared some wine for his guest tonight.

It was eight o' clock. Silvia was walking into the front door of Nathan's house.

"You look wonderful, Silvia. I'm so glad you came."

"Well thank you. I'm happy to be here."

"Come on in. we can sit and talk on the back deck. It's enclosed so you don't have the bugs to worry about. How are things in Law?" He asked as they walked back through the house to the deck off the back of the house.

"Things are good, but could be better. But I don't really want to talk about Law. Let's talk about you." Nathan took a drink of his wine and then returned the glass back to the table.

"Well, my life has changed so much that I wouldn't even know where to begin."

"What do you think you will do now that you're in this whole new situation?"

"I guess really just try to understand who I am now. And just what my purpose is."

Silvia took a drink of the wine as she looked at him smiling. "Well, I think I like the new you."

"Even the chair?"

"The chair makes no difference to me; it clearly hasn't changed who you are. Everything I've ever read about you was wonderful, and now that I've met you, to me nothing has changed."

"But there's a lot you don't know. Things that you wouldn't understand."

"But this is the fun part. Getting to know someone. The beginning, you know, square one. You do want to get to know me, don't you?"

"I'm really looking forward to that. I think it would be good to have someone to talk to. There are times that I do get really lonely."

"So what then?"

"I work or read something." The conversation stopped for a moment and Nathan led her back inside the house.

Nathan took her to a room with two chairs in it. There was nothing else in the room and nothing on the walls. He looked deep into her eyes.

"Look at this wall. Can you see the beautiful picture that hangs there?"

She turned and looked at the bare wall and said, "Yes, I see the flowers."

"What kind of flowers do you see?"

"They're roses."

"Aren't they wonderful?"

"Yes they are."

"Do you believe that I have something that will take all the pain you have in your neck and back away forever?"

"I don't know."

"Well, it will work, but you need to believe." Nathan led her to the kitchen. On the table were two clearly marked boxes. One said, "Pain reliever," the other said, "rat poison."

Nathan had her sit down at the table with both boxes in front of her. "Open the first box and take three of the pills." She slowly opened the box and took the pills. "How do you feel now?"

"I feel nothing. No pain at all." This was said as her eyes rolled up in her head and then closed, into darkness and death.

Now more time has passed. It was a Saturday morning. Nathan and Sam were on their way out the door for their workout. That's when he saw her for the first time. He stopped cold and just stared at her.

It was a woman, and she had just moved in right next door. She was the most beautiful woman he had ever seen. Somehow she was different in his eyes, special. He watched her take things into her house from behind a tree in his yard, with her never knowing she was being watched. Before long he could no longer just watch her, so he started over in his chair. But before he went, he sent Sam back into the house. He moved slowly in his chair, never taking his eyes off of her, not even for a second. She was perfect in every way.

As he got closer, she spotted him. She started to smile and so did he as he came up the drive. "Hello. My name is Nathan Wade. I guess you're stuck with me as your new neighbor."

She laughed out loud. "I know who you are, Mr. Wade. And it's an honor to meet you. My name is Sandra Jones." This as she held out her hand to shake his.

"Please call me Nathan. It's really nice to meet you as well."

"So how long have you lived in this wonderful area?"

"Oh, I've been here for a few years now. It's really nice and so are the people who live here. I think you will enjoy it here, and I think we will enjoy having you."

"That's very nice, Nathan. Thank you."

"You're welcome." She turned and picked up a heavy box.

"Let me help you with that. Put it right here on my lap."

"Are you sure?"

"No problem. Let me help you."

Nathan followed her in with the box, after she took more bags from the car.

"This is a very big house. Are you all alone here?" he asked.

"Yep, just me. But I do have family and friends in Dallas."

"And now you have more. Wow, I can see that you really enjoy art. This is wonderful! Who is the artist?"

"That would be me. That's what I do. Art is my life. I really enjoy painting because it allows me to be who I am. It's my own therapy."

"That's great. You are very talented. I would love it if you would do a piece for me sometime?"

"I would be honored."

Nathan looked at her, but not like he looked at the others. She was different. Now he felt something he had never felt before, something good and warm. "Well, I'm not going to take up all of your time. I know how it is trying to get settled in. But if you need anything, please don't hesitate to call on me."

"I really appreciate that. You're very nice. Thank you, Nathan."

Nathan left and as he did, he looked back at the house and she was there watching him go. She waved to him and he quickly threw his hand up to respond.

Nathan went back inside and closed the door. This was the first time he had ever broken his morning routine. He sat in his chair in the middle of the room, with thoughts of just the two of them together. Holding each other, kissing. He moved to one of his bedrooms. The whole room was empty. He locked the wheels on his chair and started to stand.

He walked over to the wall, and with his finger he started to paint. As he moved his hand, the colors appeared. The lines soon turned into shapes. The shapes soon turned into images. He worked and worked, moving back and forth across the blank white wall.

Then he stopped and moved back slowly with his eyes closed. It was now complete. He opened his eyes to a masterpiece of the two of them naked, lying in a beautiful pasture. Then a tear fell from his left eye. He wiped it away, leaving his face smeared with the paint from his fingers.

Nathan began to realize the power that he now somehow possessed. But how? And why now was he just starting to see what he was becoming? Maybe it was the accident? This was the only logical explanation. He was a man that had explored may unexplained things and somehow he had become one of those things. Was this a gift or a curse? Nathan had the power to choose. Had he made the choice already? What do you believe?

A few more days had passed. Nathan was in his window watching Sandra wash her car in the driveway. He felt as though she was his and sent to him from up above. He went out to her. As he did, he felt afraid, but he had to go. He had to tell her how he felt, praying that she would feel the same way.

Sandra washed the car, and up rolled Nathan in his chair. "Sandra, when you're done here, my van could use a little attention."

Sandra turned and smiled at him. "Hey, Nathan, how's it going?"

"Okay. Not too bad, just a little bored is all."

"Well, grab a sponge. A little work does the trick every time." They washed the car, talking and playing in the cold water of the hose. Nathan smiled and laughed out loud, something he hadn't done for a long time. He was soaking wet and so was Sandra. They had a good time, but to Nathan it was more than just a good time. It was something that he had never had or felt before; true happiness and love. As the water stopped, the conversation began. "Why don't you let me make you dinner tonight?"

"Nathan, you don't have to do that."

"I would really love to do it, and I wouldn't be bored if you came for dinner." Sandra laughed. "It will be my welcome to your new home gift."

"That's really nice. I accept, but on one condition."

"You name it."

"You let me bring the wine."

Nathan headed home very happy about tonight. He spared no expense for a fabulous dinner for just the two of them. And then the phone call came. It was Sandra. She had to cancel. "I'm so sorry, Nathan. I have to go to the gallery. There's some kind of mix up with the art display. And I don't know how long it's going to take me to fix it. Can we do this next week?"

Nathan didn't respond right off. "Nathan, are you there?"

"Yes, I understand. Is there anything I can do to help?"

"You are so sweet, but I'll be fine. I'll come by tomorrow so we can set it up for next week. But have to run. I'm so sorry. I'll talk to you tomorrow. Bye, now." And just like that, she was gone.

Nathan hung up the phone and looked at the table with the candles and all the food. Then he heard her door slam next door. He hurried to the window to see her rush off in her car. Nathan locked the wheels on his chair, walked to his van and drove to the gallery.

He parked out front where he could see her car. There he sat and he waited. Three hours passed. Then she came out, but someone was with her. It was a man. The two of them stopped and talked for a moment and then he kissed her and walked away. Sandra got in her car and drove off.

Nathan followed the man. The man drove to a really nice bar where he met a woman in the parking lot. Then they went inside. Nathan parked the van and went inside. He took a table, close to the back of the bar where he could still see the two of them seated at the bar. "Can I get you a drink, sir?" Nathan's eyes remained locked on the man at the bar as the girl asked him again, "Sir, may I get you something?"

"Oh. Yes. I'll have a rum and coke. Thank you." The man at the bar had his arm around this woman and was kissing her. This angered Nathan. So he waited there, drinking as he watched them and then the woman got up for the ladies' room. Nathan stood and walked to the bar and sat right next to him.

"Excuse me, but this seat belongs to a lady."

Nathan looked at him, "I'm sorry. I didn't know."

The man was very drunk and swaying from side to side. He asked, "Do I know you?"

"Well, I don't know. Do you think you know me?"

"I don't know."

"Would you like to find out?"

"I would."

"Then come with me." Nathan rose from the bar and the drunken man followed him out to his van and the two of them drove away.

"What is your name?"

"Jim."

"Do you live alone, Jim?"

"Yes I do."

"Take me to your place."

Jim told Nathan where to go. Soon they arrived at Jim's house.

"I need you to help me to take these bags into your house."

"Okay. No problem."

Once they were inside with the two bags on the floor, Jim sat down on the sofa and Nathan stood against the wall. They looked at each other. "Do you know what you have in those bags, Jim?"

Jim looked at the bags. "Yes."

"What's in the bags?"

"My two good friends."

"What happened to them, Jim?"

"I gave them something. Something that wasn't good for them."

"I see. I think you should call the police and let them know. Do you?"

"Yes, I think I will."

"Place both of them on your bed before you make the call." As Jim dragged the bodies one by one to his bedroom, Nathan walked to the kitchen and placed the box of rat poison under the sink, along with the half-filled bottle of ammonia. As Nathan came back out, he noticed Jim on the phone calling the police. Nathan passed by him and out the door to leave.

One week passed. Tonight Nathan had his dinner with Sandra planned and tonight it would really happen. At eight o'clock, the doorbell rang. It was Sandra.

"Well, come on in. I hope you're hungry?"

"Yes, I brought my appetite with me."

"Good, then you're in the right place." Nathan had the whole place decked out, candles—the whole nine yards. Sandra took one look at the layout and saw right away that maybe Nathan had the wrong idea about their friendship, but she didn't want to hurt him, so she played along.

"Nathan, this is way too much. You didn't have to go through so much trouble."

"Trouble? What trouble? This is nothing. Wait till you see what I do for you next time."

Now she knew for sure he had the wrong idea.

They sat down to eat, with light conversation, having a good time. "How do you like the wine, Nathan?"

"It's the best. Thank you for bringing it."

"It's the least I could do after all of this."

"You know, Sandra, I've been alone all my life. Not that I had to be, but I chose to be. Some may say it's strange, but it's the truth."

She took a drink of the wine and cleared her throat. "It's not strange at all. Everyone decides for themselves with whom and when the time is right."

"Sandra, I really feel that you're an incredible woman, and I would love to spend more time with you."

"You mean exclusively?"

"Well, I mean yes, just you and me."

"Nathan, I'm really flattered, but we don't even know each other that well. And I'm really not sure if I'm ready for such a serious commitment. But I do think you're a wonderful man. I just feel we should concentrate on being good friends."

"I'm sorry. I didn't mean to put you on the spot. It's just that I've never met anyone like you before."

"You're beautiful," he continued. "I can see your goodness through your eyes. With you, there would be no games, no deception, just truth. The way things are supposed to be."

"How can you be so sure?"

"I know. I just know. And I don't know how I do, but you do have these qualities in you."

"Nathan, the only sure way to know someone that well is by spending time with that person, learning about each other over time."

"For everyone else, yes, I would agree. But for me, I do know. I know it all too well."

Sandra began to feel a little uncomfortable with the whole conversation. She took another drink and decided it was time to go. "Nathan, this was really nice. I had a wonderful time, but it's getting pretty late and I should be going."

"Sandra, I believe I can paint you a picture and make you see whatever I want you to see."

"I really should be going." She got up and tried to hurry out the door.

"Sandra, but it is up to you to BELIEVE."

She stopped and turned to him. Nathan rolled around the table and stopped his chair in front of her. "But with you, I want you to believe for yourself." He locked the wheels on the chair and stood up. Now Sandra was terrified. She didn't know what to believe, or just what his intentions were. She was frozen stiff, unable to move, or maybe Nathan just wanted her to believe that.

"Follow me, Sandra." And she did, back to one of Nathan's room; the same room where he painted the wall, but really only in his mind. "Look at the wall. What do you see?"

"I see you and me naked together."

"Isn't it beautiful?"

"Yes it is."

"Is this something you want?" he asked.

Sandra stared at the blank wall. She started to cry. "Sandra, don't you understand that the way I feel for you is real? I don't want to make you feel this. I want you to feel it for yourself. I love you, Sandra." Nathan held her there with his mind, but didn't make her feel something for him, that she didn't on her own.

"Come with me, Sandra." She followed him down into the basement where he showed her things he created that would certainly make them rich beyond her wildest dreams. She could have anything her heart desired. "Stay with me, Sandra. I need you now. Can't you understand that?"

Sandra is trembled in fear, not knowing what he would to do to her. She cried out, "Help me! Please, somebody help me!"

Sandra sat on a chair close to the table with all Nathan's work on it. Nathan stood across from her, up against the wall. She had thought she couldn't move, but she could. She needed only to believe she could. "Do you believe that I need you, Sandra?"

She started to understand this game, as she sat in great terror because of this man. She said, "I do believe that you believe you do, Nathan."

He started to feel a little confused. "Wait! What do you mean?"

"I believe this is a game you're playing with my mind. But only if I believe, right Nathan?"

"What? What are you saying, Sandra?"

"You know what I'm saying, Nathan. I believe only what is real and true. Would you have me to believe anything that wasn't?"

"Well, no." Nathan grabbed his head in great pain. "Stop! Stop it!"

"I played this game when I was just a little girl, Nathan. We called it MAKE BELIEVE!"

"You don't know what the hell you're talking about. YOU DON'T KNOW!"

"Yes, Nathan, I do."

Nathan screamed out at her and ran over to her. He grabbed her by the arms and she kicked him in the groin. Sandra jumped up and ran for the stairs. Nathan ran after her. Sandra made it halfway up and Nathan reached out to catch her when he slipped, just giving her enough time to reach the top of the stairs. Now Nathan was back on his feet and coming to the top of the stairs. Sandra quickly grabbed his wheelchair at the top of the stairs and shoved the chair down onto him.

Nathan crashed down with the chair, twisting and turning to the hard basement floor.

There lay Nathan, with his neck broken and his chair on top of him with one wheel still spinning. It was over.

Sandra sat down at the top of the stairs staring down at Nathan's dead body. She couldn't take her eyes off of him. It was a real game of Make Believe. She closed her eyes and now she too believed. For when she opened them, Nathan was gone!

Now, what do you believe?

Chapter Two

Hand of My Brother

Today I sit and tell this story, although it is a very hard story for me to tell. I always loved my older brother, but he and my pop never could seem to see eye to eye. So it was hard growing up in our house, with my pop and brother always at each other's throats.

It was funny to me how my brother would complain about how my pops treated him, and how he would never let him be his own man. Because what my brother didn't realize, is he was just like my pop in every way, often treating me the very same.

I remember a Saturday morning we sat down to have breakfast. No one was doing any talking. It was silent as I poured the milk over my cream of wheat. My pop looked at me, then my brother, and then he said, "What are you going to do? Keep working at the store or find yourself a real job?"

My brother kept eating and did not look up or respond. I looked at my pop with pleading eyes not to start what I knew was going to be very bad fight. Then my pop said, "If you call yourself a man, then you should have a man's job that earns you a real paycheck, David."

My brother hated when Pop used his name after putting him down the way that he did. It made my brother crazy. Then David said, "I am a real man with a real job if you can see it or not, but of course you can't, so what else is new, Pop?"

"What kind of example are you setting for your brother Johnny here to follow?"

"Pop, Johnny is your son, not mine. You set the example for him, not me."

"You're his big brother. It's your responsibility to not be an asshole. He needs you just as much."

"And why the hell would you want him to follow me, Pop, when everything I do in your eyes is always the wrong thing? You're driving me crazy. I can't take it anymore."

David got up from the table and rushed out the door. It was this way every day it seemed. I always hoped that things would change, but they never did. My brother worked at a shoe store. My pops hated the fact that David would settle for such an unrespectable job.

I think David only kept the job to get at my pops. This was some type of game they played with each other. I never could understand it.

I went to my brother's store that same day to try and talk to him. I don't know why because he would never listen to me anyway. But I tried. I figured it was worth a shot. I walked in. David was in the back putting some shoes away, so I went back there.

I said, "Hey, Dave, you got a minute?"

"Just about that. What I tell you about coming down here when I'm working?"

"I know, Dave, but I needed to talk to you."

"Okay. What's on your mind?"

"It's about Pop."

"Look, Johnny, I told you, don't go sticking your nose in. You're too young to understand anyways. I'll handle Pop. It's my problem, not yours. You understand me?"

"I just thought…"

"That's the problem. Just don't think. Mind your own goddamn business." Then he walked out. So much for my big idea. No matter how much I tried, I could do nothing.

About a week later, me and David were coming home from a movie. It was late, but not that late.

Pops had been up drinking all night, so I knew as soon as we hit the door what was going to happen. And just like clockwork, "David, you and your brother get in here."

I looked at David and said, "Look, David, he's drunk. You know that, so don't start with him tonight."

"Look, you shut your mouth. I told you to mind your own, let me mind mine."

We walked in. My pops was really wasted. He looked like he had been drinking for hours.

I said, "What is it, Pop?"

"It's late. You boys know not to come home so late. It's disrespectful. You should have more respect for my house than that."

"I'm sorry, Pop. We lost track of time." I said, trying my best to keep the peace.

"And you, David, you should know better. What kind of man are you?"

David said, "What the hell are you talking about? I'm not the one here drunk off my ass. What about you, Pop?"

"David," I said, trying to get him to just stop.

"You think you're showing Johnny anything he needs to see?"

My Pop tried to stand up, but he was too drunk. He said, "Who the hell do you think you're talking to? This is my house here. I put this together. You've never done a damn thing in your whole life, now you got the balls all of a sudden to try and tell me?"

"That's right, Pop. It's always a double standard for you. So what, you don't think we see what you are? You're a drunk, that's all you are."

My Pop just looked at David. Then he looked at me how he always did. Then, all of a sudden, he pushed the lamp off of the table next to him and jumped up after David. I don't know why, but I jumped right in his way, trying to stop him from grabbing David.

He pushed me out of the way, and I fell hard to the floor and up against the wall.

He grabbed David by the shirt, pinned him up against the wall and got right up in his face. Then he said to him, "So you think you're man enough to talk to me like that in my own house? Drunk or not, you'll never be half the man I am, and don't you ever forget it, boy. "Then he let him go and staggered out of the room.

I was still on the floor, frozen stiff. I felt like I couldn't move even if I wanted to. I just looked up at David. He was scared shitless too. It was strange. I had never seen fear in his eyes like I saw at that very moment.

David looked down at me on the floor like I was a frightened puppy. He said, "Get up and go to bed," and walked out of the room. David had a look on his face that I had never seen before. It scared me even more.

After I sat there alone for a minute, I got up and walked down the hall to my room.

As I walked down the hall, I passed my pop's room. I slowed down to see if I could hear anything, but it was quiet. So I moved on down the hall. I felt as if I was floating on air with my feet never touching the floor beneath me, and I felt this way because I was lost, even though I was in my home with my family. I still felt very detached and not connected at all.

Even though the hallway was short, this night it seemed as long as a football field to me. Then I reached David's room, so again I slowed down to see if I could hear anything. David's door was cracked, so I knelt down in the hall and looked in at him.

David was sitting on the side of his bed. He had tears coming down his face. I couldn't believe my eyes. I couldn't remember the last time I had seen him cry. I looked closer. He had in his hand a picture of me and him with my mom and my pop. My mom had died when we were very young. We never had the chance to know her. Even though we never talked about her, we still always loved her.

David sat holding the picture and crying. I didn't move. I didn't even breathe.

Then he took the picture from its frame and began to tear it, leaving only me and him and my mother together.

I slowly moved away from the door, and went to bed.

A few weeks had passed. David and I were having breakfast. I had just graduated high school, and my Pop had gotten me a job at a local factory. It was a real good job, and it paid a lot more than what David was making.

I really think that's why my pop wanted me to take the job so bad. He was trying once again to stick it to my brother.

I thought that maybe after that night, things would settle down some, or at least I hoped as much, but it didn't. Things were the same, and always seeming to get worse.

So we sat having our breakfast and in walked my pop. David got right up and grabbed his things and out the door he went. Pop poured his coffee and sat with me at the table. He said, "Johnny, I'm proud of you, now you're a man. You have a good job and I want you to do the best you can."

I said, "Thanks, Pop, I will."

"You're not like your brother," as he took a sip of his hot coffee, "He never understood anything I ever tried to tell him. I want you to know that all I ever wanted was the best things for you and your brother, but somehow things never worked out with us. But with you, it's different. I love you, Son."

And then he got up from the table and walked past me, and he put his hand on my head as he went by.

I was shocked and confused all at the same time. My pop never used the word "love"; at least I couldn't remember the last time he did. And did he mean he just loved me and not my brother? Even if that's not what he meant, every day of our lives that's what it felt like.

At that moment I started to feel sorry for David. We already had no love from a mother, but for David, he had none of his father's either.

That had to be why he was the way he was. David felt like my pop only had love for me and never for him. He resented me, but my pop, he hated.

I started my new job and was doing well. I even liked it. When I was at work I felt okay, it was coming home that I had a problem with. I remember one day as I walked through the door, I heard the two of them screaming at each other in the living room.

I walked in to see what was going on. They saw me come in, but didn't stop; they kept right on screaming and carrying on, like I wasn't there.

I said, "What's going on?"

"Stay out of it, Johnny; it's none of your business."

Then my pop said, "What, you afraid for him to know how stupid you are with your money?"

I said, "Pop," trying to calm him down.

"You're right about one thing, Pop; it's my money, and I'll do whatever I want with it."

"Johnny, I want you to know your brother brought a used motorcycle. Spent all the money he had on a piece of shit, can you believe that? He makes no money at this fucking job of his, and this is what he does. I want you to know this, Johnny, so you don't make the same mistake."

"What I do with my money is my business," my brother said.

"What, you think you're a man with this type of attitude?"

"I'm tired of you trying to tell me I'm not a man, Pop."

"David, a man manages his money and makes good, smart decisions with it. He don't piss it all away."

David walked out of the room, and I was thinking, "Good, it's over." But then he comes right back for one last word.

He said, "Pop, you've never known a damn thing about me, or who I am."

Then he walked out the front door.

I looked at my pop and said, "Pop, why do you fight with him so much? Why can't you talk to him like he's a man?"

"You think your brother's a man? I see he's got you brainwashed too. Listen, Johnny, David's no man. He's got a lot to learn about being one. And at the rate he's going, it looks hopeless. So don't be fooled by him, he needs to know responsibility."

"But, Pop, how could he learn it if you guys are screaming all the time?"

"Johnny, he's no baby. I'm not going to baby him. Maybe that's what he wants; well, he's not going to get it from me. No fuckin' way."

Then he stormed out of the room.

I knew then that things would never get any better between them. For me, it was like watching a ship at sea go down very slowly. There was nothing I could say or do to ever change things.

Why David stayed in my pop's house was a mystery to me. I often thought he would just not come home sometimes, but he always did, and my pop never asked him to leave.

How could people who carry the same blood treat one another the way they did? I guessed I would never know, and neither would they.

Our life together was always very dysfunctional, to say the least. We never knew how it felt to have love. David and I started grow farther and farther apart. Some days he wouldn't even talk to me. I felt bad and all alone.

I wanted my brother to love me as much as I loved him, but he never knew how to love. He had never been loved from the one person in our lives who would have made a difference.

My pop's drinking problem was getting worse. I knew something bad could happen anytime. I found myself trying to keep the two of them away from each other. I know that's crazy, but I didn't know what else I could do. When David came home some nights, I would take my pop out for a drive, hoping the night air would sober him up some, so I could get him back in the house and into bed peacefully.

Sometimes I'd take David out for dinner and a movie, just killing time and praying Pop would be asleep when we came back home.

This had somewhat become a normal routine for me, but I was getting tired of it. Why should I have to be the peacemaker? These were two grown men who were just alike in every way. Neither of them could see it, but it was so clear to me.

One weekend, David and I were invited to a party. This is when I really started to see just how much we were growing apart. There was this girl that David was really crazy about. Her name was Silvia. She was beautiful and every guy in town wanted her, but she was into David.

Anyway, Silvia came to this party. My brother went without me. He left before I got home that day, even though we were supposed to go together.

I was mad that he had just up and left without me. So I got dressed and went anyway. Once I got there, I saw David with some of his friends. He had been drinking and drinking a lot.

And to me, just for a second, when I looked over at him from across the room, I saw Pop instead of David. That's just how much they were alike, and when David was drinking it started to be hard to tell them apart.

But I didn't go over and say anything then, I just started talking to some cute girl named Wendy.

Wendy and I had just started to like each other. I had told her I would see her at this party. Wendy could tell something was not right, then she asked, "What's wrong, Johnny, you seem like something is on your mind. If you want to talk about it we can." I thought that was really nice of her, it made me like her even more.

I said, "I'm sorry, Wendy, it's my brother. He's being a real ass to me lately, and for no good reason."

"Have you talked to him about it?"

"No, it's not that easy with him. I've tried, but he's got this bug up his ass and he's being impossible."

"I know what you mean. I have an older sister too and she sometimes can be the same way."

We smiled at each other and entered the dance floor to dance. It was a slow song and the first time I had ever gotten that close to her, and it felt great. We danced and as we did, I saw Silvia walk up to David, and they started to talk.

After our dance, Wendy wanted to get something to drink, so we started over to where the drinks were, and David and Silvia were standing right over there.

As we walked up, I saw David glance at me and then look away. As we were getting our drinks, I heard Silvia say, "Hey, David, isn't that your brother Johnny?"

He said, "Yeah, it is." with this condescending look on his face.

"Hi, Johnny." Silvia said.

"Hello." "I don't think I've ever seen you guys at the same time before." which really struck a nerve with me because we where supposed to come to this party together.

I tried to keep my mouth closed, but it just came out anyway. I said, "Yeah, me and my brother don't do much together anymore. Even when we plan to, it just never seems to work out."

Then David said, "Why don't you just get your drink and get the hell out of my face?"

"No, why don't you get your drunk ass out of mine?"

"You're an asshole, Johnny."

"Well, it takes one to know one, Brother."

Then Wendy pulled my arm and said, "Come on, Johnny, let's get out of here."

So we did.

Wendy had come to the party with friends, so I told her I would drive her home. As we drove, I was very upset. Wendy moved over close to me trying to make feel better, and she did. I said to her, "Thanks for getting me out of there. I owe you one."

"That's right, you do, and I won't let you forget it either."

We smiled and laughed out loud, then she put her head on my shoulder, and just for a second, I felt normal, happy even.

I dropped her off and gave her a big kiss goodnight, and I knew then it wouldn't be the last one.

But as I drove home, reality had set back in. I was pissed at David. Him and Pop had started to turn me into what I hated that they were; miserable people.

I made it home and went straight to bed, but David never came home that night. I knew he was with Silvia. I was glad he didn't come home. I didn't care to see him that night anyway.

The next morning, I was in the kitchen having my breakfast, Pops was in the bathroom, and David walked in. I didn't say a word to him nor him to me. He got a cup of coffee and sat right at the table.

We sat without talking, and then we heard Pops in the bathroom coughing really badly. He sounded terrible and right away I was concerned. After a few more minutes, I didn't hear anything, so I got up to go see if he was okay.

I went to the door. David kept drinking his coffee like nothing was going on, like he didn't hear Pops in the bathroom.

I knocked on the door and said, "Pop, are you okay?" But he did not answer, so I hit the door harder, "Pop, are you okay?" But he still didn't say a word.

So that was it. I started to shove on the door to get it opened. I pushed and pushed and then it opened, and Pops was out cold on the floor.

I called 911 and they came and took me and Pop to the hospital. David went into his room and closed the door. He never once came and looked at Pop, even before the ambulance arrived.

Now he had really pissed me off, even worse than last night.

I waited for hours for the doctors to come out and tell me something, and finally they did. They said my pops was really sick, that his liver was bad from all the alcohol he drank, and he would need a lot of care at home for a long time, if he lived through this.

I asked the doctor if I could see my father. He said okay, but for just a little while.

Before I went in to see Pop, the doctor asked if we had insurance that would cover a home nurse for Pop, because that's how much care he was going to need.

I looked at him for just a second, and said, "Me and my brother will take care of my father." and then I walked into the room.

But I was no fool. I knew then it would be me; David could care less what happens to Pop, at least that's how he acted. So as I looked at Pop lying there sick as he was, I prepared myself for what I had to do.

I got real close to him and said, "Don't worry, Pop, I'm here. I'm going to look after you now. I love you, Pop." I laid my head on his hand crying.

Later that night, I made it home and sat right at the kitchen table. I was exhausted. Then I heard David open his bedroom door and start down to the kitchen. I wanted to get right up and go down to my room, but my legs wouldn't move. I was too tired.

David walked in and went to the icebox for something to drink. He said, "So, how is he?"

I just shook my head and said, "Since when do you care anyway?"

He looked at me and said, "I don't," and started to leave the room.

"Well, that's just great, David, so what the hell do you stay around here for? Why don't you just get your shit and leave? Nobody needs you here if you don't give a damn. I sure don't."

"You trying to put me out of my own house, Johnny?"

"This is not your fucking house. This is Pop's house, David. Pop was right about some things about you, and I'm just starting to see it now."

"You don't know a damn thing about me."

"You're wrong, David. I know plenty. I know you feel like Pop loves me and never did you, but is that my fault David? I always loved you no matter what Pop said."

David started to cry, and said, "No you don't understand, Johnny. It's Pop's fault. He did this to me. Always pushing me and ever once encouraging me. I was never any good to him, even before I had a chance to prove that I was." I moved to him, but he pushed me away.

I said, "David, I'm still your brother. You just have to let me be." David started to wipe his face he was very upset, more than I had ever seen him get before.

Then he ran to his room and started packing. I walked in his room. He said, "Don't worry, Johnny. Everything's going to be okay," as he cried, packing his things. "Pop never wanted me, and now he's even turning you away from me. I won't let him do it, Johnny. Just remember, I love you."

David grabbed his bag a walked out of the house. I said, "David, wait! Where are you going? David, don't just leave like this! David! DAVID!! DAVID!!"

I had followed him out the door and into the street. I didn't realize I was screaming after him as he got on his bike and sped away.

I was very upset. I went back into the house, and sat on my Pop's bed with my eyes bloodshot from crying. I looked over and I saw the picture that David had in his room that night that he had torn Pop out of it. It was the same picture, but only now it was taped back together and on Pop's nightstand.

I picked it up and looked at it, and once again, I started to cry.

Two weeks had passed. I hadn't seen David since that night. I was really worried about him. Pop was coming home the next day, and I had the whole house ready for him. Everything we needed was going to be there for him.

I was lonely, so I called Wendy, "Hi, it's me, Johnny."

"Hey, how are you doing? You holding up?" I had told her what was going on and she had been there for me.

"I guess okay, it's really hard with both of them being gone like this. It's quiet; nobody is fighting. I know it sounds crazy, but I kind of miss it now that they're not here."

"Well, you're not crazy; you just miss your family. So you know what I'm going to do?"

"No. What?"

"I'm going to come over and cook you dinner."

And she did. We had a great time, and Wendy was a great cook.

After dinner, I told her, "You're the best thing that ever happened to me, Wendy."

"Ah, you say that to all the girls, don't you, Johnny." We kissed and then went down the hall to my room, and she spent the whole night with me. It was wonderful.

The next morning, we overslept, and the hospital drivers were bringing Pop home. They were at the front door, ringing the bell. "Oh shit, Wendy, get up! My pop is home." I put on my pants and went to the door. Wendy was hurrying to put on her clothes.

As I came down the hall, there was Pop in a wheelchair, with a paramedic pushing him into the house.

I didn't know what to say. Then Wendy came down the hall. I said, "Hey Pop! How you feeling?"

"Tired, really tired. And who is this?"

I was shaking. I had never had a girl sleep over in my pop's house before. I thought for sure he was going to have a fit, but he didn't. I said slowly, "Pop, this is Wendy. Wendy, this is my pop."

"Nice to meet you, Wendy, have you had breakfast yet?"

My pops was always big on having breakfast. No matter how we were getting along, we would always have to go to the kitchen and have breakfast together.

Wendy said, "No, sir. Not yet. I was going to fix something for you guys."

"Well, none for me, thank you, but you two enjoy."

Then the paramedic said, "We need to get your father in bed. Can you show me to his room?"

After I got Pop all settled in, I went back to the kitchen. Wendy had a wonderful breakfast waiting for me. She said, "Is he okay?"

"He's sleeping right now. I'm sure glad he's home."

She kissed me and said, "You eat your breakfast. I'm going to get cleaned up."

"Wendy. Thank you. I mean for everything. I couldn't have gotten through this without you."

She just smiled and walked back down the hall.

Another week had passed, and still no word of David. At this point, I didn't know what to think.

Pops was really sick, and taking care of him was hard, but Wendy came by all the time to help me out. I was falling in love with her with every passing day. She meant the world to me. Late one night, before I went to bed, I stopped to check on Pop. When I looked in, he looked like he was asleep, but as soon as I started to close the door he said, "Johnny, come on in here for a second."

So I did. I sat right on the side of his bed. He said, "Johnny, I know things haven't been the best here with me and your brother, and I want you to know I'm sorry, son. I never meant to hurt you."

"It's okay, Pop. You just get your rest; that's the most important thing now."

"Johnny, I need to tell you something that I promised myself I never would, but now I know I have to."

"What is it, Pop?"

"When you and your brother were very young, I mean like two and three years old, your brother David got really sick, and needed a kidney transplant to live."

"Pop, are you for real?"

"Listen to me, Johnny. Now your mother and David had the same exact blood type which made your mother a candidate for a donor for your brother."

I couldn't believe what he was saying to me. Pop had never talked to me about my mom ever.

Then he continued to say; "Now I wanted to wait, and see if there would be another donor soon enough to save your brother's life, only because I was afraid of what might happen to your mother. Not that I didn't care about David, but your mother didn't want to wait. She was too afraid of losing David. And she went ahead and did the operation. She was upset with me when she went in, because she thought I didn't care about David. But that wasn't true. I did care, but I also cared about her. And I never got to tell her the truth. I never got to tell her anything, ever again. Johnny, your mother died on that operating table to save your brother's life."

I looked at him with tears running down my face, and he looked back at me through the tears in his. I let out a wail of a sound as I grabbed him up and held him in my arms.

We stayed just like that, holding each other for hours. Then we let go. I laid my father back down on the bed and he looked up at me, with his own bloodshot eyes. He said, "Johnny, I've always loved you, but after that, it was always hard to love you both."

I went to my room with a feeling of emptiness. I had that feeling of floating once again. I was hurt and nothing could ever ease my pain.

I couldn't sleep. I tossed and turned till finally I decided to go for a walk. It was late, about three am. I got dressed, and as I walked back down the hall and passed my father's room, I heard something, but I didn't know what, so I stopped right there outside his door to listen.

I moved in close to the door, and I heard it again. So I quickly pushed open the door.

To see my brother David standing over my father's lifeless body with my father's pillow in his hand.

I don't know if you remember, but I told you this was a hard story for me to tell. You see, I loved my family, but I never had a chance of them loving each other.

So my mother and my father were both taken from me, in one way or another,

By the HAND OF MY BROTHER.

Now my brother David is in prison; locked away for the rest of his life, for this terrible thing he did.

Inconceivable Escape

I am surely captured, bound tightly with no hopes of escape to save my life, riddled with scars, ran deep with actions that cut and sever sharp as a jagged-edged knife.

When did this happen? So unaware I must have been. Visions of pleasure and of course, money would filter in concealing the clarity desperately needed to avoid the sin, which is controlling and barring the way to freedom; a place I've heard of but yet have never been.

This is hell. Every day that I live here on this earth, is my life my own? Or was it sold the day of my birth? Like a bad dream, I scream without the presence of sound. I run ever faster, but my movement as well as the scene is slow motion, as I can never seem to gain any ground.

My situation starts to get to me, although my efforts do not reflect the concern. This muddy field in which I walk is redundant and shameful to bear. A lesson of choices in this place seems inconceivable to learn.

This person has me and is not willing to let me go. How can I survive?

How will I ever know?

This person is consistent and seems to know my every move; cunning and methodical, and unwilling to lose.

My life is not my own. I feel it never was. How to break free is the question I ask to the heavens above. But without an answer or a sign, I find myself alone and running out of time, as my concerns grow stronger. How can I save this life in time?

Another day passes. Yes I'm still here; my eyes grow swollen and reddened from my tears. I fear it is hopeless, this escape I so desperately need, as this person on my integrity continues to feed.

Why is this so hard? There must be a way, although I've tried before. I continue to pray.

Give me the strength, the strength to overcome this person who controls me, who holds me captive to the needs which this person shows me.

I am not a slave, although I feel like one. This is not a life I would wish on anyone.

The sun continues to shine, but perhaps just not on me. Although it may be bright outside, for me it's growing very hard to see. I try to reason with this person who holds me, but it's just a waste of time. Although this person feels the pain, but still pays me no mind.

Why must you be this way? As I plead looking deep into this person's eyes, not a word is spoken, always with no reply. I try again to get free, but I am pulled right back in. This is shameful and life-threatening to all men.

I do know what is right, although I am very muddy from the fields. I am infected by this person, but long for freedom I do still.

Nevertheless, this person still holds me and controls my life, forcing me to continue on this path that can realistically take my life.

My body and spirit start to break down; I can't think clearly. No longer is there any firm ground. How much more can I take? I fear not much more. My heartbeat is weak; my whole body is numb and so very sore.

I've done all I can to defeat this person, this enemy. I know by now you must know this person is ME.

As I stare in the mirror at my captor, how could this be? But no longer does it matter.

I cannot run and hide from myself. There is no way I can. I am human, just an imperfect man.

I am my worst enemy. How will I find the way? Creator of my own fate.

How to save myself from my self—My Inconceivable Escape!!!

Whispers of Wind and Rain

Jordan played alone most of the time, enchanted by his own imagination.

Transforming his enclosed backyard into another world, how deep and uncharted is the mind of a twelve-year-old boy. He was an only child blessed with wealthy parents who loved him, they knew how gifted he was at a young age. Far advanced he was. His IQ was far higher than normal.

But his parents were troubled that his imagination grew as he did. His father was an engineer with great success and his mother was a former model, but now running her own clothing line. Jordan's mother continued to worry about him after his father's fatal accident. It was a ski trip that John Baker never returned from.

Jordan was younger when he lost his father and it didn't affect him greatly, but he knew that his life was somehow different now. Five years had passed. Now he was twelve years old and sharp as an eagle's eye. The world would be his playground, but for now it would be the confines of his gigantic backyard.

They worried about him because his mind was so sharp that it took him from reality it would seem. He was a loving boy, mostly appearing normal, though at times you might question his actions or words.

Distant as a memory and as close as tomorrow at times, they lived alone, Jordan and his mother, with all the money they would ever need and more. As Jordan continued to grow, his mother Ellen worried about him more, though most of her time was spent on her new line. It was hard to be a mother and the head of a new clothing company.

Jordan would spend most of his time in the backyard, in this world and the next. Jordan was colorful, warm, and friendly; all who met him really came to love him. He never had many friends after he was taken from school a few years ago to be home schooled, as Ellen thought it best.

Jordan had no say in the matter; he would find a way to be happy, that was his simple way though he was very complex. Their home was beautiful, surrounded by other beautiful homes. The rich flourished and no expense was spared by anyone to make their homes a paradise.

There was always someone there to care for Jordan while Ellen was mostly away working. Although he would never need much looking after, because once he was in the back yard he had all he would need for hours at a time.

This week it was Lynda. With beautiful blue eyes and long blond hair she was lovely, but she was not well. She was a good friend of Ellen's who also worked for her.

Lynda was heavily into cocaine, and spent most of the time using while Jordan played out in the backyard. It probably would have been better for Jordan to be left alone than with Lynda, something that Ellen overlooked time after time. Jordan came in for really no reason; it even caught Lynda off guard, even though that wasn't hard to do.

"Excuse me, Lynda." Jordan said as he walked into the room, catching Lynda with a small mirror up to her nose.

"Jordan, what are you doing in here?"

"Just thought I would come in and see how you've been feeling lately. You haven't been looking very well."

She turned, sniffing and wiping her nose and face, still leaving white powder on the tip of her nose.

"What the hell do you mean? I'm fine and how in the hell would you know anyway?"

"Don't be offended, Lynda. I care that's all—if there's anything you need, you come out and let me know."

She stopped and just looked at him, and he smiled and turned and walked away. But just before he left the room he stopped and said,

"Oh and Lynda, you still have a little of that on the end of your nose."

He left as she sat motionless with cocaine still smeared on the end of her nose.

—In the city across town from their beautiful home, Ellen sat behind her desk in one of the city's tallest skyscrapers. Looking over the latest drafts of her new line, she was very angry as she flipped each page holding her head in one hand in disbelief.

"What in the hell is this?" As she screamed at the executive who brought the drafts into her, the girl stood without saying a word, knowing that at that moment her job was at stake.

"This is nothing like what I asked for! What the hell is wrong with you? I gave you instructions, right?"

"Ellen, to my understanding, that was what you wanted"

"Well you didn't understand at all. I don't have the time for bullshit like this! We have deadlines to meet, understand now?"

"Yes I do."

It was clear that the young girl was very uneasy with Ellen, most workers are when it comes to their employer, but this seemed like something else.

Ellen closed the book and sat back in her chair looking at the young girl.

"You know if I were to let this go out like this, I could stand to lose millions of dollars."

As Ellen got up from her desk and started walking slowly around to the young girl, you could see in her face the anxiety that Ellen was causing.

"You like your clothes to fit your body nicely, and the colors to go along with your skin tones, am I right?" As she now let her hand run down and over the blouse of this young girl who stood frozen stiff by Ellen's actions.

"Yes I do."

"Fashion is a lot like life, it's very personal—don't ever forget that," as she walked back around to her desk—"That's all for now."

The young girl turned and walked out the office as fast as she could without running. Ellen sat with a blank stare on her face, with a hint of a smirking undertone.

Money always seemed to change people, make them think different and do things they most likely would have never done. But is that true? Or does it just appear this way to people who don't have a great deal of money?

It also seems that the important things in life suffer, and good decision-making turns bad. It would seem money would be the answer to most all of our problems, though it appears to bring more problems in so many cases.

From one world to the next, Jordan having money never would be a problem for him. He cared about people and so many other things. One of the great things about him was he didn't have to know you to care about you. He needed only to meet or see you and you would be forever welcome in this world and his.

Lynda once again was home with Jordan; she wandered into the backyard to see what kept him so captivated all the time. Lynda started out the back door which led to the middle of the yard. She had never been out there before, even though she had been in this house many times before.

As soon as the doors opened, she couldn't believe her eyes; it was incredible to say the least. Jordan had constructed a great structure intertwining thought the trees on the left-hand side of the yard, made with PVC piping and wood.

The yard was like another world, like a small city and this great fortress was the center of it all. There were so many things all over the yard it took Lynda a few moments to take it all in. She walked slowly to the structure in amazement. Power lines ran out to it, powering computers on the inside. Lights and food and the things Jordan found interesting were also inside. The yard was huge, like a small park with lots of trees, bushes, a waterfall and rocks. It was wonderful and Jordan had put most of it together. She looked around inside the structure, but saw no sign of Jordan.

From outside the fort Lynda started to hear voices. It was Jordan but she heard more than just one voice. It was the voice of someone older, like a man's voice. She walked out and started around back through the trees to the edge of the yard next to the fence separating their yard from the next. And there, sitting on a rock up against the fence, was Jordan. He didn't know she was there, so Lynda moved around a tree so he could not see her. He was talking to what looked like the fence. She listened quietly.

"My Mother seems very indifferent about this man. She hasn't let me meet him before, but she plans to bring him home tonight to meet me for the first time."

"Well, what's strange about that, Jordan?"

"Well, considering the fact that she really doesn't like men, for some reason she feels the need to interact with this man."

"I don't think it's fair to say she doesn't like men, Jordan."

"I wouldn't want to sound unfair, Wadley, but—she's changed. She doesn't look at me the same, and when she does I can see the rain and wind behind her eyes—and it scares me Wadley."

"Jordan, your mother loves you greatly; even I know that. She always has, even more since your father's passing. Give her a chance, young prince; she is going through a lot as well—remember."

Wadley was taken even more than usual by what Prince Jordan had just shared with him. He called Jordan the prince, because he was very special, not just because of whom he was, he was just very special to Wadley.

Wadley was an old professor who lived next door and never left his house. He lived alone and spent most of his time painting and having great intellectual conversations with his only friend in the whole world, Prince Jordan, right across the fence.

His beard was white as snow and he pulled on it regularly, as he concentrated on his art and or the conversation he would share with the prince. His eyes were light green and bright as the day's sun and often Jordan would say he carried the sun behind his eyes.

Jordan loved Wadley. It was very plain to see that they loved and trusted each other in every way. Wadley was from England and spoke with a strong English accent that Jordan loved to sit and listen to, his great stories educating him even further.

Lynda took it all in, every word. She was amazed once again, this time by the conversation this elderly man was capable of having with such a young boy.

She thought maybe by knowing all of this; she could draw Ellen even closer to her and somehow benefit from it all. This is the way she was, addicted to drugs and money, she was beautiful, but who she was made her ugly and vindictive.

On the way home Ellen engaged in conversation in the back of her black stretch limo with Don Campton, the man she had been seeing and had told Jordan about. Don was a very wealthy and important man. He could very well be the next governor of the great state of California. Don did enjoy Ellen's company, but he was very into his campaign, plus she was pushy and moving just a bit too fast for Don's taste. The phone rang in the limo; it was Lynda.

"Hello."

"Ellen, it's me Lynda. I'm sorry to call you but—will you be home any time soon?"

"Actually I'm on my way as we speak. Is everything alright with Jordan?"

"He's fine—but there are a few things I think you really need to know about."

"I won't be alone. Don is coming with me, and whatever it is, it'll have to wait until later. We're having dinner."

"I understand. That's fine, we'll talk later."

"Is everything alright at home, Ellen?"

"Nothing for you to worry about. We'll have a wonderful dinner and then spend some time alone, just the two of us."

"I thought you wanted me to meet Jordan tonight. I was really looking forward to that."

"More than being naked alone with me in my Jacuzzi?"

"That's not the point. I just thought—"

"Let me worry about everything; let me take care of you," as she pulls him to her, kissing him passionately.

"Lynda, I didn't know you were out here."

She jumped. Jordan startled her walking up from behind.

"You scared me Jordan.—I just came out to us my cell phone. I don't get good reception inside."

"That's strange. Mother never has that problem. Would you like me to look at your phone?"

"No, Jordan. It's fine. It works fine out here."

"Everything has its nuances I suppose, Lynda."

She turned and walked back into the house without another word.

A dinner fit for a king filled the table by candlelight, as Ellen entertained her guest. Lynda stayed in one of the guest rooms lining her mirror with her drug of choice. Jordan lay asleep on his bed from all the day's excitement.

Into the night Lynda lay restless, sweating, tossing, and turning as she heard the sounds of lovemaking coming from Ellen's room. Slowly she walked out and down the long darkened corridor, closer and closer to Ellen's bedroom door. Slowly she cracked the door, and watched as Ellen made love to Don on the floor.

It excited her as she looked at them. She stood sweating and breathing heavily, still intoxicated by the drugs. She closed the door softly and wandered crazily farther down the hall to Jordan's room. She opened his door and found him asleep on his bed.

She looked at him, as she touched herself, and started to walk into his room.

But then she heard Ellen's bedroom door open, and out walked Ellen. And in the shadows of the dark corridor she closed Jordan's door and ducked down in the shadows. Ellen walked right by her, never seeing her there, and after she passed, Lynda ran as fast as she could back to her room and closed the door.

Early the next morning, Jordan was up and heading down the hall. Passing his mother's room he opened the door, and Don lay asleep on his mother's bed. He closed the door and walked to the guest room, to see if his mother was there. As he opened the door, he saw a body of a woman on the bed. He thought it was his mother, but as he came closer to the bed, he saw that the woman naked and asleep was Lynda.

Jordan turned and left out the room and went down the stairs.

And as he headed for the backyard, his mother called to him from the dayroom.

"Jordan, come here please."

"Mother, I've been looking for you this morning."

Right away she knew he went into her bedroom. She tried to think of what to say, but she was at a loss for words.

"It's alright, Mother. You need companionship. You're a beautiful woman. But there's something wrong, Mother."

"Jordan, honey, I'd like to get someone for you to talk to, someone who could help you, but it would mean you would have to go away for a while."

"Really, Mother I'm fine. I have Wadley to talk to and who better than that? I am worried about you though, Mother."

"What in heaven's name for? I'm fine, my son. It is my job to look after you. Jordan, I don't want you to go outside today. I'd like you to stay inside; you can play in your room."

"Please, Mother there's things I must attend to today. Please, Mother!"

"Jordan, I didn't want to have to tell you, but there will be a rainstorm today."

"Not the rain, Mother!"

He turned white as snow and ran fast as he could back up to his room, almost knocking Don over coming down the stairs.

"Hello. You must be Jordan?"

He didn't answer. He just looked at Don, and flew fast as he could up to his room and slammed the door.

Don looked down at the bottom of the stairs at Ellen,

"I'm sorry. Bad timing?"

"It's not you Don. Are you hungry?"

Over breakfast Ellen thought it to be the best time to tell Don what she planned to do with Jordan so they would be able to spend more time together.

"Jordan needs special attention and I want him to have it. Then you could move in here with me. Can't you see how wonderful it would all be?"

"What about what Jordan wants, Ellen?"

"Don, my son doesn't know what he wants, but I know what he needs. I know what we all need."

"Ellen I'm very fond of you, but I don't think you've taken enough time to really think this thing through. Why don't you do that—take some time; we don't need to rush things."

"Is that how you feel, like I'm rushing things?"

Just then, slowly down the stairs came Lynda, taking in every word.

"Even though I haven't had a chance to talk to him, as far as I can see this environment, this yard, is what he needs. What is it about the rain that scares him?"

"The wind and the rain, it not only frightens him, but it makes his problem of coping with reality ten times harder. And we've never known why. Do you want to be with me, Don?"

"Ellen, just think about what I said, and we'll talk about this again."

Then Don stood up to leave.

Lynda entered the room after Don had gone, and sat down at the table to talk to Ellen.

"Ellen we need to talk about Jordan."

Ellen is uninterested as she drinks her coffee, "I don't see what we need to talk about, Lynda. I've made up my mind, and he's going to Vinton Falls."

"I just thought you would like to know about the conversations Jordan has been having with some man across the fence."

"Ha, ha! You mean Wadley? "

"I don't know his name, but I think he lives next door."

"Lynda, it's no big deal. Jordan has been talking with this man for years. His father and Wadley were friends."

"Jordan was talking to this man about you. That doesn't concern you at all?"

Ellen got up from the table and walked slowly over to a window overlooking the back yard.

"Lynda, come over here. I want you to see something."

Lynda stood and walked over to her at the window. They now both looked out at the back yard. Ellen came up behind her really close and spoke into her ear.

"Can you see what is happing here? All this is over, it's all coming down."

As they watched workers tearing down all that Jordan had made and redoing the whole backyard.

"My life is changing and this doesn't matter anymore. Soon, me and Don will be married and we'll start a new family together—the way it was meant to be."

"What about Jordan?"

"Lynda, don't be silly. Jordan will be just fine."

DING DONG!

It was the doorbell; Ellen moved away from Lynda, as her eyes opened once again. Ellen had captured her in that moment.

Lynda pulled herself together and started walking to the front of the house. She wanted to see who was at the door, and it was Wadley Winfred from next door. She stopped when she heard his unforgettable voice. She wanted to listen; she wanted to know what he wanted.

"Miss Baker, how are you?

"I'm fine, Mr. Winfred. Come in—what can I do for you?"

"I promise not to take too much of your time, but there is a concern I have with your son Jordan."

"Well have a seat. Would you like some tea perhaps?"

"Well that's kind of you, madam, but no thank you as it were; I've had my two cups for the day."

"Very well, so then right to it. What seems to be the problem? Has he bothered you in some way?"

"Bother me? Jordan? Heavens no, madam, nothing like that. I'm sure you know how I feel about the young fellow. He and I had a bit of a talk the other day and frankly, what he said bothered me."

"Well, what did he say?"

He now had her attention for the first time. "He seems to feel that the relationship between the two of you as changed. The boy feels quite alienated, frankly—Madam, I'll have you know I tried to get through to him, but you know that isn't always easy to do."

"Mr. Winfred, I'd like to thank you for coming by and don't worry, I'm taking care of Jordan."

She practically pulled him up out of his seat and rushed him right out the front door. She was upset and couldn't believe this man could come over and pry into her life like this.

As Wadley left, he could feel what Jordan was trying to tell him about his mother. Something was wrong and maybe it wasn't just Jordan? But there was nothing he could do.

The evening was on its way, but rain had fallen as Jordan stared out his window over-looking the back yard. His world had been destroyed by this day's end, and then a lone tear ran slowly down his face. Clutched tightly in one hand was a framed photo of his father, John Baker.

Ellen was on the phone talking to Don, telling him all her plans she had made for the both of them. She felt he would understand. He felt the same way she did, why wouldn't he?

"Don, don't you see? It's what we want to start our life together."

Don could not believe Ellen, how she made all these plans for them without even talking to him first. It was plain to see he had to let her know that this was not going to work out between them.

"Ellen, you're a wonderful woman, but my life right now is very complicated. You have to understand that. I'm not ready for a major commitment. Timing is very important right now, you understand don't you, Ellen?"

Her face went numb with no expression with her eyes cold and fixed just like Jordan would describe them to appear.

"Ellen, are you there?"

"—Yes, I'm here. I understand, Don. You're very busy. I should have known better; it's all right."

"Look, honey, you have to know I do care for you—look, I'm on my way to you right now, don't move. I need to talk to you about this face to face."

Then Ellen just hung up the phone without another word.

"Hello? Hello? Ellen, are you there?"

Don was on his way.

Jordan felt very alone as he sat on the floor by the window. He wanted his father, but his mother was all he had. So Jordan got up and walked out of his room to find his mother who he desperately needed.

As he came to her bedroom door it was cracked open, and he could hear talking coming from the room. He got closer and he listened.

"Look, Lynda, I'm not asking you to do this; I'm telling you."

"Are you out of your mind, Ellen? There's no way we can get away with killing a man! What's wrong with you?"

"You're the one on drugs. You're going to be a part of this if you like it or not."

Lynda started crying. She felt stuck with no real way out, so she went along.

"He will be here any minute, Ellen. We're not ready!!"

"Well, you better get ready."

Jordan heard everything; the plan was to poison a drink.

Jordan ran out and headed straight to the backyard. As he opened the door, the wind blew hard and the sky grew dark. The rain was coming. He stopped. He was afraid to go any farther, but he had to. Someone was going to die. Slowly he moved, trying to go through the doorway. He fought his fears as now he was outside and the wind slammed the door closed behind him.

A Mercedes Benz rolled to a stop out front of the house. It was Don. He walked around the car fighting the wind to the front door and rang the bell.

Slowly Jordan pushed on deeper into the backyard. Now every image, every tree, and every shadow moves in the wind: his worst nightmare. But he must go on! He can't let someone else die.

"Let me take your coat, Don. Would you like something to drink?"

"Why are you acting like nothing is wrong? We need to talk."

"Don, don't be upset. I told you I understood."

In strolled Lynda with a drink and very provocative clothing.

"I'm not upset, Ellen. I'm just worried about you."

"Don, you've met my girlfriend Lynda before, right?"

"Hello, Don. I've heard so much about you, it's like I already know you."

"No, I don't believe I've had the pleasure. It's nice to meet you, Lynda."

"Here I made these drinks for the both of you. I hope you like them; I call them "sex on me". I hope you like it, Don. Do you think you will?"

Don looked around. Ellen had a crazy look on her face and Don had no idea what the hell was going on as Lynda started to undo his tie.

"Wait a minute! I don't know what is going on here, but…"

"But what, Don? You don't like it? You want Lynda to stop?"

"Yes I would like her to stop! What the hell do you think you're doing, Ellen?"

"Don, just have a drink and relax."

"I didn't come here to have a drink!!"

Lynda began to feel like it was not going to work and she got a little nervous.

Jordan made it to the fence; he beat on the fence calling to his friend

"Wadley, Wadley! I need you. Can't you hear me?"

Then the rain slowly and softly began to fall.

"Ellen, I'm leaving right now if you don't stop this and talk to me."

Then Lynda spotted Jordan out of the window beating on the fence, and she panicked thinking he would bring attention to what they were trying to do.

"Oh God, Ellen! It's Jordan outside beating on the fence."

Right away she knew he must have heard their plans and was trying to get to Wadley. Then Don started to get suspicious.

"Ellen, what in the hell is going on in here?"

Ellen and Lynda hurried, putting on coats and shoes, trying to get to Jordan.

Don looked out the window and saw the boy and decided to go out and see if he could help him.

He opened the door. It was raining hard now, and wind was gusting harder.

Jordan still banged hard on the fence.

"Jordan, don't be afraid! It's just me, Don, a friend of your mother."

"No! Go away!!"

"Look, Jordan, let's go inside. We can talk about this—hey, I know you don't like the rain. Let's get out of this. What do you say?"

"Go away please—Wadley, Wadley!"

Then out came Ellen and Lynda, both with flashlights. Don was still calling to Jordan. It was even harder to see with all the wind and rain. The girls came out with the lights flashing in every direction; the wind was so strong it blew them off balance, and the lights strobed through

Wadley's window. This made him look out, and he noticed something going on in the backyard.

"Jordan, please come in, buddy. We really need to talk."

As Don is talking to Jordan, not getting too close, the girls came up behind Don. Ellen pulled out a butcher's knife and plunged it deep into Don's back.

Jordan saw the whole thing, and he screamed.

Wadley heard the scream and came running out to the fence.

"Prince, is that you? Prince is that you, old boy?"

"Wadley, help! My dad is going to die! Please, Wadley! My dad is going to die."

Now Don lay down on the ground, but he was still alive. Lynda stood there in disbelief, and Ellen now moved toward Jordan, holding the bloody knife.

"You killed my father! Why did you kill my father, Mother?"

"You ruin everything! But not anymore."

Then Lynda grabbed her, "No, Ellen! She screamed, fighting her.

Ellen straddled her. The rain poured down. She raised the knife to stab Lynda, and from behind her Jordan slammed a flashlight into the back of her head, just as Wadley came out the back door of the house.

Jordan sat without a word over his mother. Wadley walked up close, but not too close, "Prince, are you all right?"

"I never liked the Rain," as the rain then came to an end.

Blue Psych

I'm a psychiatrist. My job is to help people, to help them to understand things the way they truly are. If beauty's in the eyes of the beholder, then what about truth? Or just the plain way some people understand things? It's like the thought of this starts at one point in time, and goes in a complete circle, right back to where you began. How do you make a person see something they can't see on their own? Or how do you tell someone that what they see, they really don't see?

The mind is much more than we know it to be. Never under estimate its power, its worth, or its compassion.

My practice was new. I was new and very excited to get going healing the world. I felt like superman after flying around the morning sun. I could do anything. I was empowered and ready to take on the whole troubled planet. Helping people; is it really possible? I believe to some degree anyway, but I also believe a person can only be helped if he/she really wants to be helped. You would hope that you would have a period in the beginning to get comfortable with your new arrangements, your clients, and all the idiosyncrasies of your psyche future. But for me, nothing could have been further from the truth. My first client I'll never forget for a lot of reasons, and without naming them all one by one, I'll tell you a story.

As I sat behind my desk, I was ready, focused on the task at hand, and ready to listen and learn all I could about this woman. She would be my first and I wanted nothing more than to help her. I wanted to understand her problems and help her deal with them. This had to be a success; I needed this to be. Two minutes to one, and my secretary Sue came over the com.

"Dr. Blue, I have a Tina Gamble here to see you."

At first I didn't say a word as I tried to swallow the huge lump that had lodged in my throat.

"Dr. Blue, are you there?"

Then I said, "Yes, Susan. Send Miss Gamble in, please."

As she walked in, these are the things I noticed right away: she wore all black with jet black long hair pulled back into a pony tail, a long black trench coat and tall black boots, by the looks of her wet hair and shoulders of her coat; it must have started to lightly rain on her way in. I stood and walked around the desk to meet her. I said,

"Hello, Miss Gamble. It's my pleasure to meet you. I'm Dr. Blue."

She didn't smile. She said,

"Hello, doctor."

I looked at her for just a second,

"Please. I'm sorry. Have a seat."

And then the other thing I noticed; she was beautiful. This may or may not be the order in which I noticed these things. She sat without removing her coat; she fumbled around looking at everything but me. She fought to get herself together and for a moment I let her, and then I said,

"Can I get you anything? Tea, water or coffee?"

She said, "Well Tea if it's no trouble."

I smiled "Tea it is and no trouble at all—Susan, some hot tea for Miss Gamble would be greatly appreciated."

I hit the com, as if it wasn't the first time I had done so. I looked at her and said, "How are you feeling? I understand you've been feeling very fatigued."

Her eyes still had avoided contact with mine, it was clear she was uneasy and not sure of what to make of me at this point. She said as she fussed with a scarf around her neck, "Yes, I'm more and more tired all the time it seems—Dr. Blue, I know I requested these visits, but the truth is I'm very aware of my own situation. I'm not crazy; this I can tell you for sure."

As her eyes rolled up from her lap to meet mine for the first time I said, "Well, I can appreciate how you feel, and I'm very happy you let me know right in the beginning. I think this would be a good place for us to start getting to know each other. What do you think?"

"Very well, if you say so, doctor."

"If I were to ask you what's bothering you the most, what would you say it is, and why?"

"Well, normally it could be any number of things, but right now I would just have to say the way I feel about things, my thoughts. And as for why, well everything we believe as individuals; what we feel to be right or wrong. Maybe just what I think is right, but you may think it's entirely wrong—do you understand what I'm trying to say, doctor?"

"You say the way you think about things. This way of thinking; do you feel it's wrong to think the way you do?"

"—No, I don't believe it is wrong, but when I explain it to you, I'm sure you might."

She started to open her bag and take out a gold lighter that must have cost a few hundred dollars, and then a gold plated cigarette case that was just as expensive. Then she looked at me and said, "Do you mind if I smoke?"

As she lit the cigarette and started smoking, I never answered one way or the other.

"Do you mind if I call you Tina?"

"I would prefer it actually."

"All right then, Tina, let's talk about the way you see things, right or wrong."

"I've been thinking about meeting with you today, doctor and I have trouble understanding the reasons one should believe that another human being who has studied certain behaviors can then best mentally treat them, based only on sessions such as these. And don't get me wrong, doctor; I do believe you can be helpful, but only to the smallest extent."

She then unbuttoned the top button on her still wet black coat, still not ready to take it off completely, like she may at any moment jump up to leave. I must admit I was somewhat surprised by her topic, but she would never see past my exterior. I was ready for this. Hell, I was born for this. I looked at her and had to go deep past her beauty and into her mind. Here is where I would begin my work; the psyche that fuels the human mind.

"Well, Tina, my job is not to judge you based on the things you may tell me, but to hear you and help you understand all those things that trouble you along the way."

"So you don't think you can help me, really help me?"

"Yes, I think I can help, if you would like me to."

"How could this be possible if you have only just met me? The mental state of any individual is completely independent from any other. No two people are the same. So with no prior knowledge of this person, how could you really help, even if they wanted you to?"

She was passionate about how she felt. It meant something to her, but I didn't know what. It was like she was waiting for me to say the right thing, the perfect answer she was looking for, but I was still trying to figure this out for myself. She was smart and her mind was like a steel trap. I didn't want to get caught inside, because then anything could happen. And right then I knew, this was real my first true test. She was ready, but was I?

Then it was right back to the gold box; a chain smoker. Her teeth were perfect with not a stain or blemish anywhere. Her scent was strong, almost as strong as the tobacco; it too was wonderful. She was heavenly even though she was a smoker. I was enchanted by her; she set off a feeling of warmth inside of me, but she would never know. I was ready.

"Anyone can be helped if they truly want to be helped. You are unique, different in every way, and your emotional make up may be different from my secretary you met on your way in today. Tina, I focus all my observations on only the information you present to me at that time. I will only give counseling on the information given to me by you."

"I would still consider that information incomplete at best with no real way to really know someone in such a short period of time, doctor."

"How much time do you believe is needed for one to truly evaluate a patient, in your opinion?"

"I would say that would depend on that individual."

"I understand."

"Do you, doctor? Understanding is the whole point here. How can we really understand?

The true difference of right and wrong; is there really a way this can be done?"

Then Sue came over the com,

"Doctor, I have Miss Gamble's tea."

"Bring it right in, Susan. Thank you."

She came in and sat the tea down in front of Tina. She said,

"Thank you, Susan. You're very kind."

"You're welcome, Miss Gamble. Anytime."

Susan looked at me as she walked out. She was very impressed with Tina as I was, but in that womanly way.

This was a war. Who would win? She didn't believe in what I did, but why was she here? Just to make a point to me? But why me? It all made no sense.

She was very together, and I was starting to think she didn't really need my services. But there were signs of things that I paid attention to.

She sipped her tea, still never putting down her cigarette. I never asked if she would like me to take her coat. I knew she wasn't ready.

"I would like you to feel like this will be worth your time. I am here to help in anyway I can. I do understand your position. Maybe we can find ways through our communication to help each other better understand the things we can't for lack of time spent."

"I am impressed with you, doctor. You are trying to find away to reach me. We could talk all day, but your point of view will never be mine or mine yours; they may appear close, but still never the same."

"You're right, but who's to say yours would be right, and mine wrong?"

"Now you're starting to understand, doctor."

"I'm trying. I feel this is important, and I really feel we can help each other here today. It's not just me helping you, Tina."

"But only if you want to be helped, doctor—Do you, a doctor, really want to be helped?"

"Yes, just as much I would like to also help. This is a good thing. I feel I could learn a lot from you, but do you feel you could learn from me as well?"

"There are always things to be learned from everybody, doctor. You should know that."

"Tell me more about the things you think about."

"Someone like you I don't think could ever really understand; you're so focused on helping me and proving to me that you know more than I do. You're more normal then I am. It would be clear that I am here to receive help from you and not the other way around."

She stood and walked over to the window looking out; she started to unbutton her long black rain coat, one button at a time. From my desk I could only see the back of her. Her hands moved down slowly, undoing the coat as I watched from my desk. Then she dropped it down off her shoulders, and placed it over the back of her chair. She then reached into her bag for the golden cigarette case and golden lighter. Her body was beautiful; she wore a long, black, clinging dress that hugged her body just right revealing every curve and every line.

"I believe your only weaponry to fight against people with mental problems is that of medication; drugs to stimulate the mind in another direction other than the way it's headed. This is not a fix, doctor; this is a true cover up. To bury the problems by masking them over, like a watered-down drink. Doctor, if you filled a glass half full of Jack Daniels, and then filled the rest with water, the two would mix, but only for a short time.

You look like a drinker, doctor. You should try this sometime."

She walked back around to the front of my desk, smoking the cigarette, and said,

"After a while the water would separate and rise to the top, and the Jack would surely settle down in the bottom of the glass. Now as they mingle, the potency of the drink would be weakened. But when you weaken the effect of the Jack, you weaken many other things; things that were never meant to be weakened. You call them side-effects; I call them life-changing effects, and to which there is no return. These are the things I think about, doctor. This is what troubles me. When you help someone, do you truly help them? Or is it the band aid over the gunshot wound?"

Inside I was confused, but I would still never reveal the truth. I was perplexed, although I felt I was ready for anything. But the truth was I wasn't sure if I was ready for Tina Gamble. She was even more confident now, not like when she had first walked into my office; she was stronger now, like it was she who had just flown around the morning sun.

She was empowered and ready to destroy me and the entire world.

My mind raced, trying to find ways to undo all the wrong I felt this woman was cursed with. I knew everything I needed to know and it was just the matter of presenting it in a compassionate and psychological way. I would not lose, I could not lose, and my success was the only way.

"Have you ever taken medication for any of these issues that trouble you, Tina?"

"I have always refused. I understand what it truly means to be helped, and that doesn't help me or anyone else for that matter."

"All medication is not the same, and I will say it is very important to know the individual in need of medication, matching him or her to a drug that will help their problem. This is a very difficult thing to do. Every person that I choose to see, I understand that they are an individual. One is completely different than the next. They all have their own unique characteristics. So what may work for some, won't work for others. It is my job to make these different connections. And I do not believe this is an overnight process. It takes time, Tina, time that I am more than willing to spend in order to truly help someone.—Now I really want to help you. Help me to be able to do that."

"Have you ever helped anyone else before, doctor?"

"I would like think that I have."

"Have you ended their problems, or have they learned how to better deal with them?"

"Sometimes learning to deal with problems is a wonderful relief. It can and has changed peoples' lives in ways that they never thought possible."

"Anything is possible, doctor. Wouldn't you say so?"

"That is a fair statement, Tina. Now I'd like to focus more on you. You are here today. Why did you choose to see me over the other doctors with long careers? Don't you believe they could have shined a little more light on these topics better than I?"

It was time for another smoke; she started to smile as she lit up. She looked at me as she did. She was looking to see if she was making the new doctor nervous in any way. She said,

"Starting to think you shouldn't have taken my case—is that right, doctor?"

I will not break or bend. I might be new, but I am good at what I do, and I had to stay in control. I would never let her beat me!!"

"Not at all. Like I said, I would really like to help you."

"Still think you can, do you?"

"I still will do everything in my power to do so."

She was impressed with me. I could see it in her eyes; it was starting to become a game like chess, one careful move after another. Her eyes were hypnotic, so careful I had to be, or they would see right through me.

"Well, now that I am here, I know I have made the right choice."

"And what makes you feel that way?"

"You, doctor. I feel like you want to help me, but it will take everything in my power to make you understand that there's no way you can."

"If you felt that I couldn't help you, why did you still want to see me?"

"I'm not here for you to help me, doctor. I'm here to try and help you."

My eyes started to give me away, but I caught myself quickly before it was too late.

What was this? Had someone set me up? This had to be some kind of a joke.

But there was no way for me to know for sure. She wasn't breaking.

She must be waiting for me to, but I won't. I'm in for the long haul. Whatever this is, it can't beat me. I refuse to lose.

It was getting late and I had one more patient to see, but this wasn't over. I wanted to know what she meant by helping me?

"You know, I have really let the time get away from us. I hate to end our session, Tina."

"Well, don't. It was just starting to get interesting, doctor."

She pulled the clip out of her hair that held the long black ponytail in place, letting all her long, beautiful hair fall down and around her face. For just a moment I froze, then right away I hit the com, "Susan, could you come in here please?"

"Certainly, doctor."

She never took her eyes off of me as she walked back to her seat, and then lit another cigarette. And I could just feel that lump starting to form back in my throat. I was in for something, but what, I wasn't really sure. But for whatever reason, I was willing to find out. I knew this wasn't the right choice to make, but I did. I wanted to ride this whole thing out. Then Susan walked in, "Hey, Susan, would you mind telling my next patient I would like to reschedule for tomorrow evening and to please excuse this inconvenient timing."

She looked at me as if to say, what the hell are you doing? This is our first day.

"I certainly will, doctor"

She smiled as she turned to leave the office, and Tina stopped her. She said, "Susan, excuse me." As she stood and walked over to her close to the front of my desk, I was still seated behind my desk looking up at the two of them. "That is a very familiar scent you're wearing. Very beautiful and sensual woman of the orient use this same scent. Venice, am I right?"

"Oh my god, you are the first person who has ever been able to recognize it! I love it. I never wear anything else."

"Well I'm not sure if you're aware that the maker of Venice has recently marketed its successor, Venice II."

"My god, are you sure? Oh, I'm sorry, doctor."

"No. Its okay, Susan."

"Come here. I have some in my bag I would like you to have."

She turned and walked back to her bag and started looking through it. Susan looked at me and I shrugged my shoulders and raised my hands. And Susan started walking over to her. Tina pulled out this bottle and started to unscrew the top. Susan's eyes lit up like a Christmas tree when she saw the bottle.

Outside my office window it was now evening. My office was dimly lit as the setting sun's reddish orange made its way in through the lofting clouds from all the smoking Tina had been doing. The scene was hypnotic. It seemed as Tina turned up the bottle and touched it to both sides of Susan's neck like Susan's eyes closed for just a second. Susan is very beautiful as well with wonderful womanly curves. Then Tina waved the bottle under Susan's nose, as she looked over at me watching them.

Susan said, "That is heavenly!"

"Take it. I want you to have it."

"Thank you. That is very kind of you. I can't accept, but I do thank you again, Miss Gamble."

Susan turned to look at me and smiled, walking to the door of my office. Tina watched her going, putting the top back tightly on the bottle of perfume.

And then, before Susan could reach the door, she stopped and started to place her head in her hands as if she was dizzy, and then she fell to the floor.

"Susan, my god! Are you okay?"

I ran over to her and she was just lying there, face down and not moving. I grabbed her shoulders and turned her over. She wasn't breathing. I shook her as I screamed her name.

Then I turned and looked at Tina. I screamed at her to call 911.

She walked past me as I started CPR, but she didn't go to the phone on my desk. She walked to the door and turned around, looking back at me as I was breathing into Susan's mouth. I was in a crazy panic when Tina screamed, "Doctor!!"

I looked up and saw her pulling her long black dress up, hiking it up higher and higher until her upper thigh and black panties were exposed.

But there was something else; it looked like a black garter around her upper thigh. But this had a digital read out and it was counting down; it was a bomb. I froze; she looked at me smiling, and said,

"Don't waste your time. She's dead. And if I were you, I would be worried about myself right now. This is a bomb, doctor, and it will go off one hour from now. So do you still feel you can help me? This is all the time we have, doctor, so whatever you do to fix people's problems, you need to fix mine in under an hour, or we both die."

My eyes were wide open with a look of disbelief hung on my face; Susan was dead on the floor right in front of me. What was happening? How did this happen? I had no idea, but it did, and one hour from now I could be dead as well.

"Why—why are you doing this?"

"Are you ready to continue, doctor? We don't have all night, and just so we understand each other; yes I killed her, and I will kill us next if you try to do anything but what I tell you to do for the next hour. All I have to do is squeeze my legs together and it's all over. But if you can really help me like you've been telling me since I've come through the door, now would be a real good time. Unlike most people, doctor, I really want to be helped, so according to you this should be no problem, right? Come on, doctor, you're not at a loss for words. You're my doctor. You deal with people like me every day, right? Well then help me, doctor. We're running out of time."

I folded Susan's hands over her waist, and then I slowly got up back on to my feet. Now without a shadow of a doubt, I knew this woman was crazy, paranoid schizophrenic. I had to collect myself; I needed to get it together fast. If this was real, and the fact that Susan was dead on my floor was proof enough for me to believe it was, I knew I had to play this game with her to live.

"Doctor, I would like you to have a seat on the couch over here closer to me."

So I walked to the couch, and she pulled up a chair from across the room. She sat down a few feet in front of me and lit another cigarette. I said to her,

"It seems you have your mind all made up. Is me trying to help you now senseless? I know you feel this would never be enough time, am I right?"

"This is why I picked you, doctor. You are very smart and I knew you would be. But there is always a chance. Anything is possible right, doctor?"

"I would have to say that is a fair statement, Tina."

This was real, and I was just about to lose it. I fought with everything I could to keep my composure, but I didn't know how long I could keep it up. We only had an hour.

"Why the bomb, Tina? Why must people die for you to make a point?"

"People die every day, doctor; some because the help they receive is worthless. They never really had a chance, even though they felt they did. People should always have a chance, a real chance, doctor. So come on, fix me. Give me my real chance to be better. Help me like you have helped all those other people. I want you to feel like you did all you could. Isn't that right, doctor?"

She sat right in front of me with her legs waving open and closed underneath her long black dress, but keeping them apart enough so the bomb wouldn't go off.

I loosened my tie; I had started to sweat. The room was hot, smoky, and dimly lit. Susan was still dead on my floor over in front of my desk. My head started to spin, but there was no time to pass out. Not now. I reminded myself I was ready, hoping that would work and snap me back. I really did want to help this woman. That's what this was all about anyway. No way was I going to lose; no way was I giving up.

"Do you know why you want me to feel like I have done all I could not only to help you, but we both need help right now. The reason is that you are starting to get to know me. In just this short time, you know something you can use to help motivate me in one way or another. Isn't that right, Tina?"

"This bomb is your motivation, doctor."

"That is only one of the motivation tools, Tina. There are more. Let's talk about them."

And for the first time, she put out the cigarette before she had smoked the whole thing. I was onto something. Not much, but something.

"You said you chose to see me over the other doctors because of me, something about me. Do you remember what that was, Tina?"

"I said you were smart."

"And you also said you knew I would be. Is that what you said, Tina?"

"—Yes."

"How did you know I would be so smart? And I was the right doctor to choose for this?

What did you base this on, Tina? And how long did it take you to really know I would be?"

Her legs stopped waving; she looked away and then got up and walked over to the window. Still she didn't say a word. Was this it? Was she about to kill us both? I was scared to death. I felt like I'd be dead before that damn bomb had a chance to blow anyway.

It was quiet. She was just standing with her back to me, looking out the window.

I made a valid point, but I didn't know how she was going to take it. Would she see the logic and understand how you could learn things about people in short frames of time if you paid close attention. Or would she still be blinded, unmedicated and not diluted or masked over, buried with no hopes to return? We were running out of time. Not another word. I was afraid to speak. Would it be too much? Would I push him over the edge? Time was running out fast. So I reached over and picked up my gold cigarette case and my gold lighter and just as I was about to light up, he turned around at the window with his hand on the black device strapped around his waist. Ten seconds and counting down.

"I guess you can learn things about people in short frames of time, doctor, if you pay close attention. Is my time up, doctor?"

I looked at him as the final seconds ticked off the counter around his waist and I said,

"Yes, Tim, that's all the time we have."

He looked at me as I put my lighter and cigarette case back into my bag, and then I walked back around my desk and had a seat. Just as the counter hit all zeros, Susan came over the com, “Yes Susan.”

“Doctor Blue, you have a Mr. Tim Gamble here to see you.”

“Yes. Give me five and send him in. Thank you, Susan.”

It was over and just about to begin; my first case. And I was ready. In my mind I had gone over everything. And being a woman made it all harder, but I would never let them see me sweat. I play these scenarios in my mind all the time. I’m a doctor, a psychiatrist. What makes the way I think any different than you? Maybe we can save the world or maybe we can only in our minds.

Understanding Nelson!

My name is Solomon. I am seventy years old. Now my weekends are spent here in the park, enjoying the sunshine and watching the people go by living their lives. Here I sit on my favorite park bench, just as I do every Saturday. I am alone now, but I am very happy, as I have spent a very full life with all the people that I loved and cared the world for.

My life has been full. I have seen and learned so many things in this life, and the world indeed is a funny place. As I watch the young ones play, I smile, and as I watch the older ones, I scratch my head and just try to understand.

Normally I spend my Saturdays alone just watching, but today something happened. A young man sat down beside me, and began to talk to me.

"I hope you don't mind me sitting here? I really don't mean to bother you, but I don't have anyone to talk to and nowhere to go. I'm not asking for a handout or anything. I'd really just like to talk to you, if you don't mind?" I looked at him. Water was starting to fill his eyes. He was hurting, it was very clear to me. And right away, my heart went out to him. His pain was coming from deep inside. Something had really wounded him badly.

"My name is Solomon. What is your name, young man?"

"I am Nelson. Nice to meet you, Solomon."

"I can see you're very troubled, son. I'd like to help, if I can."

"Well, I don't think anyone can help me, but thank you for trying. I feel my life is over. I'm only twenty-five, but I don't feel the desire to live anymore. My wife and I had our first child three months ago, and I thought my life was complete; my baby girl was the key to life for me. Then a month later, she died. My child died; before I could even begin to know her, she was gone. Now how am I supposed to live? How can I go on? Her name was Anna. She was beautiful. She meant everything to me and I loved her."

He broke down crying uncontrollably. I put my hand on his shoulder and turned him around to face me.

"Nelson, it's okay to cry. It hurts to lose the ones we love. There is no easy way to get through this, son, but you can get through. As you sit here crying for Anna, the love you have for her is so strong inside you that when I close my eyes, it's as if I can see her, or I knew her. She will always be with you."

He slowly started to pull himself together, and began to speak again.

"My wife has a drinking problem. I knew she had this problem, but I never tried to get help for her, even after we found out we were going to have a baby. She needed me. Anna needed me, and I let them both down. I should have been there for them, but I wasn't. Anna was born with a rare disorder of her kidneys. The doctors say the drinking could have caused it, but sometimes it happens to children whose mother never took a drink. But that makes no difference to me now. She's gone, Solomon." He began to cry once again. "I left home. I couldn't bear to look at my wife anymore. It hurts too much. She's stopped drinking, and wants to try and have another baby. What does she think? That's going to make everything better? Anna is still gone, and there's nothing that could replace her."

"Your wife is hurting as well, Nelson, and probably is feeling just as responsible if not more than you. But what I do know is that you need each other more than ever right now."

"That's what she said to me before I left. I love her, but I feel afraid now. The thought of going through that again is more than I can handle. How could she even want me anymore?"

"Nelson, she doesn't blame you for this, so neither should you. No one is to blame for this. Life is just what it is, whatever it is, and we accept the good things as well as the bad."

"Solomon, how could I ever have another child and look into his or her eyes and not think of Anna?"

"You should think of her. She would be a part of them just as she is a part of the both of you. This life is forever changing. We must continue to change with it, and it is all we can do, as we pray for the day of understanding."

"Do you think there will ever be such a day?"

"I know there will be. You just believe, and that day will come."

"I'll never forget her, Solomon. If I live, my life will never be the same."

"No, it won't. But life should mean more to you now, not less. Don't be afraid to be a father again. Be the best you can be. It's what you must be. That truly is the best way to heal your heart."

Nelson looked at me and started to cry. My heart once again went right out to him. It was as if the pain he felt, I somehow suffered. Then he said to me, "Thank you, Solomon; you've helped me when I thought I couldn't be helped. I never knew my father, but when I dream of him, I'll dream he was a man like you."

"That's very kind, Nelson. Thank you, you are a good man. Go home and pray with your wife. Be there for each other, that's the most important thing. Sometimes people lose their way. When things go bad, we lose focus, and it's hard to see clearly. And at those times, we need to just slow down, find some peace and some UNDERSTANDING, NELSON."

That day I left the park was the first and last time I ever saw Solomon. I returned many times to find him, but I never could. Now five years have passed, and I still come to this same park on Saturdays. I sit in the same spot where we sat that day five years ago. I scratch my head as I watch the older ones go by, and as I watch my son Solomon play; I smile.

The Coffee Shop

The shop was crowded, and I had just sat down with my laptop and a hot cup of Joe. It must have been my lucky day; I got the last table over in the corner, out of the way, just like I liked it. The Coffee Shop was the most popular spot for our small community of people. Mostly intellectuals and artsy types hung out there. I loved coming here. See, I'm a writer, and maybe it's just the smell and nuance of this place that stirs my creative cup of Joe.

And it's always so damn good.

This had become a daily routine for me; I live right around the corner. My home is also my office, and lately it's just become dark and tight to me. I was starting to feel closed in and I needed some space.

But really, how I ended up here was strictly by chance. I got up one morning and started feeling that way again, so I went for a walk, and walked right into the **Coffee Shop!**

So ever since, at some point in my morning, I grab up my laptop, and head out.

This place is a creative gala, full of intricate holes that lead to wonderful situations and events that you must know and hear.

And when I'm here, it takes me there, and I sit and write, hoping to discover something intriguing enough to pull you right in.

Maybe the people here are starting to get to me? I'm starting to sound like them. But I must say I'm hooked,

"And I really don't like coffee all that much."

Coffee of all kinds released their magnificent scent into the air, mixing gently as the ceiling fans spun slowly in sync with each other.

Pastries and cakes lined the glass counter as well, making it hard to pass them by. The leather of the sofas mixing with the wood of the cocktail tables added their presence to the shop, and each man or woman coming in also exposed their own scent to this captivating atmosphere.

Today I'm trying something new. I'm doing what I call feel free writing.

What I do is write about whatever I see, and how it makes me feel, and in here is the best place I could be.

The sofa across the room is empty now; the man that was there left behind a paper, and his coffee mug stained on one side, maybe as he sat down shifting the coffee over the side. In front of me is a heavyset woman eating cake; she appears to be in a hurry, with crumbs of icing and cake flying from her lips as she rushes to finish the slice. As I look around the shop trying to find the next wormhole to enter, there the bell rings; it's the door to the coffee shop. And then I see her.

This woman is wonderfully made with long, black, straight hair hanging down just past her waist. My eyes fix on her black high heels, as she walks slowly over to the counter.

Typing I am, as my eyes make their way up her long beautiful legs, all the way up to her seductive face, and every inch of the way is incredible.

She is different, not the kind of woman I would see here in the shop, but here she is. Why?

She got her cup and now turns to the seating. She's looking around, and she's looking at the sofa, but not moving to it. I don't think she wants to sit there. Now she sips her cup of coffee as she stands there, looking around and moving her hair from her face seductively.

She could sit anywhere; why is this such a hard decision for her?

A man and his wife are walking past her and she smiles. The man returns the smile back to her, but not the wife. She is not impressed.

Now she is walking toward the sofa. I think she is going to sit there, but now she stops right in front to look around again. Now she is looking right at me.

I'm looking right at her, and she is looking right at me as I type this. I feel like looking away, but I can't. Why doesn't she?

She's powerful, in that womanly way. She is not intimidated by me at all. She now knows I'm looking at her.

She's walking to me right now. Her face is still, no smile, but still very beautiful. Now she right in front of me at my table. She's speaking to me,

"Do you mind if I sit with you?"

But I don't stop writing; I can't, so I answer,

"It would be my pleasure."

Now she is sitting down and slowly places her coffee on the table behind my laptop. I can see the steam from her cup coming up over my screen as I write, and she is still looking at me.

My fingers slow to a stop as my eyes roll slowly up over the top of my screen. Now they start again, as her beautiful lips begin to move.

"What are you writing?"

"Well, everything."

"What do you mean everything?"

She picks up her cup to sip her coffee.

"I think I'm going to call this, **Coffee Shop."**

She almost smiles, and says, "That's not very original."

I'm smiling, "There's something about this place I really love, and it's very captivating."

"It is nice, but I don't care for coffee all that much."

She sips once again.

"How far along are you in your story?"

"I'm right here, at this table right now."

She's looking at me puzzled.

"You mean you're writing this, right now."

"Yes I am, every word, and every thought."

"So what happens now?"

"Whatever the coffee shop wants, I guess."

"So whatever the coffee shop shows you, you write?"

"Something like that."

She's sipping again, and my coffee is completely cold.

"Do you come here and do this every day?"

"Mostly, but normally I just write, but not like this."

"What made you do this today?"

"The coffee shop."

Ann is at my table, warming up my cold coffee,

"Thank you, Ann."

She said it was no problem, like always.

"Did you write that, what just happened now?"

"Yes I did."

"What's the point? Why would I want to read this?"

"Because you have questions, and you need answers."

She's moving her long hair back again, as a few more people make their way into the shop.

"Is there a plot?"

"There should always be, but you will have to be sharp to find it."

"Will there be clues?"

"Certainly, just look around you right now."

"This is just a coffee shop, that's all I see."

"But there is so much more, more than even I can see."

"I can tell you only one thing about this coffee shop; maybe this will help your story."

I stop—I didn't see this coming, and she's sipping again.

"I own this coffee shop, and this is the first time I've been here since it opened."

I'm stopping and sitting back to sip my coffee.

I'm back, I can't believe this.

"Why did you sit with me?"

"Now you have questions."

She smiles for the first time.

"If you don't mind, you know, for the story."

"No, I don't mind."

"Why a coffee shop?"

What was it about her? It fit that she owned the shop; she drew me as much as it did.

Then she took the last sip of her coffee and said,

"If you really want to know all about this coffee shop and me as well, be here tomorrow, same time, and this same table."

We look into each other's eyes, as she slowly stands, and now she's turning and walking away. She's almost to the door…and now she's gone.

You see what I mean about this place; it never lets me down. I can't wait until tomorrow.

Well, I guess I should be going. Looks like I'll be back at this again tomorrow, so now I'm going to go. I'll pack this up, and head for home.

Walking Home!

I'm home. I know I was supposed to wait until the coffee shop tomorrow before I got back to this, but I think this is important.

When I came through the front door to my house I went to the kitchen, sat my laptop on the counter, and opened it up to write what you're reading now. And in she walks, the lady from the coffee shop,

MY WIFE.

"Hello, honey."

"What are you doing now? You told me only in the coffee shop."

"I know, but don't you love a good plot twist?"

THE COFFEE SHOP!

Full Capacity

I'm going to ask you just for a second to think about the human mind, the most powerful instrument known to mankind. No computer of any kind will ever be able to match the power of the human mind, simply because the human mind would be the creator of any such computer or apparatus.

Now think about all the breakthroughs in technology that the human mind has conceived; what a power and ability to conceive and create. We as human kind, continue to amaze ourselves with unbelievable accomplishments.

So now let's ask ourselves; what would it be like to be able to tap into the human mind's **Full Capacity**?

What a wonderful gift this would be, or should I say curse?

John Blake was just an average man, twenty-three years old, trying to find a way to build a life that was worth living. New York City was a hard city to get ahead in with no skills or education. But John was determined to find a way to make his dreams come true, and be a successful man, and a husband and father. He was simple, not in ignorance but in demeanor, and he was alone, finding it hard to capture the heart of a woman.

John's life was about to change in a way that you and I could never even dream of. He would soon know more than any other man alive; the only man ever to have a mind of **Full Capacity**.

May 29th 2004, John had just spent the day looking for employment, without any luck. As he drove back to his one bedroom apartment in the lower side of Brooklyn, he was perplexed by his situation. As he arrived home, a hot shower was just what the doctor ordered. He placed all the contents of his pockets on the cocktail table, and undressed, turning the water temperature to a hot steaming high.

Soon he was totally engulfed in steam, soothing his mind and body in the heat of the hot water. As he stood in the shower, his mind would not let him escape his reality. He was safe as long as the steam and hot water surrounded him, but right outside was a world of troubles awaiting his return. Not ever wanting to leave his peace and security of the bathroom, his body began to prune. Slowly he turned to shut the water off and do what he knew he had to do; return to the brutal world outside.

But as he moved, it happened; he slipped and fell hard hitting his head on the wet shower wall. Now he was out cold on the shower floor, with the water continuing to pound him with its hot steaming spray.

Slowly his eyes started to open, to massive white steam clouds all over him. "What happened?" he said, as he reached over to turn off the water.

I must have fallen? I can't believe it. He said to himself as he sat on the floor of the shower. *But I guess I understand why. I wasn't paying attention. My thoughts were somewhere else so I fell.* It was strange, but it all was so clear to him; not just the fall, but also his perception of everything. He could feel this running through him like fire in his veins.

John put on his robe and left the bathroom. He started a pot of water for coffee and went to get dressed. After he was dressed, he walked back to his living room, where he noticed the contents of his pocket he had placed on the cocktail table before. There was some loose change, some keys, and a folded piece of paper. He stopped in front of the table, looking down at the things from his pocket. He looked at them all. The paper was the only thing that drew him in, but why? This too was strange; he knew what it was, but why now does this piece of paper mean more somehow? *It's the bar code on my receipt from the health store in the mall today; it's not right. Someone has corrupted the computer system; this is an act of terrorism. I have to warn them. They're all going to die.*

He grabbed the phone and called security in the mall. He had to try before it was too late. As the phone was ringing he thought *how do I know this? Am I going crazy? What's happing to me?*

"Midtown Mall security. Jackson. Can I help you?"

"Get out! Get everybody out as fast as you can."

"Who is this? Is this some kind of joke?"

"My God no! You have to believe me! Everyone is in danger; you must get all the people out now!!"

"Calm down sir; let's start from the beginning.""No! There's no fucking time! Get them all out now!!!"

He knew there was no way to get this man to understand he knows all this because of a bar code on a mall receipt. He slammed the phone down and ran out the door headed back to the mall. He drove frantically though his mind was clear and sure. He knew what this was, and there was no way he could be wrong.

Now the mall was in sight. He parked his car across the road and jumped out running, screaming, "Everybody get out! Stay out of the mall!"

And as he came close, it happened. He stopped dead in his tracks, looking at the mall, and then it blew up in one big massive explosion. John was blown back at least 30 feet as the debris began to fall everywhere all around him. Now he lay covered in dirt and ash crying, *I knew, I knew this was going to happen! Why did I know? WHY?*

He must have blacked out; the next time he opened his eyes he was in the hospital. In walked a doctor and nurse, looking over him. "How are you feeling, Mr. Blake?"

"I'll be just fine. I no longer need to be here, but I do have information on this matter for the police."

"You mean the mall bombing?"

"Yes, something like that. Can you get the police for me please?"

"Yes we can do that for you, Mr. Blake, but I must be sure you are okay before we do anything."

John looked into the doctor's eyes and he said, "I need them now, please."

And without another word, the doctor left the room to find and bring back the police. John slowly opened his hand to find the piece of paper from the mall still smashed in his hand.

Now in his room stood two police officers, taking a report from John who was an eyewitness.

"So, Mr. Blake, what is it you think you know?"

"I know everything, all the things you don't know, and I don't think I know. I really do know."

"You know then that a lot of innocent people died today, and you were almost one of them. Can you tell us anything about this?"

"I'm going to tell you everything, but know this before I do; I had nothing to do with this happening; I just know how and why it did."

"Do you feel you need a lawyer present?

"That won't do me any good. You will understand soon enough, and then you will see I speak only the truth."

The police didn't know what to make of John, but they had nothing in the way of answers. Why did this happen? John slowly opened his hand and unfolded the small piece of paper. "This is how I know. The bar code on this receipt has been encrypted, and it came from Midtown Mall earlier today."

"You say it's been encrypted. What does that mean?"

"Only a few groups of people are capable of this type of infiltration; this knowledge is not widespread. The bar code has been changed; which made the system overload and explode."

"And what makes you knowledgeable, if you don't mind answering?"

"No, I don't mind. The truth is I don't know, but that is the only thing I can't answer for you."

"Can't or won't?"

"Just get your experts this information, and then you can answer that one yourself."

Then it all started; the investigation into it all. They couldn't believe what John Blake knew and could explain. He showed them things, things they would have never known, but how did he? That's what they wanted to know next.

For weeks they probed him, trying to understand how he knew all he did.

The information John gave on the terrorists was accurate, and they all were captured and sentenced to death. The FBI watched his every move, never letting him out of their sight. But this didn't bother John, he knew he could do whatever he wanted to do at any time, and no one could ever stop him.

As he sat alone still in his one bedroom apartment, he began to see just how different he had become. He could see everything, things that he normally could never imagine, but now it was nothing to his mind's eye.

His capacity was powerful in many ways. One night he sat at the table drinking coffee, looking out the window at the unmarked police car across the street. He looked back to the table to see for the first time his new great power.

He had sat for so long the coffee started to go cold, as he stared into the coffee slowly a light steam began to rise from the cup. His eyes opened wider with a surprised glare, but then right back to a more focused stare. Now without touching the cup, the now hot coffee started to stir. John did all this; not with his hand, but with his mind.

He stood up from the table and walked into the other room, still in a state of disbelief from the coffee moments ago. *What is this? Why do I know how to do these things?*

I can do anything, and have all I ever wanted to have; no one could ever stop me.

He sat down on his sofa looking at the television that was turned off, so with his mind he turned it on. Then he turned down the volume, and picked up the phone next to him, and made a call to a local car dealer. He ordered a car with a credit card number he made up in his mind only moments ago.

His mind flooded with ideas, manipulations, deceptions and scenarios.

All the things he could do, and all he would gain, *this is the best thing that ever happened to me, and I deserve it and more. All my life I've had nothing, but all that is about to change.*

John sat contemplating his next move. The FBI out front, he needed to leave, so he thought of reasons the cops would have to leave. He showered and dressed and was ready when the car salesmen rang his buzzer.

John went to the window to look out after letting in the salesmen, but the FBI for some reason was gone. The salesman filled out the paperwork for John's new vehicle and was on his way, leaving John with the keys to a very expensive sports car.

Off he went in his new car, looking for whatever came his way as the day turned to a slow faded dusk. The streetlights marched one by one over the cherry-red paint of John's new car in a steady stream as he rolled up New York's nightlife. Soon he found himself at a club, at the bar when a beautiful lady sat down next to him.

He looked over at her and said,

"Hello my name is John, let me buy you a drink, but just as a social gesture, because I'm sure you really don't need anyone buying you anything."

"That's nice of you. Thank you."

"I find it really hard to meet women in places like this; there are always so many preconceptions on what you or the other person has on their mind. So from now on I will always let the situation dictate all the interactions."

"I like the way you look at things, it doesn't seem you would have any problems meeting women."

"It's true; two weeks ago I would not have been able to have this conversation with you."

"Why not?"

"Let's say my life has drastically changed, and now I'm able to see things more clearly. I'm more confident. I know what I want, and I feel now, for the first time in my life, I can get it."

"So when you look at me, what do you want, John?"

"I want to get to know you better, even though I feel like I know already."

"What is it that you think you know?"

"I know you find me interesting, and I think you would like to know more. You like conversation, but it must be the right kind. You're good at spotting someone who talks a lot of bullshit, but you already know I'm not one of them, so I think you should trust yourself like you always do."

"That was incredible! How did you know that?"

"I know a whole lot more; let's go somewhere quiet so I can tell you all about it."

Her name was Gwen, and she was everything John had ever wanted. She was smart and beautiful; kindhearted was her personality. She was just right.

They left the bar together, it was close to morning, and John drove her off in his new car, thinking to himself, *my life has changed so fast. Is this a dream? This is the life I should've had a long time ago. Now I can make my life whatever I want it to be, just like I've dreamed, just like I've prayed.*

"So where are we going?"

"To a very nice place not so far away, right outside the city, just trust me, you will really love this."

"I don't know why, but I do. I feel like I've known you forever."

"That's a good thing, which means we understand each other, so getting to know you better is something that I hope you will let me do?"

A beautiful lake with paddleboats for rent. It would make the perfect first date. Gwen was very excited as John opened her car door to take a better look at the lake. As she emerged from the car, John's face turned to stone.

"What is it John? You look like you just saw a ghost."

"I don't know, something's not right and I'm not sure what it is."

"Well, let's not think about it now, let's just enjoy ourselves."

"You're right, that's what we're here for."

The lake was surrounded by different vendors: foods and sunglasses and all kinds of things. The boats were the main attraction. It was a haven for lovers to share the day together, leaving the troubles of a hard world behind, if only for a short time. Whatever was bothering him, it was getting worse by the minute. But John didn't understand what it was, so chose not to say anything at the moment. He took Gwen by the hand and headed for the boats, but she wanted to eat something first. This bothered John as well, but he did as she wanted and took her for food right around the lake.

John sat looking at Gwen from across the table as they waited for their food.

He thought to himself,

This is not real? This woman is here with me for what? I am the same man I was yesterday. Maybe I'm not. I don't feel the same, I feel better. I can handle anything and do anything. I know she wants me.

"I am so ready to eat, John, are you?"

"I am. And I am ready to kiss you."

"That's just what I was thinking, it's like you can read my mind."

"I can."

John kissed her for the first time; a long passionate kiss. Gwen was taken by him; he seemed to be everything she ever wanted. John had never felt the warmth of a woman's lips this way, he fell instantly and deeply in love with her.

Then the food came. Gwen had seafood and John had a salad. As they sat eating and trying to hold a conversation, the man at the next table was looking at them trying to talk to them, and being very loud. Every time John tried to say something to Gwen, this man had something to interject.

John tried to smile and not let this man upset him, or this wonderful time he had waited his whole life to share with the right person. But there was a limit and this man had crossed the line.

"Excuse us sir, but we are on our first date and would like a little privacy if you don't mind?"

"Just wanted to know how your young lady friend likes the fish? I've been eating fish here for the last five years, and I'll tell you right now, it's the best."

Gwen looked at him and smiled, then said,

"It's great, it's very good."

He smiled back at her, but John's face had the look of a lost boy.

She said, "What is it, John, you okay?"

"Yes I'm sorry; this guy I guess is just getting to me, that's all."

John had that same strange feeling he had back at the car, but he was into Gwen too much to let anything get to him, even this asshole.

But the man didn't stop; he kept talking to them, bothering their meal every few minutes. By now John was going crazy. Gwen thought the whole thing was funny so she just smiled. "I've ask you nicely a few times, sir, to please leave us alone, but you can't seem to do it."

"I'm sorry; you're just such nice people. I don't get to talk to nice people like you and your girl."

"Just leave us alone!"

As his voice demanded the attention of all the tables, John's anger continued to mount as he looked at the man talking and spitting fish everywhere with his mouth wide open.

John peered at him as everything slowed down, and no sound but John's heartbeat was present.

Hateful thoughts made their way into John's mind, as he looked at the fish flying and falling from his huge mouth.

I hope that fish kills your ass, you damn fool!!

Then Gwen called to him and brought him back from his mind's captivity with this man.

"John, it's alright now; let's just go to the boats."

John returned smiling at her, as he took her hand and walked away to the boats.

He looked into her eyes and said, "Nothing can spoil this day, the day my every wish came true." Soon they were on the boat, just the two of them. John was rowing the boat; it was wonderful. But soon John started to feel strange again, and looked over to the side of the lake and saw the same man who had pestered them at dinner; he was on the ground with a bunch of people standing over him.

Gwen said, "Oh my god! I hope he's alright?"

Then all at once, John knew what that feeling was that pulled on him, telling him that somehow something was very wrong. He was frozen, as he looked at this man dying from food poisoning. It was the fish!

I have killed this man with my thoughts. I wanted the fish to be bad, and it was. This is what I have done, "Oh my god! Gwen? Gwen?"

But there was no response. Gwen was now motionless on the floor of the rowboat.

She had the fish as well.

Chapter Three

Good Boy, Mason!

This story is about a dog: a dog named Mason. Now just what is it about this kind of animal that draws us so close to them to the point of caring for them, and even loving them, as much as a family member?

It has been said that a dog is man's best friend. Why is that? If you are among the ones who feel this way, maybe after the events of this story, you may feel somewhat different.

Anthony Wilcox was just about to receive his degree in law, at Harvard University. Then, tragically, he received word that his father, Peter Wilcox, had died. This was more than devastating to Anthony; he was his parents' only child. His thoughts turning directly to his mother, he worried that this would affect her, in ways that may be too difficult to recover from.

So, without a second thought, he left for home to grieve with his mother. Peter Wilcox had been a judge. Serving for many years, he was loved and respected by all who knew him. Anthony's dreams were to be like his father, a lawman, and a man that would be true and just, all the things he had learned from him.

Upon returning to their beautiful home in Palm Springs, Anthony found his mother alone, sitting quietly, looking out of the beautiful patio doorway. This huge two-story ranch was magnificent; it appeared over-whelming to even Anthony, as he looked at his mother sitting all alone.

"Mother!" He cried as he went down to one knee to embrace her, as she sat still looking out at the beautiful garden, that she and Anthony's father had grown together. She held onto him and as he cried on her shoulder, she said,

"It's all right, my Anthony. It's all right, my son. He will always be with us. We will never be alone."

Anthony continued to cry, as he squeezed his mother even tighter.

After they cried together, the two of them made tea, and sat by the huge fireplace that Anthony and his father had built together. Anthony took a sip of the honey tea his mother made for him that he loved. He looked at her and said,

"I can't believe he's not here with you. Every time I have come home, he has always been here with you. But when I walked in here today, for the first time, I felt just how big this place is."

"This is still our home, and this is where we'll be; right here where your father wants us to be."

As Anthony looked around the huge colonial-styled room, he shook his head.

"How can I leave you here all alone? I won't do it."

"I belong here, Anthony. I'll be fine. You have unfinished business. You must go back; it's your whole life."

"But how can I?"

"You think your father would want you to stop now? He loved you, and wanted this for you as much as you do."

"I feel different now. I don't know if it's what I want anymore."

Ann Wilcox looked deep into her son's eyes, and then she put her tea down on the antique wooden coffee table, and said,

"Don't say that. This is what you were born to do. Your father and I have known this for a long time. Don't let us down, Anthony. We have always loved you, and we know you will succeed."

Anthony sipped on his tea without another word, and soon he led his mother up the winding staircase to her room, to settle in for the night.

Now the Wilcox home was quiet. As Anthony burned candles in his father's study, he looked through his pictures. Seated at his father's desk, he now sipped on a stronger drink, his dad's fine brandy. And he cried himself off to sleep.

Now about a week had passed, and Anthony's father had been lowered into his final resting place. He thought his mother was taking the whole thing better than he thought she would. But still he was torn, not wanting to leave his mother all alone. Ann Wilcox was not a social person; she didn't have any friends that visited regularly. They were private people. They always had been.

Anthony was running out of time. If he were going to graduate, he would have to be back in the next few days. He had tried talking to his mother, trying to make her understand that he didn't want to leave her. But she would not listen. To her, he had no other choice; he had to go.

So the morning he was to leave, he got up early and went out to take a walk and think about everything.

As he walked across their twenty-acre spread, he knew he should go back, but he also knew his mother needed him, even if she would not admit it.

He loved this place, his home where he grew up. And now with his father gone, how could he leave his mother? But as he walked back, he knew he had to go. It would hurt his mother worse if he were to stay.

Just as he walked up to the front of their ranch, he had what he thought was a great idea. Ann Wilcox watched from the front window as Anthony jumped right into his SUV, and drove away.

As she watched him drive away, she thought that this was strange; he never just left without saying where he was going, or when he would be back.

But soon she was off to the kitchen to get started on dinner. This would be her last dinner with Anthony before he left for school.

Now dinner was done, and the wonderful meal she had prepared had filled the whole house with wonderful aromas. A beautiful flower centerpiece, with candles on either side, enriched the meal's appeal to that of a king's spread. Now Anthony was late, and she started to worry. But before long, she could see the lights of his SUV, pulling up to the house.

She waited for him in the dining room. As he opened the front door, then made his way to her, he said, "Mother, I'm sorry I'm late. I had to go pick up something just for you," as he stood there empty-handed.

"I started to worry. Is everything all right?"

"Everything is going to be fine now," he said, as he smiled for the first time since he had been back home.

"What is that? It smells wonderful, but before we eat, I'd like you to meet someone."

The pleasant look on her face suddenly faded, as she said, "Anthony, now is not a good time for guest. Tonight is just for me and you."

"I know, Mother, but I have already picked him up, so just come with me."

Anthony knew how she felt about people coming to the house, but he thought this was something she needed. As they made their way to the other room, Anthony could see how much she didn't want to see anybody. He just smiled as he led her by the hand.

Now, as she stood there with her mouth open, in a state of disbelief, he continued to smile.

"Mother, this is Mason, and Mason, this is Mother."

She couldn't have been more surprised, as she looked at this huge four-legged shepherd.

"It's a dog!"

"He's much more than just a dog, Mother. He's the smartest I've ever seen."

"But why is he in my house?"

"He's yours, Mother. I got him for you."

"Why in God's name would you get me a dog? You know how I feel about pets."

"Well, Mother, you know how I feel about leaving you all alone, so this is what it comes down to."

"There's never been a dog in my house before, Anthony. This is not a good idea."

Mason sat quietly, not moving or making a sound, just watching the two of them as they talked. Ann knew that Anthony was not going to take no for an answer. As the back and forth between the two of them slowed, Anthony made his mother promise to give Mason a chance. He then hurried from the room, so she wouldn't have time to change her mind. Now she was alone with Mason for the first time. Mason was still in the same spot, sitting looking right at Ann, and she was looking back at Mason. The room was silent. Then she said to him,

"Well, are you going to say something?"

Mason responded with a hefty "WOOF!"

This came as a surprise to Ann, and she nearly jumped out of the chair she was in. Mason was a huge black and gray-haired shepherd. To look at him would send a message of fear to someone who didn't know him, but he was gentle and extremely smart. Ann started to laugh, as she thought, "This dog just answered me." She sat back in her seat, looking at him again. Still he didn't move. She said, "Can you stand up?"

Mason right away stood to his four legs. She was impressed. Now he appeared even bigger when he stood.

"Can you walk over to me?"

Mason started over to her slowly.

"Whoa, stop there, that's far enough."

Mason immediately stopped, just as she said. Ann couldn't believe this dog was so smart. She stopped him because she was still somewhat afraid. He was so big. Then she looked at him and said, "Have a seat."

And Mason sat promptly. She smiled; Ann had never seen anything like him before. Then Anthony walked back into the room. Ann took the smile off her face, and she didn't want Anthony to know that she was this impressed with Mason.

"So, you two are getting along?"

She said, "I've never seen a dog quite this big before."

"Mother, he's the sweetest thing in the whole world. Plus he will keep you safe. Why don't you pet him? Go on, try."

Ann sat up to the edge of her chair nervously and said, "Come here, Mason."

And Mason got up, and walked right to her, and sat back down. She slowly held out her hand to pet the top of his black head, and as her hand landed on top, she felt how soft he was, and so gentle. She began to smile, and Anthony knew this was going to work out. He smiled back at his mother, now petting and hugging Mason. She said, "Good boy, Mason."

The next morning, after Anthony showered, as he packed and got dressed to leave, he could hear Mason's deep bark, and his mother's laughter. He couldn't believe she was up so early, but there they were, out in back. She was walking with a big stick, as Mason jumped all around her. They were having a great time. Anthony stared out his bedroom window at them, as he fought to keep the tears from coming down his face.

Anthony made his way downstairs and found a freshly brewed pot of the best coffee you could find anywhere.

And before long, the two of them made their way back into the house. It was a wonderful day. Ann was so into Mason that the fact that Anthony would be leaving today seemed to be all right. And this was just the way Anthony wanted it to be for his mother.

They began talking, as Mason lay on the floor not moving, or taking his eyes off Ann for a second. If she went to another room, so did Mason, and when she sat down, so did Mason.

Ann smiled at her son. She said,

"Thank you, Son. This is wonderful. I love Mason, and you know me so well."

"I love you, Mother, and I want you to be safe."

"Well, my Mason will see to that. Isn't that right, Mason?"

Mason let out another deep "WOOF."

They both laughed together, as they held each other, saying their goodbyes.

Mason watched, as Anthony and his mother walked from the room, and out to the driveway. Mason, not wanting to take his eyes off of Ann, got up and moved over to the closed screen, so he could see her in plain view, as she kissed Anthony goodbye. Mason, looking on with his great black face and black glossy eyes softly "WOOFED," to show his discomfort with their embrace.

Now Anthony was gone, and Ann turned to walk back into the

house. Mason stood up on his hind legs at the door as she came back into the house.

"Good boy, Mason." She said as she hugged him upon entering the house.

"Are you hungry, Mason?" Mason answered with a great "WOOF", as they went into the kitchen.

"We are going to have some very good things to eat, nothing but the best for my Mason, and after we eat, we are going to take a walk to the fruit store.

Doesn't that sound good, Mason?" He ran to her legs, wagging his tail happily. They had their food, and were soon on their way.

As they walked, Mason was without a leash; he didn't need one. He knew to stay right by Ann, and he would never run off. As they walked up to the storefront, the owner was out front putting up new prices for the fruit; he smiled as he saw Ann coming. He turned and said, "Wow, Ann, who's your new friend?"

"Well, this is my good boy Mason. Isn't he wonderful?"

"He's incredible."

As the storeowner moved towards them to pet Mason, Mason lunged at him, with a mad snarl. The man was terrified and stumbled back; Ann was shocked as she screamed,

"Mason NO!" Mason stopped on a dime, and sat down at her side.

"I'm so sorry. I don't know why he did that, but I am sure he won't hurt you. Will you, Mason?" And then Mason responded with his deep "WOOF."

The man was still shaken, and still thought he should back away. Ann looked down at Mason, and said, "You stay here, and I'll be right out. You don't move, and don't woof at anybody else." Mason just wagged his tail as she walked into the store.

Mason sat in that spot, and didn't move or make another sound, and when Ann came out, they walked home.

About a week had passed, and Ann started to see how protective Mason was of her. One afternoon, Mason was taking a nap on the living room floor, and Ann had been waiting on a package all morning. There came a knock at the door; it was the postman.

Ann went to the door, happy her package had come, and Mason still looked to be asleep. This was the first time anyone had come to the house since Mason had gotten there.

Ann greeted the man and took the package from him, then all at once up ran Mason, pushing past her, almost knocking her to the floor, and jumping on the man out the door. It all happened so fast that Ann didn't know what it was at first. "Mason!" She screamed, and he stopped and let the man up. The man then ran as fast as he could to get back to his truck. Ann closed the door, looking at him, as she rubbed her shoulder she had banged against the wall because of Mason's foolishness.

"What has gotten into you? Why did you do that?" Mason stared at her with his black glaring eyes, walked over slowly, and sat right in front of the door.

"Now what does that mean?" she said, still mad at his behavior. Mason didn't move. He just looked at her. "Go lay down away from that door." She ordered him. But Mason didn't move. He just sat there looking at her.

Ann started to feel a little odd at how Mason was acting. She slowly moved away, not taking her eyes off him, but Mason still sat motionless, watching her every move as she walked from the room. Ann was very upset about what Mason did to the mailman, and wanted to call the office to see if he was all right.

Mason still sat at the front door not moving. Ann was now in the kitchen making tea and looking up the phone number for the post office. The house was silent as she found the number and started to dial the phone. And as she did, Mason slowly got up from in front of the door and started into the kitchen.

The phone started to ring as she stood by the stove waiting for an answer, and Mason was making his way down the hall slowly and was almost to the kitchen.

Between the front door and the kitchen, a large old-fashioned grandfather clock sat in the hall, and as Mason passed it by, it started to pronounce the hour with its golden chimes. The sound now filled the house as Mason came into the kitchen. Somehow she knew he was in the room, without even turning around to look. Now he stood there watching her make the call.

"Hello, my name is Ann Wilcox. I'm calling about the postman who handles the Oakwood Pass. Is he there?"

As Mason moved a little closer to her, she turned to him, just as the corners of his mouth started turning up to a snarl. Ann was frozen stiff, her eyes fully dilated, and locked on him. Mason's snarl soon turned into drooling as the man on the phone started to speak to her.

But Ann was now locked in on Mason, scared to even make a sound.

"Hello, hello? Miss, are you there?"

Ann, still in shock from Mason's behavior, tried to speak.

"This is Ann Wilcox."

Just as she began to speak to the man on the phone, Mason went crazy.

Jumping and WOOFING at her, he was out of control.

He was so loud she could no longer hear the man on the phone, so she put the phone down. And all at once, Mason stopped.

It was quiet again. Mason sat down right in front of her, not making another sound. Ann was breathing heavily as she held onto the counter for balance.

Masons eyes fixed and locked on her eyes, and hers were on him.

"What's wrong, Mason?" She said with a shaky voice, trying her best to calm herself down, but he was still and not moving; his black glossy eyes watched her. Ann slowly moved over to the table and sat down. Mason watched her every move as she went, but still did not move himself.

Ann was still very upset. She tried to think of what to do, and then she said,

"Mason, why don't we call Anthony? Yes, that's a good idea." And as she started over to get the phone, Mason jumped up and started WOOFING at her again. She quickly sat right back down, and then said, "All right then, Mason. I won't call." And just like that, Mason was calm once again. He sat back down and just watched her.

"Are you hungry, Mason? I'll make you something to eat." As she slowly tried to move again, this time Mason didn't make a sound, so she went to the cabinet and began making him his food.

Ann looked over at him as she made his meal. She tried to smile, fighting back the tears that so badly wanted to come running out.

"This is going to be good, Mason. I know you'll like this."

She put his food down right in front of him, and then moved back to her seat at the table. Mason was still not moving, just looking up at her as she sat back down. Not even once did Mason look down at his food.

"Go on, Mason. It's good. You eat it all." She said, trying to stay calm.

And Mason slowly lowered his huge black head down to the bowl, still keeping his eyes on Ann.

"That's it. Good boy, Mason." She said, as he snatched up all the food like he hadn't eaten for days.

After Mason had finished all his food, Ann got to her feet and picked up the bowl and put it away. She then started into the living room to have a seat and do some reading. As she went, Mason followed close behind her, and sat down right in front of her as she opened her book to read. Ann tried her best to stay calm, so she would not upset Mason, but this was hard and getting harder by the minute. She held the book up, covering her face so he could not see her expression of terror, as her eyes filled with tears.

Ann sat there for hours holding the book; afraid of what was going to happen next. Then Mason got up, and started looking around, then back at Ann, "What is it, Mason?" She said, bringing the book in her hands down to her lap. Mason then walked up to her, and with his big black head nudged her leg, once and then again. Now she started to understand what he wanted; Mason wanted to go outside. Then she started to think, "This is my chance to get him outside and lock the door. What else can I do? I need to call for help." All these things started running through her mind; finding a way to get to the phone, getting Mason outside of the house.

This was it. She had to try.

Slowly she reached over and put the book on the coffee table, then she rose to her feet and started to the front door, and Mason started right in behind her.

Now she was just about to open the door, and Mason closed the gap between them. As she opened the door, she pulled it back and as she stepped back, trying to clear a path for Mason, he came to the door right behind her. He just lowered his big black head, and rammed her from behind, pushing her first, right out the door.

She screamed as she flew out of the door. She wasn't hurt, just surprised at how it had happened. Now she turned to look at him, "Mason, that wasn't nice." Mason just turned up the sides of his huge mouth to the craziest snarl you could ever imagine. Then he moved to one side of the front door, never taking his eyes off of Ann, squatted right there, dropping a hot steaming pile right next to the front door.

"Mason, why right there? You could have gone out in the grass."

Once again, she had missed her chance, or Mason had taken the chance from her, by never moving far enough away from the front door.

Now he was done and was ready to go back inside, but not without Ann going first. He WOOFED at her, and she knew what he wanted her to do, so slowly she walked up to the door past Mason, and into the house.

Once they were both inside, Mason pushed the door with his head, closing it hard. And as he turned around, he saw Ann making her way up the spiral staircase to her room. Looking back at Mason closing the front door, she couldn't believe her eyes.

Ann lay across her bed on her back, with a look of horror on her face, trying to understand what was happening to her and why.

She gazed up, staring at the ceiling fan, as its spinning blades reflected the moonlight from the window down across Ann's tired old body. There were no phones on the second floor in the Wilcox home and there had never been. But now, as Ann realized this, she wished the tradition didn't exist.

Mason walked around the first floor of the house, as his long nails, with each step he took on the hard marble floors, rang out screeches of terror to Ann's ears, all the way up to her room. She lay there, hoping to fall asleep and tomorrow it would be all over, she prayed.

She did fall asleep, but she woke well before morning. It was Mason. It sounded like he was running in the house, and knocked something over. This noise woke her.

"Anthony, is that you?" but all was silent once again. She looked around the room, which was dark, but dimly lit from the moonlight.

Then she heard the noise once again. Now she was scared and starting to panic.

No longer could she sit in this room. She had to try to get help. It was driving her out of her mind, thinking, "This dog is holding me hostage! Right here, in my own home!" The phone was what she needed to call Anthony and he would come and take care of her, she thought as she cried, putting on her house shoes to walk down to the kitchen for the phone. But where was Mason?

She opened the door to her room very slowly, peeked her head out and looked down one way, and then back down the other way. No sign of Mason, so she stepped out, and headed to the stairs. Ann moved slowly, holding onto one side of the railings as she came down, praying Mason was still asleep and didn't hear her coming down. And as she came to the bottom, still there was no sign of him anywhere. It was very quiet. The only sound that could be heard was the tic-tock of the old grandfather's clock in the hall.

Now she was at the bottom of the stairs. Ann was so afraid that her legs had stiffened up, and were not willing to move her any further. She whispered,

"Please, not now! Please, not now!!"

Ann stood there crying, trying to get herself to the kitchen, before Mason would hear what she was trying to do. Then somehow she got her legs to move, still very slowly, but at least she was moving. Finally she was in the kitchen,

And on the counter was the phone. She had made it, and started to dial the phone. Very shaky, she was trying to calm down long enough to get the number dialed.

But just as she was done dialing, the phone went dead.

"Hello, is anybody there? Hello!!" It was dead. She slowly put the phone back down, and heard something coming from the other side of the counter. She slowly pulled her way down the cord to the end and around the counter. Looking down, she couldn't believe it. She saw Mason with the phone cord in his mouth, looking up at her with his insane snarl once again. Ann started to freak out. She fell back and almost to the floor, saying,

"There's no way. He can't do that?" then from around the counter, Mason came running at her. She fell to the floor, screaming in pain with both her eyes closed. And as she opened her eyes, she saw Masons mouth wrapped around her ankle, her blood mixed with his white saliva running down and out of his mouth, and down her pale-skinned leg. Mason was not biting down hard, just enough to break the skin. Just to see this bloody, foaming mess was enough to send her into shock. Ann passed out.

When she came to, Mason was gone. It was still night and her leg looked worse than it really was. She got back up the stairs to her room and cleaned it up before she went back to bed. Ann thought, "What kind of dog could this be? And why would he want to hold me here? What am I going to do?"

The night passed. It was the next day. Ann came down with an old cane that Peter used to have for a knee injury a long time ago. As she came down, Mason was at the front door, so she knew what he wanted her to do. Today she would do just that. She didn't know what he might do when provoked this time. So she opened the door and walked out first, then he came right to the side of the door to drop another pile, and then waited for her to walk back past the stinking mess into the house.

She came in and Mason closed the door behind her. Right away she started his food as he lay down in the hall, so he could still see her in the kitchen.

As she was putting Mason's bag of food away, she saw in the back of the cabinet a box of weed killer for her garden. "Maybe I could give him just enough to make him sick to the point he can't run after me," she thought to herself. "It's worth a try." So she got the weed killer and mixed some into his food and called him in to eat.

"Mason, come in for your food." And right away he came; ready to eat.

She sat the food down and said, "Good boy, Mason. Eat all your food."

But just as Mason put his head down to take the first bite of his food, he smelled it. Something was not right. Mason started growling with his face still down in the bowl, and Ann started to panic.

"What's wrong, Mason?" She asked, as she moved back from him. Then he looked up at her, and lunged at her, hitting her with his big black head and sending her back down once again to the hard floor. Now she was on her back, breathing very heavily and shaking. Mason grabbed the bowl of food in his mouth, and picked it up and dropped it right next to Ann.

Then he climbed up on top of her, staring right down at her as she cried in terror. Mason started growling and foaming at the mouth. As the white drool dripped from his mouth down onto hers, she gagged.

"Don't hurt me, Mason. Please."

Mason took his right paw and moved the bowl closer to her, and let out a big WOOF. She knew he wanted her to eat the food in the bowl, she knew it all too well.

"Mason, please."

He then moved his face really close to hers, and opened his mouth and placed his fangs right on her neck, and started to apply pressure.

"All right, Mason. All right, I'll do it." And then, just like that, he let her go.

Mason moved off of her, giving her room. Ann was shaking as her hand moved towards the food. She scooped up a bunch in her fingers, as Mason started growling, and then put it into her mouth. She started to gag, but he was watching her, so she swallowed all of it. Mason then turned and left the room. Now she started to stand, crying and still gagging from the dog food mixed with her very own weed killer.

Now it was late, and Ann made it to her room. She felt very sick and could barely make it into the bathroom to vomit up the poison in her system. Mason sat right outside her bedroom door, listening to her heave violently.

After a while it became quiet again, and Mason got up and slowly walked to the stairs.

Mason decided he still couldn't trust her, so he walked down the stairs, urinating as he went down, leaving each step wet.

Ann was still very ill, sitting on the side of her bed, trying to think of what she could do to escape this mad dog. She then remembered there was another phone in Peter's study, if only she could get to it in time. Her stomach was in knots, excruciating pain striking her every time she moved. She needed medical attention fast; she felt she wouldn't make it till morning. So with all the strength she could muster, she made her way to the door.

She looked out to see if Mason was anywhere in sight, but the coast was clear, so she made her way to the stairs.

Now she started down. It was dark and she couldn't see Mason sitting at the bottom of the stairs, watching her struggle trying to make it down. Every step he watched, she was almost halfway down now, stepping in the urine with every step.

Then with her next step…. she fell.

As she twisted and turned, falling, her leg broke, then her arm, and just as she hit bottom…her neck.

She fell face down, right in front of Mason, as he sat there, looking down at her dead twisted body.

Mason's big black head lowered to her. He smelled her.

And then he raised his head once again and the smoky whites of his eyes appeared surrounded in his darkness.

Victor's Spoils

I always loved the great outdoors; it seemed I belonged in it, like one of the wild. It was home.

My passion was not to kill, but to think like they did, in their environment.

I wanted to smell it and see it from their point of view. I'm just a man, but when I'm alone out there, I'm more.

I'm a deer hunter. There was no man more dedicated than me.

I always hunted alone, it was personal to me as going to the bathroom or punching in my code at the ATM, and something I wouldn't want others to see. I respected my prey. I believe the deer could feel this from me; they felt the goodness in me. I thought they all feared me, but I was wrong!!

It was late fall and the cold winter was just starting to make its presence felt as the wind sharply made its way down and around the Rocky Mountains. The first snow was still holding off, with the exception of the snowy caps on the mountaintops high above me.

I was there, alone at the heart of it all, like every year this same time.

What would be the outcome? Just like always the spoils would be mine.

My custom-triggered 22 with scope was ready. I trusted it and it had never let me down. I had just arrived and just stood there in the middle of this field, looking all around, taking it all in, like I do every year.

I knew this place like the back of my hand; every tree, every path, and every lake. It was like going home, and smelling the scent that reminds you of something you knew well, or just a place you have been before.

Now I was home, and for the moment anyway, I felt safe.

I readied my gear from my truck and headed in. I had driven all night to an early start. This was perfect; I was very excited. It was colder this year than most, but no matter, I was a hunter who could brave all the elements, and more for the spoils. As I hiked to my first location I thought about how my family and I would feast, and mount the great head, and hear my stories of the hunt. I smiled under my mask as I moved slowly, deeper and deeper into the forest.

Soon I picked up tracks from what looked like a buck, but these were the biggest I had ever seen. I studied them long and hard, like something first discovered. I couldn't believe what I was seeing.

That's when I heard it.

I stopped and looked up from the tracks.

I could still hear it as I looked around, my eyes passing and scanning the trees one by one. "What is that?" I said out loud.

It was a sound that I had never heard out there before, and then it stopped.

It was dead quiet, something else I had never heard out there.

I looked back down at the tracks, and after a few seconds, the forest slowly came back to life. I thought to myself, "That was strange!" But I was onto something and so early in the hunt, so I found the perfect tree to nest in just east of the tracks I had found.

I was ready. I had never been this close so soon in a hunt before; it was like this deer wanted me to find it. The tracks were in the open and this buck moved slowly like it was not afraid. As I sat scanning the trees, I waited. I wanted to see this great buck, and I felt like it wanted to see me.

I was excited like it was my first hunt, but why? Something was different, something at the time I couldn't explain.

My eyes sharp as an eagle, I watched and waited for the prey, but there was something else. Squirrels, making there way up and down the tree I was in. More than I could count passed over me and around me like I wasn't there.

They saw me, but they were not afraid, then I heard it again.

That sound; what was it? Where was it coming from?

I grabbed up my 22 and peered through my scope hoping to see something, but then it stopped again, and as I put the gun down, all the squirrels had gone; not one was in sight.

I was starting to spook myself a bit, so I smiled and shook my head, and settled myself back down in my nest to wait.

Hours passed and from the west came a cold breeze that rocked this great tree I was in slowly back and forth. And as the wind slowed, I heard a sound I knew, something moving in my direction from the north. I readied myself; this could be it. I looked through the scope, waiting. I could see something moving, but was having trouble making it out behind all the bushes and trees.

I waited, looking, not moving at all. It was big. It had to be a buck; it was a ways from me. Then I noticed that the forest had gone dead quiet again.

All I could hear was the sound this thing made whenever it moved.

I felt like it knew I was watching, waiting for it to come out into the open, so it didn't. It stayed just out of clear sight.

I looked up to the treetops as the forest started to come back to life, but when I looked back through the scope, it was gone.

I didn't know what to think or how I should feel; this had never happened before. I calmed myself and ripped a piece of jerky to chew on and wait.

I knew this game I'd played many times. I had reason to be here, but only the strong will survive.

Man shall have the beast to do with as he pleases, but as for the beast, he is unaware of the man's needs.

That had always been my view as a deer hunter.

The day continued to pass with no sign of the buck. I was beginning to think I had seen the last of him, well, for the day at least.

Evening was now all around me. The grasshoppers and other insects were singing out in great numbers as I sat front row center, it was captivating, hypnotic in a transparent form. My eyes were heavy as the sun continued to set in the west. Deep in meditation I was, as the sound riddled me, and then I saw them; they were all over me. The sound stopped and the dusky lit area was deadly silent as black widows crawled all over me.

I wanted to jump down from the nest, but I couldn't move. I wanted to, but I was frozen. I panicked as they crawled over my face and head. And then there he was, standing right in front of me, facing me, looking at me, as I tried not to breathe so that the widows would spare my life. He was right there just looking. In his eyes I could see him wondering if I would be the spoils, and he the victor. I started to shake; I tried to hold it in to save my life!

I screamed!!!!

I opened my eyes and the great sound of the singing insects released me.

There would be no spoils, there would be no victor, and the hunter never hunted again.

The Wrong Number

It was late on a rainy night in a small town called Hampton. Roman Coal lived alone in a small one-bedroom apartment. He wasn't happy with how his life was going. His place was shitty, but it was all he could afford working as an unarmed security guard. He sat home as the rain poured down, trying to find something to watch on his old black and white TV.

Desperately needing something to work out for a change, and make his life better than it was.

He was thirty years old with no real education to speak of, trying to find a way to make ends meet in this miserable world in which he was stuck.

He was a strong, athletic, five o'clock shadow kind of man and almost always with the smell of beer on his breath. Blue jeans, white t-shirt and brown leather jacket were all he owned for his wardrobe. And on his scuffed nightstand were: mousse to slick back his black thinning hair, and a half filled bottle of Brut he would splash on whenever he was trying to hook a lady fish.

This was Roman. Not a bad guy, just troubled and in need of help in a lot of ways. He started to feel that it wasn't ever going to get any better, but then the phone call came.

He was passed out on his broken down sofa, with a can of beer still in his hand spilling as he fell deep into a hard sleep. Then the phone started to ring and ring, and then it rang again. Roman slowly moved his drunken body close enough to pick up the phone. He said,

"Hello."

It was a woman. She was upset and in a hurry, trying her best to tell Roman something.

"It's me. I'm just calling to tell you I'm on my way to drop it off right now. I can't believe you're really going to go through with this. This is crazy, you know how I feel."

Roman was still half asleep and he had no idea who this woman was. He started to sit up and get himself together fast enough to understand just what the hell this woman was talking about, so he said, "What are you saying? Who is this?"

"Don't play with me. Now's not the time. It's all set; I have all the money."

Now Roman, scratching his head, said, "Hey, I think you have the wrong number."

"I can't believe this, you son of a bitch! I'll call you back when I get the money to the store, all right?"

Roman was still trying to understand what she was going on about, but he did understand the word money so he said, "All right." And just like that, she hung up.

Roman sat there wondering what this was all about; he thought, "This woman really thinks she's talking to someone else." It was strange, but then he really didn't give a shit. "She probably won't call back." He thought to himself, and went right back to the sofa and off to sleep. About an hour passed and the phone started to ring again. He jumped up this time because the phone was right next to him and it scared him. He said, "Hello."

It was the same woman and this time she was crying. She said, "It's me. There's no fucking way I can go to the store because they're following me. I can't believe this shit! I knew this was going to happen!"

Roman was trying to think fast, but he had just woken up. He said, "All right, calm down; just tell me what this is all about."

"What the fuck do you mean? It's about this money, right? That's what you want. You don't give a shit about what happens to me."

She was right, he didn't give a shit, but she was talking about money for the second time and that's what made him play along. He said, "That's not true. Where are you now?"

"I'm at the Pub, calling from my cell phone. I came in here when I saw that they were following me."

"Who's following you?"

"I think it's one of Logan's goons, he's been on me since I left the house. I don't know what to do now. Should I come to you?"

"No! That's not a good idea. Tell me, what happened at the house before you left?" Now Roman was trying to find out all he could about what was going on before this woman figured out she called the wrong number.

"Well you know how big the place is; it took Logan over an hour to get ready and leave. I had no problems last night; you know he's putty in my hands. I can't believe what a fool Logan is. You know, at first I felt bad taking all this money for you, but he has taken money plus people's lives, so to me this is what he deserves."

Roman's hands were sweating thinking this woman just might give him the money. So he had to think, how he could do this. "How much money are we talking about?"

"I told you last night it was over one hundred thousand, and I'm not fucking counting it, so don't ask. I know how you think, Ray!"

"So that's who I am in this deal, "RAY." Roman said to himself as he began to smile. "You have all the goddamn money, right?" Roman now was trying to get into character, to totally convince this woman he was who she thought he was.

"Yes, it's all right here. Don't be mad at me, Ray. I'm doing the best I can, but these assholes are scaring me. I think they may know I took the money."

"All right, just listen. You're at the Pub. Go out the back door and down the alley, all the way to Front Street, get a cab and take off then call me back."

Then he just hung up the phone. He was hoping she would just do what he had said, but he wasn't sure, so he waited, and sure enough, the phone rang.

She was in a cab just like he had asked. "It's me. I'm going down Front right now. I don't think they seen me. Where do you want me to go?"

"You don't think? You better fucking make sure! Look around, do you see any of the same cars you saw before?"

"No! I don't, but I'm not sure if they saw me or not. Just tell me where you want me to go."

"All right, go to State Park, it's not too far from where you are right now. There's a library at the end of the park. Walk through the park to the library and go to the back, to the study area and have a seat at one of the tables there, then call me back, all right?"

"Are you sure? That's a real public place. Lots of people will be there."

"No shit, that's why you need to go there, you're safer in public than anywhere else."

"Okay, I'll call when I get there."

"Try not to panic; it's going to be all right.

"I want you to be able to trust me, because I know you don't. You haven't even told me your real name. I know it's not Ray. We should trust each other."

"Can I trust you now?" Roman was trying to find out about her, and this was his first chance, so he took full advantage of it.

"You can trust me. My real name is not Mary. It's Kim. Now it's your turn. I really hate calling you Ray, when I just know that's not your real name."

"Okay, Kim, first name only. It's Tony. Now if I'm going to really trust you, understand that you have to do what I tell you to do, so we can get through this in one piece."

"What happens when we get done? Is that it between us? You must know by know how I feel about you Ray, no I mean Tony."

"I guess I do, but right now we need to think about what we're doing, all right? Then we'll talk about us later."

The day was turning to dusk; the wind had picked up a lot as the cab pulled up to the front of the park's entrance. Kim put the cell phone into her bag as she took out money to pay the driver; the money was in a duffle bag next to her on the seat.

She got out, struggling with the heavy bag and into the park she went, but not before looking in every direction to see if anyone was following her. It looked to be clear as she hurried her pace to get to the library.

The park was big, beautiful and quiet. Tall trees waved in the evening's breeze. A few people still moved about through the park passing her by. She carefully watched everyone as she nervously puffed on a cigarette.

Roman figured he had a little time to get cleaned up before Kim would reach the library, so he jumped into the shower and dressed fast as he could before the wrong number called back again.

By now, Kim had made to the library, and was making her way through. She found a seat at one of the back tables just like Roman had told her to. She hurried to get the phone out of her bag to make the call, but when she did the cell was dead and needed to be charged. This made Kim crazy with panic. She looked around and now everybody in the library looked suspicious.

She moved fast to put the phone back into the bag and make her way back out of the library. She was making noise, which was bringing more attention than she needed.

Back into the park, she burst out of the front doors of the library, terrified, thinking that someone was watching and following her. She moved as fast as she could with the heavy bag of money, trying to get back through the park to get another cab. Then, out of nowhere, there were two men walking up in her direction. She stopped. They kept coming. She threw her cigarette down and turned to run in the other direction.

She looked back and sure enough, they were now running after her. The wind had started to blow even harder, making it almost impossible to run with the heavy bag. She tried to make it back inside, but she fell hard. The bag and the strong wind were just too much.

Roman was still at home waiting for the call, thinking she should have called by now. Something must be wrong. He thought maybe she figured out she had the wrong number and wasn't going to call back. "Goddamn it!" He shouted, as he threw his beer, smashing it against the wall.

He felt cheated. This was going to be the thing that turned his miserable life around. He needed this money, and he needed it bad.

He tried to hit redial on the phone, hoping to reach her, but it didn't work, so he sat back down on the sofa and just waited.

The two men in the park had taken Kim to a motel nearby. They had already called Logan and were told not to let the bitch out of their sight, and the money too. Logan also told his men to find out whom she was working for, because he wanted his ass dead before sunrise tomorrow.

So they started in on Kim. She was tied up in a chair with her shirt torn open. They beat her real good. She didn't want to talk, but she thought she was going to be killed at any time.

The man said, "What's his name? This is the last time I'm going to ask, and if you don't tell me this time, it won't fucking matter anymore."

She was crying. Trying to pull herself together, she said, "His name is Ray. He is supposed to meet me in the park and get the money. That's all I know, I swear it."

"Is that right? Well, what say you give this Ray a call, and tell him you ran into a little trouble, but it's cool to still come get the money."

The man picked up the phone and gave it to her, after untying her hands.

She made the call.

Roman was still sitting on the sofa, staring off into outer space when the phone rang.

"Hello, it's me. I had a little trouble, but I'm fine now. You should just come to the park and get me and the money, all right?"

Roman was no fool. He knew something was wrong. He said, "Something is wrong. If I'm right, just say okay."

"Okay."

"How many are with you? If there are two or less, just say okay"

"Okay."

"Where do you want me to come for you?"

"I'll be by the waterfall in the park. Hurry! I want to get the hell out of here."

"Okay. I'm on my way."

Roman did not want trouble with these people. He knew they had to be bad news. But the money was worth the risk to him, so he was going. One thing was still in his favor: they didn't know what he looked like, not even Kim.

At the park it was windy and dark as Roman made his way in. He cut through the trees to the waterfall, and there she was. He knew it was her sitting next to a big duffel bag.

There was no one else in sight, but he knew someone was watching. Kim was beautiful. He wondered how a girl like that could be mixed up with people like this.

He worked his way in a circle around the waterfall, looking for anybody.

And there they were, looking from behind a big statue. So he made his way back around with a pipe up his sleeve, walking straight to the waterfall.

He knew they wouldn't shoot. It was still close to the library, people might hear the shot. He also knew that Kim would be surprised when he walked up to her. She had never seen him before in her life. He just hoped she would be willing to go along. After all, he was trying to save her damn life.

As he walked up to her, she stared at him. He said, "Are you all right, Kim?"

"Who are you? How do you know my name?"

"It's me, Tony. You recognize my voice. Don't ask questions right now. I'm trying to get you out of here."

Kim was confused, but happy to see anybody at this point. She said, "They're going to grab you on the way out. What are you going to do?"

Roman grabbed the money and said, "You just start walking. Let me worry about these assholes."

They started back through the park, and out of nowhere, one man came out and cut them off.

He snarled, "How you doing, Ray? I see you found my bitch and my money. I guess I should be more careful where I leave my shit. It's a bad habit of mine, know what I mean?"

Roman looked around for the other man, but didn't see him. He then slipped the pipe down into his hand and turned fast and bashed the man in the head with the pipe, knocking him down hard.

Roman turned back to Kim and yelled, “Let’s go! Run!!”

And just as they started to run, out from behind a tree, the second man hit Roman hard in the face, knocking him down to the ground. Roman turned to Kim and screamed, “Grab the money and run! GO NOW!!”

The man put a gun to his head as the other one started to get up. They had Roman, but Kim was long gone. The man with the gun said, “Come with me, or I’m going to blow your fucking head off.”

They took Roman to their car. One was driving and the other got into the back seat with Roman. The man in the back still had the gun on him as they drove. Roman asked, “Where are you taking me?”

“Fuck you! You’re lucky to still be alive, but don’t worry, you won’t be for long.”

Now here he was, in this car, about to lose his life, when all he wanted to do was better it. “Life is funny that way. Things hardly ever go the way you want them to. Don’t seem fair.” He thought to himself as they drove.

As they crossed the Highland Bridge, the wind was blowing so hard it blew the car to one side of the road, throwing the man with the gun onto Roman.

He grabbed the gun and fought with the man, trying to get the gun from him, and then it went off, killing the man driving.

Roman took the gun and beat the other man in the head until he also stopped moving, and then he jumped from the car that had crashed on the side of the bridge, and ran for his life.

Now it was over. He was back home with his life, but no money; he was shaking and finding it hard to calm down. He was almost killed and for what? A fucking wrong number. Roman took a hot shower to settle himself down for the night, trying to forget about what had happened. As he lay on the old sofa, soon he fell asleep, dreaming of a better day, maybe tomorrow? Who knows? Asleep and dreaming he was, and then the phone rang again. Maybe it was Kim? Or just another wrong number!!

Burn

The house was old and run down; the walls had paper that had started to curl down and fade. It reeked of mothballs and rotting wood. The pipes were rusted, and shook the place when turned on, and the sunlight that streamed in from the outside revealed the lofting dust ever present in the air, but still this was home.

The outside was weather beaten as well with the shutters holding on by one remaining rusty nail. The grass and bushes were all overgrown and faded brown in spots all over the yard, and the verandah was weak to say the least, but still supported an old sofa glider and chairs. This was deep in the heart of southern Mississippi, the remains of what was once someone's wealthy life.

This area was abandoned and long forgotten, but somehow it was still home.

Now this was home to a drifter named Sam. A good man in his late forties, Sam had long salt and pepper hair that he tried to keep back in a ponytail, but he was never really successful. Long strands found their way loose to wave around in the breeze.

Sam lived off the land.

Whatever he caught he ate, and he would never go hungry. As long as he could walk, he could hunt and that's what he was best at.

He dressed in the only thing he had for clothes: an old faded pair of overalls, flannel shirt, black boots and baseball hat; the Cincinnati Reds. Sam was all alone, and that's the way he liked it. He never trusted anybody; he never would again. He had been hurt before, and never wanted to feel that pain again.

Sam had been here for almost a year now, and had not seen another living soul since his arrival, but this is just what he wanted; to be alone, away from everything and everyone.

This was Sam's world; just he and the house and the peaceful surroundings filled with animals and nature's wonder.

What he had searched to find for so long, he had now found, where he could be apart from the world and its uncaring mankind. Sam had been scarred badly, and forever changed from who he once was. Not willing to ever look back, he was happy with himself and his new found home, for all it was worth, which was the world to Sam.

The nights were black as outer space, filled with stars as far as the eye could see. It was all around him covering him in darkness, and only the moon spared him from complete blackness.

Most nights Sam sat alone on the verandah, in his sofa glider talking to the stars.

They had become like family to him; some he had even given names to.

Sam Speaks to the Stars

"Here I am once again all alone with you, all of you.

What will we talk about tonight?"

He gazed upward at their array of brilliance.

"This is a special night; this night marks our one year anniversary.

Can you remember the first night, Falcon? What about you Cullen?

Well I'm sure you do. Since then a lot has happened, hasn't it?

I feel we all have become a family. You watch over me and for that I am forever grateful.

I must tell you I have made myself a promise, one I said I would never break.

But now that I have found my family, my place, I feel I can.

Tonight I give you my trust, which is the key to all I am and have in this world.

And you don't have to say a word; I know I have yours. Good night."

His days and nights, even though he was alone, were not lonely. He was happy and never felt alone. No trust at all for mankind, yet only the stars in the night sky knew his secrets; his true story.

The next evening it was time to hunt for food, as he made his way deep into the woods of

Mississippi. Slowly he moved as a buck made its way right into a trap Sam had laid.

"Got'em!!!" He cried, as the buck was now his meal. Then he heard something. What was that? He moved away from the buck and over to where the sound came from.

Slowly he moved up to a thick patch of bushes, as his eyes tightened trying to see through them. Whatever it was on the other side, he was afraid, but he had to know what it was.

Sam had not seen another human being in so long he at first did not know what to do.

He watched him. He was still breathing; this man was alive. "Are you okay?—Can you hear me?—What are you doing here?"

"Water." The man said, in a very weak voice. Sam's first instinct was to run away and leave him there, but he couldn't do it. He was too good of a man and could never live with the thought of this man dying out here and not helping him.

He picked him up and carried him all the way back to the house and cared for him.

The man was about the same age as Sam; he was dirty and looked like he had been wandering for a long time. His clothes were torn and old and smelled like skunks had sprayed him. He was dehydrated and must have been starving to death.

The night was coming fast, as the grasshoppers and crickets rang out in great classical numbers.

The house was still fed water from an old reservoir about a half-mile away.

Sam never used the water, but he had to tonight, the man was in great need.

The pipes screamed out in pain as the rusty water slowly made its way through the old pipes into a pail Sam held in one hand, as he kept his eyes on the still unconscious man.

Sam boiled the water and cared for the man, cleaned him up and washed his clothes.

By now it was well into the night, and Sam was exhausted and went out onto the verandah, to his sofa glider and feel off into a deep sleep.

The buck is almost to the trap as Sam hides behind a big tree, trying not to make a sound. Stay low don't even breathe—he's almost there, almost there—

"Are you awake?"

The man said, as he was now sitting in one of the chairs on the verandah. Sam jumped to his feet, pulled from his sleep like a bad tooth on a string.

"Who are you?" Sam said, trying to catch his breath and calm down.

"My name is William; you must be the man who saved me."

Sam looked at him, before saying another word, "I haven't done much at all."

"You are modest as well as kind; those are things I'm not used to from people."

"Neither am I. My name is Sam."

"It is nice to meet you, Sam, and I would like to thank you for all you have done for me. I owe you my life."

"There is no need for that, I have no interest in your life, and so you owe me nothing."

William looked at him and just smiled; he knew that Sam did not trust him. It was very plain to see.

Sam said, "Well I'm sure you want to be on your way. I made you some food to take with you on the road."

"Thank you, Sam, but I would greatly like to rest up a bit before I take off, if that's alright with you."

Sam looked at him, and as he walked inside he said, "That's fine."

Sam went on with his day not paying the man any mind as William watched Sam stacking wood in the yard. The sun was hot as Sam stacked the wood with the sun on his skin, but not as hot as William's eyes that peered at him from up on the verandah.

As Sam came back up on the verandah later that afternoon, William met him with a bucket of fresh water for drinking, and they sat down together. William tried his best to get to know Sam. The conversation went into the early evening. Sam found himself talking to William and even laughing with him, something he thought he would never do again. What was it about William that made Sam open up to him?

The night was now here and too dark for William to leave, so Sam invited him to stay. He liked him.

Not just the next day, but now weeks had come and gone, and William was still at the house.

The two of them had become friends, and did things together like hunt and clean food, fix things in the house, and just enjoy each other's company.

Sam was not afraid of him as time went by. William was a good man and Sam could tell he was not like the people from his past; he was like him, insightful.

Time continued to pass, and it seemed that William was making this place his home as well. Sam never talked about him leaving and William never acted as if he wanted to go.

They started to get to know each other well never fighting. It was always peaceful and good between them.

William came with only a big bag full of old news papers and ink pens, and one day Sam was burning up some things that had no use, and as he was about to put the big old bag of paper in the fire William screamed "NO!!!" And ran out and take the bag back into the house. He never explained why the bag was so important to him; it just was and Sam never did ask.

Six months had passed. Life was still good and the two of them still together in the house. It was evening now and they were on their way out for a hunt.

Slowly they made their way through the deep woods, watching the traps they had already laid. Sam had the idea to move to the other side of the traps to move any prey in the right direction, and as he was moving out came a rattler and it had him cornered.

"Don't move Sam." William said, as he saw his friend in great trouble. He moved slowly over to him, tying to get the attention of the snake. But before he could get to him, the snake had bitten Sam.

And the poison started moving fast straight through Sam's bloodstream. His eyes started rolling up into his head; the tall trees seemed to have legs and started running around him, circling around him fast and faster as he laid on his back on the ground with William kneeling beside him, calling to him, and then it all went black!

Slowly Sam's eyes opened, to the dried and rotting ceiling of the old house. He was alive.

The peeling paper on the walls was blurred as his eyes fought to focus, then he could see him; it was William.

"I guess now we're even, thank you for saving my life."

"I didn't do much at all."

"You are modest as well as kind; those are things I'm not used to from people." He said, as he smiled at his friend.

William said, "How are feeling today?"

"I'm sleepy, I'm not ready to get up yet, and how long have I been asleep?"

"Three days now. I was starting to get worried, but last night the stars told me you would be alright."

"They told you did they," As he smiled.

"Well not in so many words, but they knew."

Sam held out his hand to his friend and William shook his hand.

Six Months Later

Sam was well, and it was all because his good friend had taken such good care of him, and for that Sam has told him he would be forever grateful.

The night had come once again, and all the stars were out, as the two of them sat out on the verandah talking. Sam said, "William tonight is a special night. Do you know why?'

"Yes I do, I been here one year today."

"This is our one year anniversary, and I'm very happy we are here together. A lot has happened since you have come and it's all been well. I must tell you I made myself a promise along time ago, never to trust any man ever again, but you have changed me somehow. I feel like I can trust you; we're close, we're family. So tonight I will share with you what I have only shared with the stars in the night skies; my secret, my true story." Sam reached his hand down under the sofa glider and pulled out a tin box with a small lock on it.

He opened the box and pulled out a document; it was a deed to property in South America.

As he shows William the deed, William sees that this is one of the richest properties in the world, overflowing with oil and gold. But this deed remains unsigned and unclaimed.

"Sam! Do you know what you have here? You could have anything you want; you do know this, don't you?"

"William, don't you see? I do have what I want right here; this is all I need. I've tried that life and I know people can't be trusted. Things are never the way they seem when it comes to people."

William sat with a blank look on his face, not sure what to say to Sam, so he said nothing.

Time continued to pass, and William never talked about that night again, although he tried to get Sam to see that not all people were bad.

After all he did trust William, and he was a good man.

Life for them was the same for a while, but it seemed that William was starting to feel restless; like this life was now getting old; at least this is how Sam was starting to feel about him.

He felt that maybe he should have never told him, but he didn't regret it, he felt it was right.

Then one night Sam came home from a hunt and William was not there. Sam didn't think much of it maybe he was off for a walk or a hunt himself.

The night passed and still no William. Now Sam was starting to worry.

It was just before dawn, and Sam was still in bed; he had not gotten up for the day yet.

He planned to go looking for William as soon as there was enough light.

The darkness started to fade, and the house was still and slowly Sam turned over in bed and there he was. William stood over him. He straddled Sam, and then raised a two by four over his head smashing Sam in the side of his skull.

Now Sam was out cold.

But Sam was not dead, even though William thought he was, as he ripped through the house looking for the tin box.

Sam slowly got to his feet and stumbled out of the room. William still crashed through the house like a great wrecking ball, but not finding the box.

Sam had now made his way out, as blood ran down his face. Onto the verandah he moved, slowly trying to balance himself, as William continued to look through the house.

Sam began to feel like he may pass out again; he was still losing a lot of blood, and then out ran William. He spotted Sam and yelled, "Where is it Sam? You tell me right now! Where?!!"

"It's not here. It's not in the house."

"Where?!!"

"It's out there, by where I stack the wood."

William looked out to the middle of the yard by the woodpile.

"It's right in the middle of the pile in the tin box, William."

He jumped off the verandah, running out to the woodpile.

Never looking back to Sam at the house, he was almost there, and there it was: the tin box.

He opened it, but it was empty.

Slowly he turned back to the house. Sam stood in the doorway of the house. William looked at him breathing heavily, without moving or saying a word. Then he said, "Where is it?"

And Sam held his hand up, holding the deed in the one hand, and a candle in the other; he slowly moved back into the house, and closed the door.

And William screamed out, "NO!!!"

Bringing a dead silence to all the grasshoppers and crickets.

He started running back to the house. It instantly went up in flames and he stopped,

And watched it **BURN**!

The Romanesque

Ancient architects of Rome and other great cities still intrigue us to this very day with their unbelievable structure with unfading imagery. The Romans will be remembered forever, and so will the great Roman Pantheon est. 27 BC. The house was built for the gods. It had to be fitting, worthy of all the gods. It stood 143ft from the ground; no steel support beams only poured concrete. Open in the very top to allow the light to enter the structure.

Pantheon; Romanesque, massive inside and out, fit for the gods, and perfect for their treasures…Present day, Rome.

A dimly lit room of men and one woman sat around a table, one still empty chair waited, it seemed, for a great man of respect and power, Numerius Octavius.

His limo pulled to a slow stop in front of this city structure, as the windy evening dust blew briskly down through the stone city streets, and away again back into the reddish evening skyline. Numerius was an older man of great size with hair as white as snow and a long white beard. His clothes were black as night and as the wind moved his beard around his neck, he walked inside.

Among this room of Romans and Greeks, there was only one American, Alex Rowed.

Alex was a well known and sought after archeologist and photographer. And then there was the only woman, Lucia Abutius. She was as beautiful as she was deadly, more powerful than half the men in the room. Also present were Titus and Gaius the Greeks, two brothers known for a number of different things. And at one end of the table was another great man who was loved by many, Appius Cassius. He was the reason this group had been called together this day.

Numerius walked in and not a word was spoken. He took his seat and looked down the table to Appius. No one really knew why he or she was there. Now more than ever they wanted to know. Numerius opened a case and slowly pulled out some very old scrolls.

And across the top of the old scrolls in big Greek writing was the word, **PANTHEON!**

(A temple to all the gods.)

The table was set, here is where we begin and end. Right before them all, lay the scroll of the plates of the gods. Appius began,

"My friends thank you all for coming here today. The fact that you are here means one thing and one thing only. And that is you have respect for the greatness of Rome…

To tell you all why I have called you here, I give you Numerius Octavius."

"Thank you, sir, you are a wise and great man, and my respect you will have always. You people were chosen because we feel you are the best we could offer Rome.

You all will be known and remembered for all times from this night on. This scroll here before you shows all the gods; it also shows each god with his or her own chest plate, which is their key to power and communication. Without these plates there is neither power nor communication. With your help, I plan to return all the plates to all the gods in the Pantheon."

Alex could not hold himself back from asking, "That is a great and noble thing, Mr. Octavius. But is the betterment of Rome your only reason? "

"Mr. Alex Rowed, how did I know I would hear from you first?"

"I was compelled to know, sir."

"The answer is no; that is not the only reason. There is another, even greater than that of Rome itself."

Lucia Abutius laughed out loud and said, "Well, please then do tell us at once. Rome is starting to bore me."

As she looked to Appius, he turned down his face, embarrassed by her comment.

Then Titus rang out, "Greater than Rome itself?"

And Numerius explained, "Yes, better for all of mankind. I have one of the plates in my possession, but after the next week passes, those other three will be mine as well. Through my years of research and findings, after all the plates have been returned to their positions with the gods, and the ancient prayer has been read, communication between the gods and man will be here."

"You mean it will be possible to speak directly with the gods?" Lucia said with a troubled brow.

"That is correct. Imagine the possibilities—all we have to gain, understanding at long last, lady and gentlemen." Numerius stood up and raised one of the plates over his head; and at that everyone was amazed; it was made of solid gold and a beautiful sight to behold.

Everyone knew Numerius was out of his mind as he explained how all the plates had to be in their rightful place with the gods, all at the same time, and then the prayer would open a line of communication with the gods.

How ridiculous it all was! But after seeing one of the plates in person, everyone wanted to see them all together. Alex knew that no one had ever photographed all the plates together in their rightful location before; this would be his chance of a lifetime.

The Greek brothers, Titus and Gaius, thought of the prestige and fame it would bring to their family name. Lucia Abutius thought of only herself, taking credit for the whole thing. That was it; Numerius did not want to be in the forefront, that was the whole reason for having Lucia involved, and Appius, a man of principles, wanted only to respect the will of the gods.

They all agreed and the plan was laid; the Greek brothers put together a very sophisticated security group to walk the halls of the pantheon for the next week. The plate Numerius had was settled into its rightful place; this made the pantheon the most likely place to be robbed in all of Rome.

Lucia would handle all the press, telling the story to all who would hear about the plates that would bring man and the gods together at long last. It was like she believed this herself to be so.

Numerius stayed close to it all but out of sight for the most part, as did Appius, praying for the best to come from all of this.

And as for Alex the American, he was to be inside the Pantheon all five days during the open hours. People would come to pray to the gods, and Alex would document everything and everyone.

The First Day

One of the remaining three plates would come the first day; there were great crowds outside the Pantheon. Numerius and Appius sat up high in the ledges, while the chest plate was brought in and placed into position. Alex was down one of the corridors shooting the priest walking with the gold plate. And then, out of nowhere, Lucia came up from behind him, very close and she said,

"They are worth more than just wealth, or is that all you can see?"

"I see many things, maybe more than even you."

"—We shall see."

As she turned and walked away, Alex watched her, and as she walked, she excited him.

In the distance behind Alex, one of the Greek brothers' men saw the interaction between Alex and Lucia and right away made a call on his radio.

The first day came to a close, and the Pantheon was silent and almost empty.

Alex was on his way out after putting away the film he kept in a locked room no one but he knew about. As he walked out, he saw a light coming from one of the rooms.

Slowly he moved closer to the door. It was Lucia and Numerius talking, but before he could get close enough to hear what they were saying, the Greek brothers came down the hall. The Pantheon was dark and lit only by candles, so quickly he moved on down the hall before he was seen.

Now there were only two more plates that need to be placed into position and everything seemed to be going according to plan. But for some reason, Numerius was not happy, and called a meeting the next day with Appius.

Numerius let him know more than he wanted to know when he said,

"There is a small problem, but it can be easily fixed if you remember what you told me in the beginning—Do you remember what you told me, Appius?"

Appius looked afraid of Numerius as he poured himself a cup of coffee and folded his hands behind the hot steaming mug.

"You told me I could rely on you for whatever I needed—you do remember?"

"Within reason, Numerius, all within reason."

"This is for the great city of Rome!! Is that not reason enough for you—my friend?"

"A friend would not ask a friend to do what is not ethical to do."

"Listen to what I ask of you, it is for all mankind that I ask." Numerius said with great passion.

Appius looked away out of the window at the city of Rome, dreading what Numerius would ask of him. Numerius stood and walked over to the window looking out, with his back to Appius. He said,

"The next plate is in the care of a man named Bannabis, it seems that he has decided not to follow through with his word."

"What do you mean, Numerius?"

"He will not give us the plate, and without that plate there can be no connection."

"But I thought everything was in order. Every plate holder agreed."

"They all did, and still they all shall—I need you to call another meeting, but this time it will just be you and Bannabis."

"Why won't you be there? I have nothing to say to this man, Numerius."

"This one will not change his mind; he will never give us the plate."

"Then why call him here? I don't understand."

Numerius turned from the window and walked over to the table. He said,

"He will not come if I am here. Once he is here you will ask him to continue as planned, and when he refuses, the Greek brothers will come in and bring him to me."

Appius was shocked, he had no idea Numerius could be so dark hearted. He was upset and asked, "What will you do to him, kill him?"

"I don't want to see a man die. I need the plate and I will have that plate."

Appius tried to reason with Numerius. Appius pleaded, "Numerius, is this the way to bring honor to the gods? There must be another way."

"This is for the good of the gods, Appius. You should understand."

"I will not be a part of this. This is not right, Numerius!!!"

Then Numerius looked at him, walked over to the door and said, "You have to do what you must, Appius my friend."

Then he walked out.

That night Appius was home alone reading up on the plates of the gods, and someone came to see him. It was late and he thought it was strange someone would call that late. He went to the door and looked out. It was someone in a black overcoat. It was dark and the hood was down over this person's face. He said, "Hello, who is it there?"

The person in black did not respond but just knocked once again. Out of frustration Appius opened the door. The person rushed in and removed the hood. It was Lucia. She said, "I didn't think you were going to let me in, Appius." She walked back past him to look out the window on the door. It was raining and a black limo slowly started to drive away, and Numerius closed the back window as the limo pulled off.

Appius looked shocked. He asked her, "Lucia, why are you here? It is very late."

"Are you not happy to see me, Appius?" She took off her coat, revealing her sheer clinging dress. He tried not to stare at her, but she was beautiful, and he was an older man who lived alone. She was clearly there to toy with him, this even Appius knew. But he found it hard not to succumb to her advances, and before long she had him eating from her hands. He asked her, "What do you want from me?"

After it was all over and she was putting on her coat to leave she said, "You know what I want. I want everybody to be happy, mainly myself."

"Before you go, did Numerius have you come to me?"

"No man has me do anything I don't want to; you know that, Appius."

She turned and walked out the door. Appius now felt a breeze of reality; there would be a price to pay for this. One he knew he did not want to pay.

Appius grabbed his robe and walked down the hall to his study and made a call to Alex.

"Hello?"

"Alex. Appius Cassius. I hope this isn't a bad time."

"No, Appius. What can I do for you?"

"I have a problem, and I need your help, my friend. There is a problem with one of the plates, in fact the one that is to be brought in tomorrow."

"What kind of problem, Appius? We were told this was already taken care of."

"There is a man by the name of Bannabis, it seems he has a problem with Numerius and will not give us the plate as planned."

"This will change everything." Alex said.

"Not if it is left to Numerius. I believe he will do the unthinkable to have all of the plates together. I have even compromised myself into helping him."

"What can I do to help, Appius?"

"You must find out what you can of Numerius and Lucia. Something is going on and I need to know what."

"What about tomorrow? Will the plate be brought in?"

"We shall see—we shall see."

The Third Day

At the pantheon, people waited to see the next plate. They all wanted to be a part of this; they wanted to be close to the gods.

Everything was ready as the third day's dusk was on Rome. The inside of the Pantheon was lit only by candlelight, as the evening's dusk hung gracefully in the air.

Alex lay back in the shadows with his camera waiting for Numerius and Lucia, trying to capture something that would bring some light to this task, as it was all slowly going bad. Then all at once, three men came running down the corridor right at Alex. As he turned around, they knocked him into the concrete wall and he fell to the floor.

As he looked up from the hard stone floor, he saw the men that the Greek brothers hired come from the other direction, cutting the other men off. They held electric tazer sticks, which they used to beat and shock the men who were trying to steal from the Pantheon. These Guards were brutal and unforgiving, almost killing the men before they dragged them out.

Just as Alex got to his feet, Numerius was being seated, and then the music started as the high priests made their way in carrying the next plate.

Somehow he had gotten the plate, but Appius was not there. Alex started taking pictures, of everything and everyone. Only one more plate and it would be complete, and Numerius would have to live up to his claim or be mocked forever.

The look on Numerius face was stern; he didn't appear to be worried about anything.

Everything went well and the second to last plate was slid into place.

It was incredible to see, so powerful, so Romanesque.

No one really cared it seemed, if what Numerius said was true. Just to see and feel the power of it all was worth it all and much more. As Alex was leaving for the day, Lucia appeared out of thin air, and asked him if they could talk. Alex had forgotten all about her by this time. He said, "No problem. Why don't you come with me? I know a great place in here where we can talk."

Lucia smiled as if she thought Alex had more than just talking on his mind, and that would be just fine with Lucia. Alex was a strong, good-looking man. Alex took her to the room were he kept his photos and lots of other things he needed for his work, and before now no one had seen this room but him.

As he closed the door behind them Lucia said, "Would you like to talk first or later?"

Alex looked at her, she was sexy, very sexy, but right now he needed to find out all he could. He said, "You wanted to talk to me, remember?"

"Yes, that's right, I do. You know the last plate will be here day after tomorrow, all that money and power, all in one place. It excites me. What about you, Alex?"

"I'm not sure what you mean by that."

"You know what I mean. You're a smart man; what would you do if it was all yours?"

"Lucia, I'm what you might call a realist. I only allow myself to ponder on things tangible, you know what I mean?"

"That's just it, Alex, anything is tangible as you say, it's just a matter of how bad you want whatever it is."

She moved close to him and ran her hands through his deep brown curly hair, and then he stopped her. Alex said, "What is it you're really after, Lucia?"

"My life and all it holds for me."

"You must remember; everything that glitters isn't gold."

"And every conversation isn't worth my time."

As she turned to leave Alex stopped her, "First tell me everything you know about Numerius, and then I'll tell you about all I desire."

"What you want to know, Alex?"

"Come on, Lucia, I see you talking to him. I'm not stupid; I know something is going on."

"Alex, you men are all the same. You should worry about you. I know about as much as you do about Numerius, and that's the truth."

And just then Titus the Greek kicked the door down, and ran in and jumped on Alex and they went down to the floor fighting. Lucia tried to stop them. She said,

"Titus, no! What are you doing? Stop this!! Stop this at once!!!"

The fight went on and they were hurting each other. Lucia ran away to get help.

They fought until they couldn't lift their arms, then Alex said, "Titus, wait!! What is this bullshit about? Why are you doing this?"

"I know you're trying to have Lucia. She has business with me, and I don't want her confused about who her loyalty should be with."

"What do you mean business? What kind of business?"

"That doesn't concern you, Alex. You better know your place and stay in it, my brother, and I have no problem taking care of things like you."

"You don't understand. I think Lucia is trying to use us, to get what she really wants."

"What the hell are you talking about?"

"Hear me out. I think she is working with Numerius. It's bullshit about the prayer when all the plates are together. Once all the plates are here they are going to steal them, and I think they want us to do the stealing for them."

"Why should I believe a word of what you say?"

"Well the hell with what you believe, man!!! She's coming on to me; she's coming on to you, she's having all these conversations with Numerius and trying to hide it. She's setting us up, Titus. Can't you see that?"

And Lucia returned with some of Titus' own men, but the fight was over and Titus just looked at Alex and pushed past the men and Lucia in the doorway.

The Next Morning

The sun came up on the great city of Rome, casting its shadows on the remaining walls of the coliseum, and right in the center of one of the window's shadows was a man's body dead on the floor of the coliseum.

The man was Bannabis, and to Alex, Appius seemed crazy with fear, like he knew it was Numerius who was responsible and now he was afraid that Numerius would come after him for not having the meeting. Appius had called Alex and he had come right over.

Appius had helped Alex in the beginning of his career, so it was like Alex owed him and would need to return the favor.

Alex could tell something was very wrong with Appius. Alex said "What happened, Appius?"

"Numerius has killed this man, and I don't want to be involved."

"Calm down, Appius. You don't know for sure."

"It must be true. The gods have turned the wind and the rain against us."

And the great storm began to build in Rome.

The storm continued to build as Alex and Appius talked. Alex said, "Appius, you are my good friend. I feel I know you well, but this isn't like you. What's going on?"

"The other night Numerius sent Lucia to me, and I tried, but I could not resist her. I have shamed myself and turned the gods against me. I know Numerius had this man killed for the plate, but everyone knows that it was Numerius' money and name that was directly involved with this man and the plate. Lucia made sure of that, telling everyone how the plates could be brought together. Now the police will speak to him about this man's death and the plate showing up at the pantheon. And then they will want to talk to me, and Numerius will expect me to tell them nothing and cover up this man's death. How can I live with this? How can I be in debt to him?"

Alex said, "If they come to you, tell them nothing, that's all. Let them talk to Numerius. Tomorrow is the last day and this will all be over. You will make it, my friend, don't worry."

And then there was a knock at the door. It was the Greek brothers.

Titus said, "Lucia said I could find you here."

"How would she know?"

"That doesn't even matter. I think you're right about what you said. I heard her and Numerius talking about some man name Bannabis, and what to say if the police ask about him."

"Well, what did they say?"

"Numerius was saying that it may have been Appius and you, Alex that had my brother and I kill this man, but they needed proof. We had nothing to do with this."

"And neither did I or my friend."

Appius said, "It's no use now. This is the beginning of the end."

Alex said, "Let's just get through tomorrow. I will find the proof we need to clear our names."

The Last Plate

Fit for the gods the Pantheon was this night, as the storm grew stronger over last night, building through the whole day and blowing hard into the night.

It was not going to let up, as rain rushed down into the Pantheon from the hole on top soaking the middle of the great room of the gods, where soon all the plates would open a line of communication. Rain poured into the middle and candles had been placed around the walls next to the statues of the gods.

Numerius stood in front of the last statue, which would receive a plate as soon the high priests carried it in. Appius sat up high in the ledges, and Alex was on the main floor with his camera, and the Greek brothers stood on both sides of Lucia a few feet away from Numerius dressed in a white robe.

It had begun; the priests sang the hymns of the gods as they slowly walked in holding the last plate. The sound from the rain and the singing was unique, something no one would never forget. They came closer and one could see the excitement in Numerius' eyes.

Alex was taking pictures of everything. This was historical, and he would capture it all.

The plate was now being slid into position, and just as it settled home, a great wind came up and was blowing all around the Pantheon. Numerius tried to start reading the prayer. The candles were starting to blow out making it harder and harder to see.

Then the Greek brothers pulled out daggers and ran them in Lucia's back from both sides, and Alex screamed, "No!!" As he dropped his camera and started running over to them, Appius came to his feet, and the priests ran from the Pantheon.

Then the Greek brothers started walking in Numerius' direction as he continued to read the prayer not knowing what was going on just behind him.

But before they could make it to him, Alex dived on Gaius, and they went to the ground fighting over the knife.

Titus kept walking, and Appius's hands and fingers dug deep into the rail around the ledges.

And then as Alex and Gaius fought, Titus ran his knife deep into Numerius's back.

The white robe slowly turned red, as he still stood in shock trying to finish the prayer before he would fall to the ground dead.

Alex was on top and about to win the fight with Gaius, then Titus turned and looked up to the ledges and Appius was gone.

Titus took one step to help his brother, and deep into his back plunged another blade in Appius's hands. Titus looked at him as he fell to his knees. Titus said,

"FATHER, WHY?"

Now a second later, as Appius turned around, he saw Alex run his son Gaius through.

Appius stood watching him, holding the knife. Alex was still breathing heavily over the dead body of Gaius. He said, "I can't believe its you, Appius. Why?"

"My friend, this is the biggest thing to ever happen to Rome, and I will be remembered for making it all happen. Not only by men, but the gods as well.

This is bigger than life. This is ROMANESQE.

AND THIS IS WHO I AM."

Alex hung his head as the rain still poured down into the Pantheon and the candles were almost all out. There was not much light left; he gripped tightly onto the knife in his hand and jumped up screaming and running at Appius.

Then Appius pulled a gun from his robe and fired one shot hitting Alex in the shoulder.

Now Alex was down on the ground bleeding badly, and Appius was holding the gun. Still pointing it at Alex, he said, "I'm sorry, my friend."

And just as he started to pull the trigger, lighting struck down from the opening in the Pantheon in a blinding flash and hit the gun killing Appius instantly. As he fell in the middle of the rain coming down, it was over.

Certainties

When they met they knew instantly. What they felt for each other was something very special. Something most of us will never find in our whole lifetime. To have someone that you can share and receive everything with is truly a wonderful thing.

As time passed, he learned he loved everything about her. And she could please him, even without words, as he could do the same for her. The key was the communication, getting to really know each other. What she liked or didn't like were things he studied, learning all that would please her, bringing him closer to her in every way. How long does it take to really get to know and love someone? Most could not put a time on it, and we all know Rome was not built in a day.

But neither was any lasting relationship. It isn't the amount of time that is most important, but even more so is just how well you communicate. What you know and love about each other.

They did everything together, from finding out what were each other's favorite colors, to how long one could hold their breath underwater. It may sound corny to us, but this is what most of us lack in our own relationships. As time passed, he knew when she needed space or when she needed him to be there, close to her. And she knew all the same things about him.

What they had was special and rare, and they knew just how blessed they were to have each other. They talked about it, their love for each other. Understanding of what the other person feels not just about life and times, the focus was on each other. This is what they had. It was wonderful, and every man and woman should know what this feels like. To love someone and have them truly love you back.

One of their favorite things to do was go to the drive—in movie; they loved the movies that they had seen a million times before. So this night was going to be great.

"Silence of the Lambs" was showing and they were very excited as they drove down and around the winding roads of southern California. She was looking deep into his eyes as he held her close. He reflected on how lucky he was to have her, and he smiled as the moonlight lit up the black sky as beautifully bright as the love they shared for each other.

They made it to the drive—in and as they found the perfect spot, he noticed that there were not many other cars. He said to her, "Wow not many people like this movie. Almost nobody else is here."

And she said, "No most people have this on DVD and can watch it when they want."

"Maybe you're right and that's fine with me because I have you and the movie all to my self, and that's what I really wanted anyway."

She smiled and said,

"You know my mother warned me about men like you getting me alone in dark cars and trying to have their way with me."

"Well that's funny, she didn't warn you I would want to take you back home and have my way with you in my bedroom as well?" They laughed together and kissed, as they spilled the wine they had brought along from home. Now it was time for the movie to start, but they still were not ready to stop feeling and touching each other to watch it. When they did look up they realized that they had missed the first thirty minutes of the movie. The windows had started to steam from all the heated romance. They fed each other fruits and cheese with the rest of the wonderful wine that they didn't waste all over the car.

They would never leave the car to go to the snack bar. After a while he looked back out the still steamed window of their big expensive automobile and now he could see there were even less cars at the drive-in than before. He said, "These people must not be enjoying this movie as much as we are."

Then she moved close and pushed her hand down the front of his trousers smiling and she said, "I don't think any one is having half as much fun as we are."

And with a high, shaky voice he said, "I think you just might be right."

So just like that, right back at it they went. The movie really made no difference; the main attraction was each other. Then she stopped him and said, "Wait I heard a car door." as she pushed him off of her so she could look out the steamed window. She wiped the window just in time to see someone's feet lifting up into a nearby car and starting to drive away. She said,

"Look, now there is only one car still here other than us; soon we should have the whole place to ourselves."

He pulled her back from the window and said, "That's just the way I want it to be." And back they went, not to the movie, but to each other. By now the movies was halfway over, and out of nowhere, the last car there other than theirs, started to lay on his horn. They looked up to see what was going on, but all they could see was the car with no lights on. The windows were dark and the sound of the loud horn nonstop. Just as Clarice Starling made her way into the house of the person she felt was the true killer on the big screen in front of them.

He said, "What the hell is wrong with this guy!!!" He was getting angrier as the horn did not stop. He said, "This is ridiculous! I'm going over there."

Then she said, "No honey I don't think that's a good idea, it will stop just wait a second alright?"

And he said, "Alright honey I'll wait, I just don't want anything to ruin our night, that's all." So he waited, but the horn did not stop.

Soon he could wait no more. He had to go see what the hell was wrong with these people. After all, they had paid for this movie and this was just not right. He put on his shoes and unlocked the car doors and slowly climbed out. He looked over his car at the car blowing the horn; still he could only see the car, but no one in or outside of it. Slowly he walked around his car to the other car, and as he came closer, suddenly the sound stopped. He stood there just for a second and then looked back at his car and his wife; she was waving him back to her, through the half steamed windows of their car.

He said, “I can’t believe this.” And then he walked back to his car, and climbed back inside.

She said, “I think I’m ready to go. Let’s go home now.”

But now he was upset, he wanted to continue the wonderful evening they were having. He said, “Honey you said that we wouldn’t let any thing ruin this evening for us.”

She said, “I know but we can finish when we get home.” He really wasn’t happy with that, but it was what she wanted, so that’s what he was going to do.

But just as he went to start the car, both back doors opened at the same time and in climbed two men and they slammed the doors closed. The one behind him said, “Turn the car off.” As he pushed the barrel of a forty four magnum to the back of his head, and she put both her hands over her mouth to keep from screaming.

He said, “It’s all right, honey. Just stay calm, it’s all right.”

He slowly turned the car off, and then the man behind her said, “Put your arms around both sides of the seat, slowly.”

She looked at her husband crying, and he said, “Do as they say, honey. It’s going to be okay.”

As tears started running down her face she looked at him with the gun at the back of his head and did what the man behind her asked her to do. Then the man behind him said, “How do you know?”

He answered, “Know what?”

The man pushed the gun harder into the back of his head and said, “That everything is going to be okay.”

At that she started crying loudly, she could no longer control her emotions. She felt the men were going to kill them both.

He said, “Well if we do what ever you ask, I hope that you would let us be.”

The man behind him said, “Hope is all we have. We hope that we know what we need to know, isn’t that true?”

He said, “Yes that is true; tell me what it is that the both of you need?”

The man behind him said, "The real question is what you need of each other."

He looked confused, and she continued to cry. Minutes passed and no one said a word, only the sound of her tears filled the car and now her hands had been tied tightly behind her seat.

Then he said, "Please tell me what it is you want from us, I'll give you anything I have."

The man behind him sat back taking the gun from behind his head and said, "Lock the doors, please." and he did. The man went on to say, "Anything we want is that right."

He looked at his wife as he answered, "Yes. Please just don't hurt us."

Then the man behind her said, "What if we said we wanted your wife?" He pulled hard on her ropes and she cried out once again with pleading eyes as she shook her head no, looking into her husband's eyes.

He said, "Please she is my wife! She is all I have. Please!"

The man behind him said, "She is not all you have, you have much more. Don't lie to us again."

At that he started to cry. He tried hard to fight back the tears for her sake, but he was starting to lose hope. He looked at his wife as she cried as the man behind her started to reach around the seat to touch her body. She looked at him through her tears and him at her through his. He knew at that moment what she needed. He felt he knew what he had to do. He started to pray she would understand even though he couldn't explain.

He said to the man behind him, "Why do you want her?"

At that the man said, "Why do you?"

"She is my wife and I love her."

The man behind him laughed and said, "Would you rather we kill her, over my friend here having her for himself tonight and right in front of you?"

He started to breathe heavily, trying not to panic, "I wouldn't want her to die—I want her to live. Please don't do this to us."

The man behind her put his hands over her mouth so she could not speak. And the man behind him said, "Do you know what she wants?"

"I think I do, she's my wife."

The man said, "Do you really know?"

He looked into his wife's eyes as her tears ran down over the man's hand that was pressed over her mouth. He said, "Please don't kill my wife!!"

The man behind him said, "I think I know your answer now.

He started to cry, and found it hard to look over at her after that.

The man behind him said, "You think you know; you think you're doing the right thing for your wife, but you don't know, you only hope. My friend, I want you to take her to the other car and I'll stay her with him. I think you know what to do."

They looked into each other's eyes as if this was the last time they would ever have. No words, only feeling passed between them, and then she was gone. Now only the man behind him remained.

The man said, "Please don't forget I have a gun on you and I will kill you, and my friend has one too. So don't try anything."

He looked over as the other man pushed his wife into the front seat of the other car. It didn't move. The car was dark and just sat there.

The man behind him said, "Strange isn't it? You can't do anything, anything but hope, isn't that right?"

He said, "I hope and I pray."

The man said, "What do you think is happening to your wife right now?"

"I don't know."

As he put his head in his hands weeping and crying, the man said, "If I asked your wife, what would she tell me you would want to happen? Would she say you would rather die or see my friend have sex with her one time? What would she say you would choose?"

He looked away and said, "I would rather die."

"Is that what she would say?"

And at that he didn't care anymore, he lost control and turned around and tried to get to the man behind him. Then the gun went off—he wasn't dead, the man had only shot him in the leg. He fell on the front seat holding his leg in great pain, and the man behind him said, "I don't think you know anything. I wonder what she knows."

And he took the butt of the gun and cracked him hard in the back of his head, now he was out cold.

The man behind him dialed a cell phone to his friend and said, "Ask her what her husband would choose?"

It was almost morning, and the two cars were still parked in the drive—in as the daylight began to appear. The movies were long over and no one was in sight. And in the car there he was, still out cold, but starting to come around. He looked around and started screaming for his wife. But his leg was bad. As he tried to get out of the car, to go over to the other car; he fell to the wet ground as it was raining. He screamed and cried as he pulled himself along the ground trying to get to the other car.

He was almost there; he was wet and covered in mud as his body slid along the ground in the rain and mud. He reached up to the door handle and somehow swung the door open, and there she sat on the front seat, but she wasn't moving and he screamed. He climbed in on top of her shaking her, telling her to wake up and then—she did.

He said, "Are you all right? What did they do to you?"

She smiled and said, "They asked me about you, and I told them."

"Told them what?"

And she said, "The same things you did."

And it was over.

How long does it take to know someone, and love them? Can you put a time on it? Or is it the quality of time that really matters? Do you know the one you say you love? Do you really know?

Are you **CERTAIN?**

Play on the Middle

I knew something was wrong. I just didn't know how incredibly wrong it was. We had been together for five years now, and it was getting harder for us to communicate or bond like we so lovingly did the first few years. I really loved Cordial, he was my husband and I knew he loved me, but somehow the love he had for me seemed to be fading.

He provided for me very well. We owned a beautiful home in California that I loved. It was perfect, everything a young girl dreams of. But I learned rather fast that money could never buy happiness, no matter how much you have. We both felt the strain on our relationship, even though we never talked about it.

The respect for each other was always there; we did the kind things for each other, smiled as we passed each other by in our home. Not really knowing what to say or do with ourselves, we just tried to keep out of each other's way to avoid awkward moments. But as time passed, we knew this would never last if we kept on this same path. I remember the day Cordial said to me, "Sandy, what happened to what we had? Do you still love me?"

"Yes I do. Things haven't been good, and I really would like to do something about it." "I was hoping you would say that, I still love you and I want us to be happy. I know I work a lot, and I haven't been spending enough time with you, but I can change that."

"Cordial, your work has never bothered me, although sometimes I can get a little lonely here in this big old house."

"Well, I say we start right now today trying to consciously work on spending more time together talking, and remembering why we are together, and trying to put the most important thing first, us."

"I think that's a wonderful idea. I know this will make a difference. I know I love you; that has never changed for me."

"I feel the same way."

It was a wonderful conversation and I felt so much better after we put all the cards on the table. So with plans to go in a much more positive direction, I thought things would get better really fast, but they didn't.

A week later, I had prepared Cordial's favorite dinner. There was candlelight with champagne chilling. I wore my black silk dress that hugged my body just right, which I knew he loved. Everything was perfect, but when he came in and saw me standing by the table, he didn't look pleased. He tried to smile, but I knew the evening I had wanted wasn't going to go the way I had planned. "How was your day?" I asked with forced enthusiasm.

"It was a long day. I'm really tired."

"Too tired to eat and maybe have some dessert later?" I said looking down and moving my hand along my silky black dress.

"Sandy, you look wonderful, and this is all great, but today was hell for me. I'm gonna have to pass." He walked over to me and kissed me on my cheek, and quickly left the dining room. I told myself not to worry and start jumping to all kinds of conclusions; maybe he was really tired and had a trying day.

So I continued to try. Our intimacy was a thing of the past, as he hardly ever touched me. To me, he wasn't really trying like he said he would. Time passed with no real change at all. We talked a few more times about it and he always felt like we could make it better, but it never was. To me it was worse; I didn't know how much more I could take. But things didn't seem to bother Cordial like they bothered me. Why not? It was his life too.

Our lives had completely changed, and I had no idea why. Cordial was always on time coming home and I never had problems reaching him at work or anywhere he was, so for me to think of him having an affair would be hard. But now I was done with this; something had to be done.

So when he came in the door, everything I had been thinking and not saying all came pouring out. This was the first time temper and emotions ran high; we really had never spoken to each other in this way. I told him I felt he really didn't love me the way he said he did, but he just told me I couldn't possibly know how he felt.

The conversation ended badly. I was crying hard as I stormed out of the room. Cordial was upset as well, and he poured himself a glass of vodka. As I lie there on my bed weeping, I heard his car start up to leave. I went to the window and watched Cordial drive away. I got undressed and ran myself a hot bath hoping this would relax me; I was very tense to say the least.

The bath helped to soothe my body, but it didn't do much for my mind. I went to bed with tears still running from my eyes, as I cried myself off to sleep. I was abruptly awakened by Cordial slamming the front door when he returned home that same night. I sat up in bed hoping he would make his way to our bedroom, but he didn't.

I listened, but heard nothing, so I lay back down and tried to fall back to sleep. The next evening I was making dinner when Cordial returned home from work. I was at the stove with my back to the door as he walked up behind me.

He said to me, "Sandy, we need to talk, not fight. I mean really talk." As I turned to him, he stood there holding a dozen red roses.

I asked, "Are those for me?"

"Of course they are. You don't think I would have roses for any other woman, do you?"

"I don't know what to think anymore. We say we love each other, but somehow we have forgotten how to show it."

"People who love each other never forget."

"So you really don't love me anymore?"

"That's not it, I do love you. Lately, work has been more than I can stand, more than you know about."

"Then why don't you talk to me about it? I need to know if something is wrong. I'm your wife. I do want to be there for you."

"That's just it, work is work, and I don't ever want to bring those problems home with me."

"But look what it's doing to us, Cordial. It's tearing us apart, piece-by-piece. Don't you see what's happening? Whatever we had is gone, and I'm starting to think we can never get it back."

"Don't talk like that, Sandy. We can save what we have and I know how we're going to do it." Cordial picked up his briefcase and placed it on the counter. He opened it and took out two tickets to Florida. "This is it; this is where we start putting it all back together. I know how I feel, and all I need to know is if you feel it's worth saving."

"I love you Cordial. I'm just afraid."

"Everything is going to be just fine; you just have to trust me."

"How are you going to leave work right now with all that's going on?"

"This is very important to me. I want you to know that. I have a way I can do it to make it all work."

"Cordial, I'm willing to give this one more try. I can't live like this anymore." "I understand. I know how hard this has all been on you, Sandy. I'm going to make up for it all. You'll see."

"When do we leave?"

"I have an old college buddy named Dan Walker, who lives out there. He's willing to help us out with this."

"You told him about our problems?"

"No, Sandy, give me some credit. He thinks we're coming on vacation."

"So how can he help us?"

"Well, in order for me to go, I have to see this merger through over the next few weeks, and fly to New York at the end of the week with our new clients. Once I'm there and all is said and done, I'm on the first plane to Florida to meet up with you and Dan."

"So you mean you want me to go without you?"

"Just for the week, Sandy. You need to get out of here right now. I'll be out of town most of the week anyway, and I don't want you sitting around here all week alone thinking about how bad everything is. Believe me, the sun will do you good, and you will love Dan."

"But I don't know this guy, are you sure it's okay?"

"Absolutely. He's a good friend. I always could depend on Dan."

"But you haven't seen him in a long time, right? People change, I'm just not sure."

"Come on, Sandy. I have been talking to Dan for months now. He's a good friend who I really trust. Don't you trust my judgment?"

"I do. Why haven't you ever talked about this Dan before?"

"I don't know. He's just an old buddy, that's all, from a long time ago."

"Okay, how is this all going to work?"

"Well, you'll fly out and Dan will meet you at the airport. Dan has huge, beautiful summer home with a guesthouse where we will be staying right by the ocean. You won't have to stay in the same house with him; we have the guesthouse all to ourselves. Now, how does that sound?"

"Really not that bad. I guess I could handle a little sunshine."

"Good, then it's settled. You'll leave first thing in the morning. Sandy, I'll be there so fast you won't have a chance to miss me, I promise, we will work all this out. I love you."

He kissed me, passionately like we used to kiss. As he held me in his arms, I was lost and falling back in love again. Cordial had a way with me; he could understand me like no other man I had ever been with. After he kissed me, he quickly left the room and I started thinking; why can't he be that passionate all of the time; if he really felt that way?

It was like he could turn it on when he wanted to, and block me out just as well. Something inside me signaled a warning. I couldn't help but to feel that way.

The next morning I was ready to take the trip. I was all packed and ready to go. Before I went to bed, I took a hot shower, and then covered my body in scented oil. I pulled the covers over my naked body in bed, where I waited for Cordial to join me. When he made it to the bedroom, I was still awake and watching him taking off his shirt. He looked at me and said, "Are you waiting for me?" I didn't say a word. I just pulled the covers off, exposing my nakedness to him. He continued undressing, but without taking his eyes off of me.

He climbed in bed naked as I was, kissing my ankles all the way up to my breasts and then to my lips. We kissed and began making love like we hadn't in a very long time. The next morning I awoke and Cordial was already up and on the phone in the other room. I got up and put on my white bathrobe, and went down the hall slowly and quietly.

As I came closer to the door, I could hear some of what he was saying on the phone. He was talking to Dan. He said to him that everything was set and not to worry, but why would Dan have reason to worry? It was strange to me. I tried to move a little closer to the door, but as I did, the front doorbell rang, so I moved quickly back to our bedroom.

As I got dressed, I started thinking, what was that all about? Why make the call in the other room? And why would Dan be worried? I don't know. Maybe it was how he said it, "Don't worry." It all bothered me, but I was still going to go. Cordial came in the room and took my bags down to the car. I was still getting ready to go as he said to me, "Hurry up Sandy, we have to leave in ten minutes."

"I'll be down in five. I'm almost ready." As we drove to the airport, there wasn't much conversation. I thought after last night there would be something to talk about. I asked Cordial if he thought this was going to be good for us. He said yes, and that everything was going to be just fine. He looked at me with what I felt was a forced smile. Now we were at the gate and it was time for me to board the plane. Cordial put his hands on my face and said, "I'll be there before you know it. This is going to work, this just what we need. Dan will be waiting for you at the airport. He will take you to his guesthouse so you can get settled in, and he will probably take you for dinner later, okay?"

"Cordial, I want you to know that I'm only doing this because I love you, do you understand that?"

"I do, I love you too, now go have some fun, and I'll be right behind you." As I turned and headed down the jet way to board the plane, I started to cry. My life was strange to me, and taking me in different directions. I didn't know how to feel anymore.

I was on my way; I told myself I was going to focus on having a good time, no matter what. The flight was very nice, smooth all the way; as we came in to land I realized that I didn't even know what Dan looked like. I got off the plane with my carry-on and headed up to the gate, looking, but for whom? Someone I had never seen. This is crazy, I thought. What was I going to do?

Then for some reason I had this strong urge to turn around. As I did, there he was with a sign in his hand that said, "Sandy Johnson." He looked at me smiling like he knew who I was, then he started over to me. As he came closer, I watched him. He was beautiful with sandy blond, curly hair down to his shoulders. He was very strongly built; his body was darkly tanned and his eyes were a perfect shade of green. Now he had stopped right in front of me, still smiling but not saying a word. Then he held the sign up closer to me, and I began to smile.

"Yes, that's me, and you must be Dan. Am I right?"

"Dan Carter, at your service, Miss. Come with me. We have to get your luggage before they send it out to God knows where. How was your flight, Sandy?"

"It was great."

"Good, glad to hear it. Are you hungry? Is there anything you need?"

"No, I'm fine, thank you."

We got the bags and left the airport. It was a beautiful day as we drove up the coast. Dan had a jeep, so the wind blew softly though his hair as he drove. I tried not to stare, but it was hard. He kept his eyes on the road the whole time, with a soft smile on his face. We made it to his place and I couldn't believe my eyes, it was wonderful to say the least. He stopped the jeep out front and said, "This is it. Welcome."

It was a beautiful house surrounded by palm trees and waterfalls, and flowers of all kinds with statuettes sunbathing throughout. "What do you think? Do you like it?"

"Like it? I love it, this is like paradise."

"Well thank you; I must let you know that you are the first angel to visit my paradise." As we walked up to the front doors, I smiled looking at him. "Thank you Dan, that's really nice to say."

"Come on in and let me show you around." And the inside was more wonderful than the outside. Inside was a Jacuzzi and outside, a huge swimming pool. If Cordial and I couldn't make things good here, we couldn't be happy anywhere. Dan showed me everything then we went out back by the pool. He pointed across the pool at a very big guesthouse. It was also wonderful.

"Why don't you go and get cleaned up and meet me later out here by the pool? We'll have a drink and talk, how's that sound?"

"Sounds good to me. I'll see you in a little while."

As I walked through the door of the guesthouse, giant arrangements of flowers met me on the other side. Dan really had a way of making his guest feel right at home. He was very nice, just like Cordial said he was. But now it was time to indulge myself. I took a fast shower and got right into my bikini, and gave a little attention to my hair and makeup as well.

I don't know why, but I was a little nervous as I walked out to the pool to have a drink with Dan. Sounds silly, I know, but I was. Kind of like a first date your best friend sent you on. I just took a deep breath and headed out.

Dan had a very nice table set up by the pool, with candles and flowers, and a small bar on wheels that rolled right up to the table. Dan must have been inside the house when I came out, so I just had a seat at the table and started taking in the beautiful view.

There was a cordless phone on the table that started to ring. I looked around to see if Dan was going to get it. After three rings, I picked up the phone. "Hello?"

"Sandy, it's Dan. I'm calling from inside the house. You have a call on the other line from a man who claims to be your husband."

I smiled, "Is that right? Is this man's name Cordial by chance?"

"Yes, I think that's what he said. You just hit line two and I'll be out there in just a minute and we will have those drinks."

"Thanks Dan, I'm looking forward to those drinks." As I smiled, I hit the line two get the call from Cordial. "Hello, honey, where are you?"

"Hi, I'm in New York. How is everything? Are you okay?"

"This place is wonderful. I love it."

"I knew you would. What do you think of Dan?"

"Dan is a very nice man; he's made me feel right at home. How long will you be in New York?"

"Not too much longer, a few more days, then I'm coming straight to you. I can't wait to get there. I think this is going to work out well."

"I'll be here when you get here."

"You just enjoy yourself. I'll see you soon. I have to go now, I love you." And as I was saying I love you too, Cordial had already hung up the phone.

Normally that would have bothered me, but today I was intrigued by my surroundings as well as my host. As I turned, Dan was walking out of the house around the pool smiling as he approached me. I returned a warm, welcoming smile; he wore white shorts with his bare tanned chest exposed. He said, "How is my good friend and will he be joining us soon?"

"Yes, he will and he's doing fine, but not for a few days yet."

"I see, so I have the pleasure of entertaining you all to myself for a while longer, and let me say it will be my extreme pleasure."

"What a gracious host you are."

"That I am. Now, let me make you my wonderful Island Passion. This is a drink that my grandfather made for my grandmother. No other place in the whole wide world could you find such a treasure."

"Well, I'm honored."

As he made the drinks, I watched him. He had a way about him that was gentle and kind, easy to be around. Even though I didn't know him well, it felt like I did. I was enjoying myself much more than I thought I would.

"Here you are. I'm dying to hear what you think." I took the glass from him as he watched my every move. I put the glass to my mouth to drink.

As I sipped, our eyes locked. "This is heavenly, I've never had anything like it before" "I'm pleased you like it. Now tell me, how is it being married to my good old friend? Is he still stubborn as the day is long?" I laughed out loud, as well did he.

"Well, yes in some ways, but probably not as bad as you remember. Now tell me about you; have you changed from what Cordial would remember of you?"

"Me, I don't think so, I've never had a lasting partner to bring about such changes in my life as Cordial has with you, and from what I could tell, no doubt for the better"

"I'll drink to that"

"Hear, hear."

"Are you and Cordial anything alike, and what made you and him such good friends?" "Well, we shared a lot of things in common. I was going though some bad times back then, and he helped me get though them. He was always there for me, a really good friend."

"Why didn't you and he stay in touch? Did something happen?"

"Well, I guess you could say that. After school our lives changed somewhat, some of the things we shared in common changed. I believe we will always remain the best of friends, and this reunion is the proof of that."

"Did Cordial tell you why we are here?"

"Well, he did mention that you two really needed this time together, and that there had been a strain."

"I do love him, Dan, but the last few years have been really hard on me."

"Cordial is a good man, although I remember him having some problems focusing on important things, but after meeting you I'm sure he knows he has a good thing."

I smiled as I took another sip of my drink, as did he. "I can't believe you are not in a relationship, you seem to have so much to offer the right woman."

"Thank you, Sandy, but the right person is sometimes hard to put your hands on. I guess I'll be okay."

"I'm sure you will."

"Well, I'm glad you're here. I really needed the company. I promise we'll have a good time, and we'll let these matters work themselves out, what do you say?"

"I think you're right." I looked into his deep green eyes. We finished our drinks and enjoyed each other's company, and then I went back to the guesthouse for a little rest.

As I lay there trying to rest, I tossed and turned trying to fall asleep, but wasn't having much luck. Surprisingly to me, my thoughts were not on Cordial, they were on Dan as I fell asleep to dream.

I was alone in Dan's Jacuzzi surrounded by candlelight, and softly playing music. In walked Dan in a white robe, holding two tall glasses of champagne. He moved closer and put one of the glasses to my mouth and I took a sip. He then stood up and untied his robe baring his naked body to me, and climbed slowly into the water with me.

He put his hands on my face moving my hair from my eyes as he moved even closer to kiss me.

And just as our lips touched, I woke up.

Breathing heavily, I sat up looking around the room, excited and ashamed all at the same time, as a small grin began to show at the corners of my face. If things weren't already bad enough, this was all I needed. I was there for one reason, and one reason only, and that was to save my marriage. But I couldn't help the way I was feeling, and I hated myself for that. It was just that Cordial had made me feel so unwanted for the last few years; I was starting to feel like I wasn't attractive or sexy enough anymore. The way Dan looked at me made me feel like I was, or maybe he made me feel like I wanted to be.

It was about six o'clock when the phone rang in the guesthouse; it was Dan telling me to be ready by seven, and he was taking me out for dinner. I frantically got myself together like a sixteen year-old schoolgirl, trying to find just the right thing to wear. Finally, I was ready and right before seven. As I looked out, Dan was walking around the pool coming to the guesthouse.

He was dressed very nicely in a black suit. I pulled back so he would not see me; I didn't want him to think I was over excited about dinner. Dan knocked on the door and I took just a second before I opened it.

"Are you ready to eat?"

I smiled and said, "You bet ya." He had a limo out front waiting I couldn't believe it; we drove down to an Oceanside restaurant, for the best seafood I had ever had.

As we sat and had dinner we laughed and talked, just getting to know each other. I felt like I was on my first date, it was wonderful. Then my thoughts went to Cordial, and I guess it showed, Dan looked at me and said, "What is it? Is it Cordial?"

"I'm sorry. I'm really having a good time, but my life right now is not good. I have no idea what is going to happen."

"That's just it, no one does. It's unfair, I know, but you have to ask yourself, what it is that you really want."

"I just want to be happy, but I feel like that's impossible. We never are on the same page anymore."

"Well, that's why you're here, right?"

"But I'm starting to feel like I'm kidding myself. I don't think I can do it, or if I really want to try anymore."

"Do you still love him?"

"I do, but I don't think that's going to be enough." I excused myself from the table and took a walk out to take in the view, and just to clear my head.

And up from behind Dan came and put his hand on my shoulder. He said he knew how it felt to love someone and not be sure if they felt or ever could feel the same for you. He said it could slowly drive you crazy if you let it. As he turned me around, he looked into my eyes, "Don't let it destroy you. You have to be strong for you. Protect your heart at all costs, because that's all you have."

It was late, so we went home. The ride was quiet. I didn't talk; I had a lot on my mind, and most of my thoughts were on Dan. I couldn't stop myself. It felt like I was drawn to him. I looked over and he looked back at me; we didn't speak, but we both felt the same way.

Once we were home, Dan walked me to the door of the guesthouse. I turned to him and said goodnight and he said the same. I walked in and closed the door, and pressed my body against the door on the inside. I could hear Dan start to walk away. I slowly opened the door again. He stopped and turned to me slowly; he looked at me and started back to my door.

Once he was inside, I moved to him. He ran his hands though my hair very slowly, looking into my eyes. He kissed me and stayed the night.

The next day when I awoke, I was alone. Dan was gone. I could still smell his scent on the sheets where we just made passionate love just last night. As I gathered the comforter up close around me, I felt surprisingly calm. A warm sense of clarity came all over me. What had I done? I no longer cared.

Then I thought about Dan. How did he feel? I showered and got dressed and went up to the house. As I walked in, I passed the study where Dan was sitting at his desk looking over some documents. I walked in and sat on the sofa. He looked at me and said, "Good morning, are you hungry?"

"No, not really. I'm sorry about last night. It's my fault. I should have never opened the door."

"You're not to blame. I know how much pressure you're under right now, but I couldn't stop myself and for that I'm sorry." He got up and walked over to me and sat down on the sofa. "What are we going to do? Cordial will be here soon, and I don't think I can face him."

"This might sound bad, but I don't feel bad about what we've done. I know it was wrong, but I also feel like I needed this, and maybe you needed it too."

I grabbed him and pulled him to me, and kissed him passionately. We spent the rest of the day together; Dan took me everywhere and showed me everything. The whole day we shared together, and not once did we talk of the fact that Cordial would be here tomorrow.

Later that same night as we lay together after making love in Dan's bed, we started to talk. "Dan, I've been unhappy for so long, searching for reasons why things were so bad between Cordial and myself. Maybe there was never a reason. Things happen and nobody really knows why they happen. They just do. All I know is right now I'm here with you, and I want to be."

"Sandy, this time we've spent together has been wonderful, and I don't regret it. But Cordial is your husband and my good friend, so we're going to have to face this."

"Dan, something has happened to me, and it's all because of you. You've made me feel like I deserve more, and I want more. Is that so wrong?"

"Sandy, I want you to be happy, but I don't know what we can do."

"We could just leave before he gets here and maybe just take a little time to figure out what to do."

"Are you telling me you don't want to be with him?"

"I want to be with you, that's all I care about."

We talked and talked for hours. Dan wanted to be with me just as much as I wanted him. As we continued to talk, Dan told me how Cordial and him talked about me, and the fact that we were having so many problems. He said that Cordial didn't know how to leave me, even though that's how he felt. This vacation was probably a way for him to let me know that we should go our separate ways, but only if he could find the nerve to tell me.

I couldn't believe it. I really knew all along it was over, but this coward just couldn't say it. He played with me, stringing me along. Knowing how much I was suffering, why would he do it?

Now I was angry, and with good reason to be. Cordial was not a man, now he was a child to me who played games, so I was going to teach him a lesson that he would never forget before I left him. I convinced Dan to play along with my plan; I was going to make sure that Cordial knew never to play with anyone's feelings again.

My plan was to let Cordial catch us in bed together, and then I would act like it was all a mistake, and that I still loved him and that I was so sorry. And when I got him to forgive me, I would then tell him I was going to leave him. But Dan didn't want Cordial to know that we were going to really be together. He said he was Cordial's friend, and that would be too much. So I agreed to leave that part out.

So it was all set, the next day Cordial was coming in around noon. Dan said that I should go shopping and not be there when he came in, and when Cordial arrived Dan would send him out to get something special for me.

So that's what we did. As I shopped, I felt good about what was going to happen. He deserved what he was going to get. All I ever did was love him and be there for him. I took a cab and headed back to the house. I paid the driver and walked up into the house.

Once I was inside, I looked around. I saw Cordial's bags by the front door. It was quiet with no one in sight, and then I heard a noise up the staircase. I looked and I saw clothes on the stairs leading up to Dan's room. As I started up the stairs, my heart started beating harder. I could hear only my heart beating as I came closer to the top.

Now I stood right outside Dan's bedroom door, and I could hear noises coming from inside. My hand reached out to open the door, and as the door opened, nothing could have prepared me for what I saw.

Dan was making love with Cordial, and my life was over.

This had been the plan all along. I was a fool. Cordial's old friend was more than just that: he had been his lover. Cordial had tried to make it work with me, but no longer could he do it, because it was Dan who he loved and wanted. I was in the middle, played on both sides.

Real Time

"Is it possible you know which way United is?"

"I think it's down here to the right."

"Thanks, if I hurry I just might make it, here keep the change." The door slammed hard on the yellow taxi as Joe Parker ran to catch a flight leaving in just thirty minutes.

"Excuse me, sir. I'm sorry, please can I get by." There had never been a more busy day than today it seemed as Joe fought his way past crowds of people, all trying to make it to where they had to go by a certain time.

But nothing was more important than Joe's flight; he had to be on this flight, no matter what. Another flight would never do. The flight time was in just over one half hour and anything more he could never make it.

It would be impossible to explain how crucial making this flight was to all these people, like their flights were not as important as his, but this was just how he felt as he pushed past, sweating, trying his best not to miss this flight.

The airport was one of the biggest in the country, and Joe had a long way to go to make it to the United gate in time. He could make it, but only if he hurried. "Please excuse me please; can you let me pass please?"

The corridor was packed wall-to-wall and almost impossible to pass on either side, he panicked "Oh, shit! This can't be happening, not now."

But it was, and there was nothing Joe could do other than to just keep pushing with the flow of people that was moving but at a snail's pace.

As he pushed he looked over to his right at the bodies of people smashed together. He noticed a man's hand was in a lady's bag right in front of him, he was taking all her money and credit cards. The man was so close to the lady it looked as though they were dancing as they moved back and forth with the flow of the crowd.

But this was no dance, this bastard was stealing from the lady and she had no idea what was going on. As he watched, it seemed as everything slowed down, no sound, and Joe could see it happening; only him. He could stop it, he could make his way right over there and tell that officer, or he could grab the guy himself. Then everything jumped back to real time again, and he turned his head and kept pushing the people ahead of him. He was running out of time.

"Let me through here please! I need to get by."

"Hey man, we all need to get by; get off of my arm!!"

"No you don't understand—"

"No, you don't understand; stay the hell off of me, man!"

The angry man turned around and Joe just looked at him like he couldn't believe this man had the nerve to talk to him this way. The man was carrying a large brown leather bag that was hard for the man to move though such a crowded space. He was right in front of Joe, he looked down at the bag and he could see this man's boarding pass hanging out of the bag. Then it happened again, everything slowed down, nothing was moving but Joe; he easily could have pushed the man's pass back into his bag, but he did the opposite and pulled it all the way out and let the pass hit the ground.

Then all at once everything jumped back to real time again and now he was really running out of time. The man looked back over his shoulder at Joe as now he had made it to his gate. Joe just looked at him, and the man smirked as Joe pushed on.

Joe was now pulling his tie off his neck as sweat was pouring down the sides of his face; he started to panic even more. It was loud and hard to hear yourself think with all the people and everything that was going on. Children were crying, and mothers yelling at their children. Men were screaming at gate agents to do something about the crowded conditions, but really no one could do anything, it was hopeless.

But even still, Joe had to make this flight no matter what. He was breathing heavy and he didn't look well; he was starting to feel kind of dizzy, but this didn't slow him down.

People started to look at him. They knew when he would bump or fall into them as he was trying to pass, that something was wrong with this man.

Then it hit him, this terrible feeling, this pain deep in the bottom of his stomach.

He stopped and grabbed his stomach, but as soon as he did, another passenger ran into the back of him sending him forward. He started looking to his left and then right looking for a restroom, but he couldn't really see one. He was still being pushed from behind; he didn't want to move, but he had no choice now, he had to.

With every step he took, the pain was stronger, harder and deeper into the pit of Joe's stomach. His face was turning beet red, his eyes watered, and with no escape the crowd now came to a complete stop.

He closed his eyes for just a second, and when he opened them he was still in great pain.

He noticed he was really close to the wall of the corridor so he pushed hard as he could to get to the wall. He was all most there and then he reached out his hand and touched the wall.

Then he turned looking back over his shoulder with people so close they now had him pinned up against the wall of the corridor. Joe moaned in pain, trying not to scream out, even though if he did, no one would probably even notice.

Joe looked back to the wall and placed his forehead against the carpeted wall and just then everything slowed down again. His hand moved down to his zipper, and he exposed himself right there and began to urinate on the wall, going completely unnoticed.

Then, all at once, everything went back to real time, as the crowd started moving again.

He quickly zipped up his pants and moved along with the crowed hoping he could still make the flight; make the flight, that's all he could think about. His pain was not as bad since he was able to relieve himself.

There wasn't much time left and he still had a ways to go, and the people were still only crawling along.

"Please, sir! Excuse me, please. Let me pass. I'm sorry, please!"

He was not going to give up, he was still in pain, but he knew he had to keep moving.

Then right in front of him was a very wealthy lady with more bags of luggage then he had ever seen in all his years of traveling. She was fighting with a gate agent.

And there was no way past her, no way around her luggage. This lady also had a dog in a large cage; all this plus her was blocking Joe's way.

"Please, lady, you have to let me pass."

"No, you have to wait just like I did and everybody else. Joe tried to move the lady's things himself and the lady lost it.

"Are you out of your fucking mind!!!? Get your hands off of my things!!!"

Joe couldn't believe how she was reacting; he wasn't stealing her things, simply trying to move them out of his way.

Joe tried to move back, but now this lady was right up in his face.

"I'm sorry lady."

The lady turned back to the gate agent and yelled at him to call security.

Joe looked down at the cage, and at that moment everything slowed down once again. He reached down and opened the cage door and this very small dog ran out under peoples' legs and moving very fast; if she wasn't caught right away, she would surely be smashed.

Now the lady really lost her mind,

"Mandy, stop!!! Come here girl! Come here Mandy!!!"

As soon as the lady lunged after her dog everything went back to real time. Joe jumped on top of the cage, smashing it as he got over it and back on his way to his gate.

Now he was moving, but still not very fast, and that pain deep in his stomach was starting to come back again. Joe knew what he needed to do, he needed to dig down deep into his black bag he was carrying over his shoulder; he had a bottle of pills he hated taking because they put him to sleep, but he needed them desperately. There was no time for stopping to find this bottle in the bottom of this bag, but every second he started feeling worse.

So he decided to reach down in the bag as he walked, pushing past the people in front of him. It was all he could do, he had to try.

Joe was dizzy again, falling into people as he reached in the bag at the same time; where the hell are they? And then he saw the first United gate.

There it is. His eyes lit up like the sun, but he was still not to his gate yet.

Still reaching for his pills, his hand hit the bottle; he looked down at the bag and pulled out the bottle of pills.

He almost smiled as he moved to take off the top to the bottle, when a man came up from behind and hit him in the back, knocking the bottle of pills from Joe's hand and down to the floor.

"Oh, no! My pills!!!"

Joe fell right down to his hands and knees trying to find the bottle of pills.

People were kicking the bottle away from him every time he got close; a lady stepped right on the back of his hand and he screamed.

"OOOOHHH, My hand!!!"

And there they were: the pills, right over by the wall. He was on the ground and people continued to walk past him, around him, and over him. Joe was holding his hand in pain and pressing it against his stomach that was also killing him.

"Please help me! Excuse me. Please watch out, and hey, move out of the way please!!!"

He was in great pain as he tried to get to the pill bottle against the wall, and he was almost there; he reached out and grabbed the bottle, and quickly opened it and took two pills as he sat against the wall like a scared child. Then it happened again everything slowed down and he heard the gate agent come over intercom saying,

"At this time all passengers flying flight 222 straight through to Los Angeles LAX, should be checked and boarded at this time. That's flight 222, to Los Angeles LAX is now departing."

Joe was there, he made it to the gate; it was right in front of him about thirty feet away.

But he couldn't move, not even to save his own life.

Then all at once everything went black.

Slowly Joe's eyes did open again. He had blacked out. He was still in pain now, but feeling better than he was.

He got to his feet. The great crowds were all gone and not a soul was in sight, just him getting up off the floor over against the wall.

Joe looked around and saw a payphone and started moving to it, as he did he reached into his pocket and took out a small card and hurried to call the number.

"Hello, hello?"

"Yes, this is Joe Parker. I was supposed to be in this afternoon. I missed my flight. Please listen to me; please, I can catch the next flight in and be there in a few hours. I…"

"No, you just can't say—what about me? You're sorry? You're sorry?!!!"

Everything slowed down again as reality set in. Slowly he fell to the floor next to the phone, with a blank stare on his face as a single tear fell from the corner of his eye.

Then the card with the number he called fell from his hand slowly to the floor, face up.

It was a card for the heart and kidney donor association.

He was next in line, but ran out of, **real time.**

Horse of Another Color

Part 1

I'm Mark Rhymes and what I'm about to tell you is true, believe it or not. And even though it happened to me, I still have a hard time believing it myself. Things like this don't usually happen to people like me, but maybe now they do? At the time this crazy shit all started, I was a young black man 26 years old living in Cleveland Ohio. I was a contractor for a local cable company, which paid me shit, plus it was wintertime in Cleveland, and most of my work was outside. I don't know if you have ever been through Cleveland, but gray, freezing cold and wet, is putting it mildly. I was married, but had recently gone though a divorce.

I had become the proud father of one very wonderful little baby girl, and once me and the ex separated, it was hell for me not being able to put my baby to bed every night, as well as welcome her each morning. The weekend thing was cool, but not what I wanted for my first child and myself to know as our relationship. This was very hard for me. So there I was, trying to build this new life, outside of what I had just built with the ex and my baby. Money was a big problem, and caused me much grief and devastation. I was beginning to feel like a failure, like I had played my last card and it just wasn't good enough. I really wanted to be able to do all these wonderful things for my little girl that I really had no way of doing. Money was such a problem that I had to move in with my sister Jackie and her two kids, this was the straw that broke the camel's back.

I had nothing to feel good about, and desperately needed something. A few months had passed, and then one evening after a hard cold day installing cable, I got a phone call from my other sister Edna; out in San Diego, California. Edna asked me how I was doing. I told her how hard I was struggling trying to make ends meet. She told me how I should concentrate on what I did best, writing. I told her how hard it was to be creative with my work with all that was going on in my life. Then she suggested I come out there with her for a while and work, to see if I could get something going. She said I had a lot of talent that I shouldn't let just go to waste.

So after a lot of encouragement from my sister, I started to think about the possibilities of me going. I really did need a change and something to look forward to. The only thing stopping me now, that would hold me back from just picking up and going, was my baby girl.

It was hard enough just being apart from her in Cleveland, but now I was talking about the other side of the country. But I knew that if I was going to make a difference in her life, I had to do something, something big.

So the plan was that I would go for about five months, to see if I could get a bite with my writing, get something going that could ultimately change the outlook on my baby's future. So as I sat there looking out at the snow falling down outside my sister's window, I made up my mind, I was going to San Diego.

Just like that, screw the job and this cold-ass city that had only brought me sorrow for this last year of my life. I deserved to be happy, and too, able to support my child. But I knew it wasn't going to happen for me here. I had to go and bring it home. More than anything, I wanted to be a father to my little girl. Edna had plans of coming home to visit me and my other sisters, who also live here in Cleveland, and I would return with her when she left. This would all take place in the next three weeks. It seemed that soon as I hung up the phone from Edna, I was on that plane to San Diego. Yes, I was on my way. As I flew high over

Cleveland, looking down at the weather-blown city, I started to cry. From this moment on, I would not be able to see my child until I returned, that cut me hard and deep. This was my home where I was born, and had never left it before. I started to feel like I gave up on this place, like it wasn't good enough for me and for that I also felt bad.

I needed to pull myself together; I had a lot to do in a short period of time, but it was one of the hardest things I had to do. I was hurting and felt very alone.

I made it through the first thirty days. I spent almost all my time writing when I wasn't out looking for some outside work. Then came my first break; I found a job that I could walk to from my sister's house.

Since I didn't have a car, this was great, part-time at a cellular phone store right up in the big plaza near where I was staying. I had plenty of time to write with this part-time job, and the best part was that I wasn't outside, even if the temperature was in the seventies. I made a lot of long distance calls on my new cell phone that I got from working at the store, talking to my baby, telling her how much I loved her, and missed her over and over again. I began to submit my work to a lot of different publishers and agents alike, not yet having much luck, but I was determined to be successful.

Keeping my nose to the grindstone, I kept writing, and submitting my work, and working at the cell phone store. I was starting to get a little burnt, working as much as I was, but I was driven by something bigger than me, the love I have for my child. The cell phone store wasn't a very busy place. Each day I could only expect to see a few people. So lots of days I had plenty of time to think about my writing, my child, or just how well I was doing out here. After a while, when I didn't hear word from some of the people I sent work to, or letters saying that what I sent is not what they're looking for right now, I started to worry. I knew my stuff was good; it was my best and others who looked at it thought so too.

So what the hell was wrong with these people?

One particular day, I was sitting behind the counter at the cell store, just looking out the front window, hoping a customer would come in to take my mind off my situation. The next thing I saw was this big Land

Rover truck pulling up very fast coming to a tire-screeching halt, right in front of my store. And my first thought was, "What the hell is wrong with this asshole?" I would learn shortly afterwards that my first reaction was the right one.

The driver's door opened to this big truck, and out climbed this little Italian man. The look on his face clearly showed what kind of mood he was in as he slammed the door to his truck and made a beeline into my store, right up to me. Then he took his cell phone, threw it up on the counter in front of me and began to explain.

"This fucking phone doesn't work! I've called and talked to people over the phone about this piece of shit, tried everything they told me. The damn thing still doesn't work. I'm wasting valuable time being here right now. I'm a businessman. Ever since I've had this thing, it's done one thing. You know what that is? Lose me money. That's the only fucking thing it's good for! Now, I need somebody that knows what the fuck they're doing to help me. Who are you? So can you handle this? Or you goanna tell me the same bullshit that dumb ass girl tells me every other time I've been in this fucking store?!"

As I sat there looking at him, I was at a loss. I couldn't believe this man was standing there cursing at me like that. I wanted to jump over the counter and slap him in his face a few times, and teach him some respect. But you know how it goes. The customer is always right,—Yeah, right.

So after I recovered from shock, I calmly said, "Sir, I'm sorry you're having these problems with your phone, but I will be glad to look at it, and help you in any way I can." He looked at me and rolled his eyes then said,

"And while you're at it, take all these, too. I don't want them. None of these fucking things work." He pulled out three more phones and threw them at me as well. I stood there, trying to figure this fool out. Then he said, "Look, I'm very important man. You think I got the time to be fucking around with shit like this?"

"Sir, I don't know what you want me to do."

"I want this shit to work!—I have to go, I have things to do. You just do your damn job and I'll call you, and when I do, you tell me you got my shit together." Then he turned and walked right back out of the store, and climbed back into his big truck, and drove away. So now I stood there with the phones, with this, "what the hell just happened?" look on my face.

I blew it off; like I do most things I really can't do anything about, and started right in on the fucking phones.

After looking at all the phones closely, I found out that they all work just fine. I came to the conclusion that Mr. Happy really is just an asshole; he just didn't know how to work the phones. This guy never told me his name all the while he was dogging me out, so I took one of the phone numbers he had taped to the back of the phones, put it into the computer, and pulled up his account.

Mr. Tony Russo. He only had the phones for two days, probably never took the time to sit his ass down and read the owner's manual.— "Some damn people!" I disgustedly exclaimed to myself, moving on to something else.

Right back to this life and all my thoughts. Staring back out the front windows of my storefront. Thinking about the last story I sent in to be reviewed, in my mind I played the scene of the reader who would first take a look at my wonderful work. It went like this, as he runs to tell the editor about my story.

"Frank! You got to read this short, this is just what we've been looking for. I don't know who the guy is or how he found us, but we've got to get a hold of this guy before anybody else does."

"What's his name?"

"His name is Mark Rhymes; get this he's out of Cleveland Ohio, but he's here in town shopping this work."

"Let me take a look, you go get this guy on the phone, before anybody else does."

Yeah, something like that. I'd have them all running to me once they knew I was here. I began to smile; pleased with the way I had it all worked out, but only in my mind. For now, that was good enough for me. I knew I was one of the world's greatest dreamers.

Some time had passed. I had been dreaming a bit too long. I had some paperwork I needed to get done. And just as I started to focus back on my work at hand, the phone rang. Guess who?—Mr. Happy, Tony Russo.

"Cell store, this is Mark, how can I help you?"

"Did you take care of my phones?"

"Yes sir, I did. They're all working just fine now. You can come and pick them up if you like."

"Hey, thanks a lot. You helped me out."

"No problem, Mr. Russo. Anytime."

"Say, Mark, let me ask you a question. How much money you make working there?"

This kind of caught me off guard. I didn't really want people knowing how much money I made, plus why did this guy want to know?

"Well sir, I usually don't talk about the money I make."

"Come on, Mark! You and I know you aren't making shit, selling those cheap-ass phones!"

"Well everybody would like to be making more, right?"

"That's right, Mark, now you're talking."

I didn't know what to make of this guy. Then he said,

"Mark, I need you to do me a favor. Can you do that for me?"

"What?"

"A favor!"

"Well, I'll try, sir, if I can?"

"You're not a fucking idiot, you can handle this.—One of those cell phones, in about a half hour, is going to ring. I need you to answer it and tell the guy that calls your name is Mark, and you work for me, Tony. Tell the guy to go to stall number three."

"That's it? Stall number three?"

"That's it. Hey, asshole, this is very important, take it seriously. Don't fuck this up, you got me?"

I wanted to say fuck you, and slam the phone down, but I was still at work and I was trying to see what this was all about.

"Okay, Tony. Is it okay I call you Tony?"

"Hey, that's my fucking name! I'll call you later."

And then he slammed the phone down, without even saying goodbye.

Now what the hell was that all about? I was really tripping out now. So I sat and waited, then just like he said, one of the cell phones started to ring.

I picked it up, and said,

"Hello."

"Who is this?"

"My name is Mark. I work for Tony. You need to go to stall three."

"Number three, is that right?"

"That's right. Number three."

Then the guy slammed the phone down. He didn't say goodbye, either. Must be a tough guy thing, "Whatever."

So it was done, and it was almost time for me to close up the store. As I got ready to leave for the day, the store phone rang again.

"Cell store, this is Mark. How can I help you?"

"Did you get the call?"

"Yes I did, Tony. It's all done with no problems."

"Is that right? Good job. I'll be in to see you tomorrow."

Then he slammed the phone down. Need I say more?

I locked up and headed for my sister's house. This was some day; I was tired and ready for a hot shower and bed. I really didn't think much of what happened today with this guy Tony. Strange, but no big deal. Something I probably should have paid closer attention to. Used more caution.

So I forged ahead with my writing, determined not to fail. I couldn't fail. I wouldn't fail. Even though things weren't going the way, I would dream them up; every day as I stared out the cell store window, my dreams continued. About a week had passed and Tony hadn't come back for the phones like he said he would the very next day. But then one day, as I was putting up some new sale signs in the front window of the store, he pulled up in his big black truck.

He walked in and said, "Mark, you still got my phones?"

No hellos or goodbyes, this guy didn't believe in them. "Yes I do, Tony, right back here. How you doing anyway?"

"I'll be doing a lot better when I got phones that work, Mark."

"Here you go, and they all work just fine."

He looked at the phones, made a call, then looked at me and said, "Good job man,—here's something for you." What he did next was the strangest thing that has ever happened to me in my whole life. He reached into his pocket, pulled out a wad of money and placed it in my hand. I couldn't believe it. I started counting. I hadn't ever seen so much cash all at one time before. It was about four thousand dollars in cash.

"Oh, my god!" I said, looking at the cash, "What is this for? Do you know how much this is?"

Then, for the first time, he smiled, not a big smile, but for him it was more than he had probably smiled all year. He said, "Don't matter. You helped me out."

I instantly started to stutter, "I don't think I can take this, Tony. It's too much."

"Don't be stupid. That's more than you will make all year in this fucking place."

"Put it away." he said, looking around to see if anyone was coming into the store. I was gone, right out of my mind. I put it away without another word. I right away started to think of all the things I could do with the money. Sending money home to my baby girl was first on my list.

Then Tony leaned close to me on the counter and said, "You think you can handle a real job?"

"What do you mean?" I asked.

"You want to work for me?" Tony asked.

I wanted to scream out, "Hell yeah!" but I had to try to play it cool. Inside, I was feeling like a lotto winner.

"What would I have to do?" I said, somehow feeling like the phone call I took for him days earlier could have been the death of some poor fool.

"Do you know how to drive?" he asked.

"Yes I can drive."

"Then you should be able to do the job."

"All I have to do is drive right?"

That made him mad. He screamed, "Hell no and whatever else I need your ass to do. Don't be a pussy." The way he talked to me all the time made me want to slap the shit out of his little ass, but the money made me kiss it.

"Yes, when do you need me?' I said with a smile, paying no mind to his insults.

"I'll be here at ten in the morning to pick you up. Be here at the store on time. I'm not waiting around for your slow ass."

So now I was thinking, "How does he know if I'm slow or not?"

He then turned and walked back out of the store and drove away, with not another wordabout the money. On my way home, I picked up the best food money can buy for dinner with my sister. When my sister asked how I could afford all this food, I told her I had been given a bonus at work, for sales store of the month.

The next morning came much faster than I wanted it to. I could hardly get myself up out of bed. But I knew I had to get up. This was no time for me to be late, especially with this crazy dude. I got up there a little before ten, so I waited around looking for his truck to pull in. After I waited for about thirty minutes, he pulled up. I opened the passenger door and climbed in and he screamed, "What the fuck are you doing?"

I looked at him with this look of confusion on my face. I said, "I am going with you, right?"

"I'm not paying your ass to ride; I'm paying you to drive!"

"Oh sorry." I got right out and went around to the driver's side, and he got out and passed me going to the passenger's side. He rolled his eyes at me like I was crazy or something.

We both climbed in and headed out. I drove along with the morning sun coming into my face, as Tony read the day's paper. He told me to stay on this one road, as he never looked up from his paper. After about ten minutes, I started to settle into the drive and somewhat relax, knowing by now there would be no conversation. The relaxing drive was starting to make me sleepy, I was finding it hard to keep my eyes open, as I drove down this road that nobody but the two of us were on. Then Tony put his paper away and turned his attention to me.

"So where you from, Mark?" I was happy to hear words that I could respond to; saving me from falling asleep and taking us off the side of this road.

"I'm from Cleveland, back east."

"I knew you weren't from around here. These people on the west coast are assholes."

I guess I was happy not to be included in his latest insults, but I didn't think people were bad out here, and who was he to talk about assholes?

Tony started to open up a little, telling me about the rich man he worked for and all the money this guy had. He told me how he used to be a jockey for this guy, riding all his racehorses and winning for many years. But now he didn't ride anymore, and held the job as trainer. Tony said he had known this guy for years, even went as far to say the guy was like a father figure to him. I found that hard to believe.

Now I was starting to understand that Tony's job was to take care of Mr. S. Canto's million dollar horses, and ready them for every big race.

As he talked, it all sounded good to me, or maybe I just wanted it to. I didn't think too much about it, I just went along. Not very smart, I know.

Tony said, "Take the next right; you will see the stables on your left-hand side." And right as I was going to make my turn, on the left-hand side was the biggest and most beautiful golf course I had ever laid my eyes on. I loved the game, and wanted to play every chance I got.

Now as we pulled up to the stables I asked, "You ever play golf, Tony?"

"I'm too fucken busy to play anything. I deal with horses and motherfuckers like you all day." I just smiled. It was funny. The things he said made me laugh after while because it never fit. This little man was bossing me, this big ass black man who could break his back at any moment. See my point?

The stables were huge, very clean and very rich. Besides some of the horses, I was the only black thing for miles. As we walked through the stables, stopping and taking care of some of Mr. Canto's beautiful horses, I got the occasional unwelcoming looks.

But I wasn't going to let any of that shit bother me. I was there to make money, not make new friends. Now after our work was done, it was time to go home. On the ride back, Tony asked me what I thought about horses now that I had been around them for a whole day. I thought it was great, something I probably would have never seen or experienced if it hadn't been for Tony. For that I would be forever grateful. The horses where like gods, strong and massive. They commanded respect from us, just as we wanted respect from them.

By the time I got back to my sister's house, I was tired and felt like Tony had let the horses run all over me today. Before I got out of the truck, Tony said, "I'll call you in a few days." I went in and hit the showers and straight to bed I went.

As time continued to pass, I worked part-time for the store, and the rest of the time I worked for Tony. I was making more money than I had ever made in my whole life. It was getting hard trying to hide from my sister, where all the money was coming from. But I didn't feel like I should say anything, because inside I wasn't really sure myself. But like a horse, I was going to ride it out. My lifestyle started to change. I always had a car from Tony to drive, even when I wasn't working for him. New clothes and a whole new me. It was great.

Tony took me to parties, rich parties with people who had lots of money and power. At first I felt out of place, but soon I started to feel more like I belonged. People started to know me, and call me by my name, like I was somebody and it felt good. This went on for months; my work took a back seat. But I was still getting letters saying that what I had sent was not what they were looking for at this time, and that did bother me, but not like it did before.

Then one day I got a call from Tony, he was on one of his crazy trips that I had learned to just blow off without a second thought. The truth was he really liked me. He had really never liked anyone before, so he never knew how it worked, but I had figured out he cared. He said,

"Mark, this is very important. I need you to get yourself together right now, put on one of those new suits you have, and be ready to pick me up by one p.m. You got it?"

"Tony, I got to work at the store at noon today, you know that."

"God damn it, when you going to fucking grow up, Mark? You don't know by now what your real job is?"

I thought about it for a minute. He was right. The store was bullshit, so I changed my tune real fast.

"You're right, man, I'll be there. Don't worry about it."

"Look, man, this is big. I'll tell you the details later. Just be here and be sharp." Then he slammed the phone.

I got myself together real nice and smooth, in one of my finest suits, and headed out. I drove out to where Tony was staying, playing music without a care or a worry in the world, it seemed. Not even having a clue what he had in mind for me.

I pulled up to Tony's hotel at about fifteen minutes to one. He jumped right in and said I should take the 405 Freeway. I said, "Where we headed?"

"Hollywood." He said with a half smile only he could make.

Tony was on the phone most of the ride, making all kinds of calls. Then he finally was off the phone and he looked at me and said, "Today we see a man about a horse."

Now that I had become more familiar with the horses we dealt with I asked, "Which horse?"

He said, "Anna Virus."

"Wow, that's his money maker. That's a bad-ass horse."

"Yes she is, and you're about to see just how bad she is."

Now we were into the hills, making our way up. I said,

"Who lives up here? It's beautiful."

"Listen, Mark. This is Mr. Canto's house. We're going to go in and I will introduce you to him, and after that I want you to sit your ass down and don't say another fucking word, you got that?"

Now at this point I was looking confused. I had only heard about this man, never thinking I would meet him. And why was I meeting him now?

"No problem, Tony." I shrugged.

As we pulled in to this museum, I thought it wouldn't be right to just call it a house. Beautiful landscaping, palm trees, waterfalls and flowers of all kinds, a real piece of the world's first garden, "Eden."

Before I opened my door, Tony reminded me to speak only when spoken to. He seemed to be somewhat nervous himself. As we walked up to the front of this place, we passed the most expensive cars I had ever seen. I kept cool and tried not to stare as we went by. Two giant doors opened as we came close and a servant met us. Tony said hello, he seemed to know this person.

"Hello, Tony, how are you doing? Mr. Canto is waiting for you in the kitchen."

We went in, and followed this person through this magnificent place. I only wished I could take pictures, to capture this moment in my lifetime, to show my family the way in which some people truly live.

As we went into the kitchen, I saw three older men. They must have been in their late sixties, all with white, balding hair. They spotted us. The man sitting at the table reading the paper must have been Canto. He got up and greeted Tony with a hug and handshake. The other two greeted him with just handshakes.

I was standing there, just playing the back, feeling like a fish breathing my last breath, praying for someone, anyone, to throw me back to water where I belonged. As I stood there, I looked up at a TV monitor showing the day's stock report. This gave me something to focus on, as I gasped for air.

Then Tony turned to me, saying, "Mr. Canto; this is Mark Rhymes. The young man I told you all about."

Now I was thinking, why has he told this man about me? Why would he need to know about me?

Mr. Canto looked at me, and then walked over to where I was standing. He held out his hand and said, "Mark, I'm glad to finally meet you. Tony has a lot of good things to say about you." As he was shaking my hand, I was lost but trying to play along like I knew what the hell was really going on. I said,

"Thank you, sir; it's a pleasure to meet you as well."

"These are my business associates, Mr. Walker and Mr. Likens."

They both said hello, and I said hello to them.

"Would you like something to drink, Mark?"

"No thank you, sir. I'm fine."

"Well, just in case. Honey, come on in here." He called to his wife to come and get me something to drink.

Then Tony came over to me and said, "Sit here. I have to go talk to Sam in the other room. Have a seat and don't fucking move." I wanted to say to him, "What the hell is going on in here?" But now clearly wasn't the right time, so I waited.

I sat and watched the stock reports, wanting to grab the remote on the table and change the channel to the golf station, and catch some of Tiger Woods' tournament.

Just then, in walked this lady. She had to be fifty or better. But she was beautiful. I had never seen a woman of that age with a face and body that looked that good. She walked up to me and said, "You must be Mark."

"Yes I am."

"I'm Mrs. Canto. It's nice to meet you, Mark."

"Likewise, Madam."

"Let me get you a drink."

"Thank you."

"So we hear you're interested in our Anna Virus. She's an incredible creature."

Now I was really confused. I didn't know what to say, so I said nothing, hoping that she would let the cat all the way out of the bag.

Then she went on saying, "Tony feels like you're a really good person, and wants to help you in this business. It's not easy, but Tony knows a lot, and you can learn from him."

"Yes I think so, I've learned so much already." I said not really knowing what the hell I was talking about.

"Well, Tony is a part of this family, and if he feels good about you, we will too. So if you need anything, you just give us a call."

"That is really nice, and I greatly appreciate it."

"No problem, Mark, I think I like you already,"

She smiled at me as she walked out of the room. What the hell was that all about? Where was I and what had I gotten myself into?

Just then Tony walked back into the room, and looked at me. He said, "Are you ready to go?"

I didn't answer. Then as we were walking out, Mr. Canto caught up to us and asked Tony, "Tony, did Howard ever come and bring the meds to you at the stables?" Tony looked unsure for a moment then said,

"You know I waited that day for him, but he never showed."

Canto looked puzzled. He said, "That's really strange, I haven't seen or heard from him since."

"Okay, Sam. I'll call you in a few days." And just like that we were gone.

What was that about? I didn't know, but now Tony would have to do some explaining.

On the way back from Canto's, I was trying to think of what I wanted to say. My hands on the wheel were sweating, my mind told me I was in over my head, and I was in real trouble. Tony was looking over some papers, not saying a word as I drove.

Then I couldn't take it anymore. I snatched the car to the side of the road and came to a skidding halt. Tony looked at me and said, "What the fuck?"

"You tell me what the fuck is going on, man, right now!"

Then he sprang that half smile he had, then said, "So now you got balls? Now you want to know something?"

"Yeah, I want to know."

He looked at me, and then he said, "I thought you wanted to make more money, remember everybody wants more money, right? Isn't that what you told me?"

"Whatever, man. But I need to know how I'm making my money."

"Look, I got this all worked out, and if you play along, you could make a lot of fucking money."

"I'm already playing along. I just don't know the game."

Then he looked away, and said, "How you feel about owning your own racehorse?"

I shook my head in disbelief, "how the hell could I ever do that?'

"I got it all worked out."

"What horse, Tony? Anna Virus? I don't wanna mess with these people, Tony. I don't want any part of that. They know I don't have that kind of money."

"Listen, you fuck, let me tell you. Canto gives me money for whatever I need on a regular basis; he thinks you came into some real money through your family's misfortune. I told him you checked out. He trusts me. I'm going to take the money from him, and buy the horse for you with his own money. We get the horse, and he gets his money back. You see? No harm, no foul."

"So, why me? Why do you need me? Why don't you just do it yourself?"

"I needed a buyer, asshole. I can't play both parts."

"So you have been using me all along. Right, Tony?"

"No, you been making money all along, and not asking any questions."

"But you knew what the hell you were doing; you never gave me a choice."

"I'm trying to change your life, Mark. Some things you have to do if you want more than a cell store paycheck. I thought you would understand. All you have to do now is play the part of the owner, sign these papers stating that you are the sole owner of one horse, by the name of Anna Virus." He showed me the paperwork, all ready to be signed by me.

"So, when were you going let me in on this big money making idea?"

"I was going to tell you right now."

I thought about it as I sat there on the side of the road, looking out at miles of road ahead. I knew somehow I would be breaking the law. Tony thought I was stupid, I knew he was ripping this man who was a father figure to him, right the hell off.

And before I could tell him I wanted out of this whole thing he said,

"It's too late to go back now; we got to see it through. They know it's me, and they know it's you."

Now here I was, stuck in the middle with no clue how or when I got there. It was too late to be smart now.

I was pissed; I didn't say anything more to him as we drove back. He tried to make it sound so good, telling me, "You're going to make a lot of money, Mark, more than you have ever had or seen in your whole life.

And I'm changing the name of your horse; we're going to call her, RHYME TIME."

Part 2
Rhyme Time

Far different from all the others, now you belong to me, but how could this be? This I could have never foreseen, not even in my wildest of dreams. Now they all look surprised, as we with ease take first prize. The horse of color really belongs to some other; I cannot believe this is happening to me.

One whole week went by before I heard from Tony, but I knew I would, and when I did, it was time for me to start my new career as Mark Rhymes, the actor. I was starring in the role of my life: thoroughbred horse owner. I got myself together. Today was race day. Nobody knew we had changed Anna Virus to Rhyme Time, so if she won, we were going to make a lot of money this day.

And a beautiful day it was, as Tony and I made our way to the table with my name on it, as owner of RHYME TIME.

The place was full of excitement and money. As I sat at my table amongst all the other owners, that feeling of eyes burning through the back of my neck was all over me. "How is this young nigger sitting with us in the owner's circle?" This must have been the question of the day. By now I really didn't care anymore.

I was into it. It was my role and I was going to play it all the way out. Just then Tony said, "Look, when the race starts, don't get up and go to the fence with everybody. Stay right here at the table."

"But if everybody gets up, I won't be able to see the race."

"You don't need to see it. You're going to win it." Then the next thing we heard was the man saying, "AND THEY'RE OFF."

Now as the other owners lined the fence, jumping and screaming, we sat sipping on champagne, real cool like. And low and behold we heard,

"It's RHYME TIME, your winner."

Tony said, "Just stay cool, and toast to Rhyme Time." As we toasted, all the other owners turned and came running over to congratulate me. Just then I was crowned king, and this race world was my new kingdom. All hail the new king. It was unbelievable. We partied that whole day and night. That race brought in about fifty-grand, and we had only just begun.

The next day we woke in some hotel. I didn't even know where we were. We had breakfast and talked about what was going to happen next. Tony had already spoken to Canto. He wanted Tony to go to L.A. to pick up another horse and bring him back to the stables in San Diego. This was the perfect time for Tony to hit him up for the money we would need to pay him for the horse we already had in our possession.

He sent Tony all the money he asked for, plus living expenses. Including the money we had just won from the race, we were doing real well. But just about then, things started to go bad.

As we continued talking, he told me what we needed to do. I still went along. Like I said, I knew better, but now I was along for the long haul. So now that we had the money we could pay for the Rhyme Time, and I really wanted to do that soon as possible. I thought that would make me feel better, why, I don't know. Anyway we were on our way to get this new horse. After we got there, Tony changed the plan. He said, "Mark, I need you to go back to San Diego and wait for me. I'll bring the horse back myself. Go to the stables and move the horse from stall number three to stall number four, then go home and wait for my call."

This bothered me, I didn't understand why this was so important right now, and I really didn't want to be away from Tony right now. I was kind of nervous about it all. But I did what he wanted me to do, I went straight back.

It was late when I made it back to the stables. It was dark and I didn't like messing around out there in the dark. I went in to move the horse, inside number three; I got the horse and took him out to number four. After he was in, and I was ready to go, I saw that I left the gate open on number three, so I went over to close the gate. That's when I noticed a pile of dirt at the back of the stall.

This was very unusual. This place never had a piece of paper on the ground, and it was always spotless. And this dirt was in a mound. I couldn't see it when the horse was in there, but when it was empty it was as plain as day. So I went in slowly, looking around, and then I saw a shovel that had been used to dig in the stall. I felt like running, and getting the hell out of there, but I needed to know what was really going on. I was in too deep.

I started to move the dirt with the shovel. As I got deeper, I uncovered what looked like clothing. So I got down on my knees to get a closer look. Moving the dirt with my hands now, I uncovered a human hand.

I freaked! Jumping up, backing up, and trying to get the hell out as fast as I could. As I came out of the stalls, I ran smack into a man who earlier in the week had told me not to trust Tony.

He looked at me. I looked like I had just seen a ghost. He said, "What is it? What's wrong?"

"Nothing. Nothing. I have to go." I took off running for the car, jumped in and took off like a bat out of hell. Now I was driving way too fast, shaking and sweating. I couldn't believe what I had just seen. It all started to make sense. Stall number three, the phone call when this whole mess started. Canto had asked if this guy showed up. Tony told him no. I couldn't believe this was happening to me.

What was I going to do? Think! Think!

I had to calm down. Get myself together. I didn't want Tony to know I knew what was in that stall; I had to play it cool. I went to my sister's house, took a hot shower and lay down. My mind was racing faster than any horse ever did. Why did I do this? Why did I get involved? I didn't come out here to throw my life away with this shit. I'm a writer, that's why I'm here, but it was too late for that. This was my new life now. Finally I fell asleep off into a dream.

I was getting off a plane back home, going to see my baby for the first time in over a year. As I came down the stairs of the plane, I could see her standing there waiting for me, waving, saying, "Daddy, daddy!" I was smiling as I looked at her as I came running down the stairs. Now I was on the ground running over to her, when out of nowhere came the FBI shooting me over and over, right in front of her. I reached for her, but it was too late. I was dead.

THEN I WOKE UP!

"NOOO!"

It was morning and back to my reality.

I didn't know what to do with myself, so I went for a ride. I drove around trying to think of a way out, but I couldn't think of anything that might free me.

Then the phone rang—it was Tony, had to stay cool.

"Did you move the horse?"

"Yeah, it's all done no problems."

"Look, I need you to make a call for me. The number is in the glove box."

"Whose number is this?"

"It's Canto's wife's cell number."

"Tony, I don't want to call these people. What if she starts asking me things? What the hell am I going to say?"

"Would you stop crying like a little bitch? Just listen, Mark. Tell her I'm still on my way back. Everything is fine. Tell her you love your new horse, and her horse is in the number four stall. Tell her not to worry. I'll call her as soon as I get in, you got that?" I had to play along, at least for now.

"Yeah, I got it."

"Good. I'll call you when I get to the stables."

Then he slammed the phone down.

I really didn't want to call, but I had to. I was in deep, so I made the call.

Ring, ring. "Hello?"

"This is Mark, Mrs. Canto. How are you?"

"Mark. Good, thanks for asking. How are things?"

"Everything is good. I just spoke with Tony, and he's having some trouble with his cell phone. He wanted me to make sure you knew what was going on. Everything is fine. He is still on his way back with the horse; your other horse is in number four. He should be here before long, and will call you when he reaches the stables." I did that well. She bought it with no problem.

All I could do now was wait for Tony, so that's what I did. I waited. I waited for hours. Still no Tony. I was starting to panic. It was almost dark now; I couldn't wait anymore. I was afraid if he never showed, they would come for me. So now it was time to dance to the music. I drove all the way back out to the stables; I don't now why, but I felt like this is where I needed to be.

By the time I reached the stables, it was pretty dark, and getting darker by the minute. I pulled in and turned off my lights, and waited. Then I saw what I thought was Tony going into the stall. I grabbed my golf club and headed in behind him.

I moved slowly so not to be heard or seen. Now at the gate of the stall he had his back to, I jumped out and said, "Tony, what the fuck is going on?"

But to my surprise, when he turned around it wasn't Tony, but the man who had told me not to trust Tony, the same man I ran into last night, but why was he here now? When he turned around, he had a gun in his hand, pointing it right at me. "Drop the club or I drop you."

I put the club on the ground; I thought, "This is it. I'm going to die here." Then from behind, a car pulled in. I was thinking it was Tony, but again I was wrong. It was Mrs. Canto and three men dressed in black suits. They all walked into the stall. Miss Canto walked up to me. "We know all about Tony, Mark. Are you going to tell me where he is?"

This was it. I had no idea where his ass was, and she was going to have these guys kill me, and drop me in another hole in the back of one of these stalls never to be heard of again.

"No, Madam, I really don't know where he is. Are you going to kill me now?"

"Mark, remember when I told you I liked you?"

"Yes, Madam, I do."

"For some reason, I still do. If you ever run into Tony again, if I were you, I would go the other way."

"Yes, Madam, I will."

Then just like that, they were gone, and by the grace of God, I was still alive.

Did I learn anything from this? I think I did. Will I make better choices in the future? I think I will. I should have stuck to what I do best in the first place, writing. But I was really not getting anywhere with the work I was sending in. It wasn't what they where looking for. Somehow I think this story may be what that something is? Unexpected and truly moving.

What if it is? What if this is the one?

They say everything happens for a reason. Let's see what they think about this.

WHAT IF IT WORKS?

"Now that would be a horse of another color!"